IDAHO CITY

Book Five of the Joe Beck Series

C.J. PETIT

Copyright © 2022 by C.J. Petit
All rights reserved. This book or any portion thereof may not be reproduced or used in any manner whatsoever without the express written permission of the publisher except for the use of brief quotations in a book review.

Printed in the United States of America

First Printing 2022

ISBN: 9798434531023

CONTENTS

CHAPTER 1 2
CHAPTER 2 59
CHAPTER 3 109
CHAPTER 4 140
CHAPTER 5 168
CHAPTER 6 203
CHAPTER 7 233
CHAPTER 8 295
CHAPTER 9 358
TRANSITION 381

CHAPTER 1

September 12, 1863
Southeast Corner of Idaho Territory

Joe was riding alone as he followed the wagons. They were just two miles ahead but were out of sight as Duke climbed another pass. Faith had argued with him each morning since they left Fort Bridger, saying that she wasn't too tired to join him. But her eyes told Joe a different story.

But it was when the folks were picking up their supplies at Fort Bridger that some also picked up an infection for a disease that medical science could never cure. While desertion was a problem for all of the Western forts, Fort Bridger's was more acute. But it was the cause of their desertion problem that infected some of the men in the wagon train. Gold had been discovered near Idaho City and some of the less dependable soldiers had run off to seek their fortunes. That news had infected some of the men with gold fever and it had been spreading wider each day.

It was also the reason Bo had asked him to ride behind the wagons. He was concerned that a group of deserters might be trailing them in the hope of acquiring the stake for a claim. It made sense as they hadn't been paid in four months, so they

IDAHO CITY

couldn't afford to buy a few pounds of coffee, much less a piece of land.

Joe hadn't seen any deserters since they left and doubted if he would. But Bo had given him the assignment, and Joe wasn't about to argue.

Soon the wagons would be crossing the extensive volcanic ash and lava flatlands, then a few days later, they'd reach the Snake River. As Duke climbed the upslope to the pass, Joe wondered if the gold fever would be strong enough to make some of the wagons stay in Idaho City rather than going on to Oregon. But it wasn't just the gold that might make some families choose Idaho City as their destination. It was a large town already and offered many services that the settlers hadn't seen in months. But they were farmers and not miners, so he hoped that not many decided to leave the train.

He knew the ones who were most infected by the fever, and two of them weren't farmers. He'd been stunned when Faith told him that Marigold and Becky said that Chuck and Herm believed that the gold strike was the opportunity of a lifetime. Faith said that while Marigold seemed pleased with the idea, Becky was far less enthusiastic. Joe hadn't been able to talk to them since Faith told him about their condition, but he believed he'd have a chance long before they reached the road to Idaho City.

Idaho City already had reputation that was to be expected in any town that was suddenly inundated with hundreds of men desperately hunting for riches. The soldiers had told them of the rapid increase in the number of saloons and bawdy houses to relieve the successful miners of their gold.

In an odd twist, they said that there were also a plague of attorneys setting up offices in the town to provide expensive legal help to the miners on both sides of claim disputes. While the town had a glut of lawyers, it didn't have nearly enough lawmen to keep the peace. The soldiers said that the town had built a large, fancy jail and a brick courthouse, but had a difficult time finding men who were willing to toss lawbreakers into their six stout jail cells. Joe had expected the unsavory reputation might be enough to cure the gold fever, but it hadn't seemed to have nearly the impact he had hoped it would.

But that was a problem that was beyond his control, so he concentrated on the one that was still beyond his control but was more immediate. He was wearing the heavy coat that Captain Chalmers had given him as well as the warm gloves. It was technically still summer but seemed more like early winter. While he was grateful for the heat generated by his big stallion, the powerful, whirling winds still made him shiver. To make things worse, the thick, ominous dark clouds were threatening to soak him with sheets of icy cold water. The weather wasn't bad when he started out this morning, but just before noon, the temperature plummeted, and the winds began to howl.

Joe decided not to wait for the first chilling raindrops to arrive, so he twisted in the saddle and slid his slicker from his bedroll. He pulled Duke to a halt before he removed his hat and placed the brim beneath his left thigh to keep the wind from blowing it all the way to Utah. When he let the slicker unravel, the wind almost yanked it from his gloved hands. For more than a minute, he and the strong gusts wrestled for control of the rubberized canvas. Joe was finally able to win the battle and get his head through the slicker's hole before he pulled it down. He then had to tuck the left corner under his saddle to keep it from covering his face. The right side of the slicker was wildly flapping as he tugged his hat back on then slid the chin strap beneath his jaw.

After he convinced Duke to start climbing the rise again, Joe tucked the right corner of the slicker under his thigh. The wind turned the back of the slicker into a cape that began to crack like a bullwhip, but at least he'd stay drier when the rain arrived.

Joe was close to the top of the pass when the precipitation began to fall. But it wasn't rain, chilly or otherwise. It came in the form of tiny ice pellets that felt like bee stings when the wind shot them into his face. He tilted his head down to let his hat's brim stop most of the frigid missiles knowing that the back of his neck would suffer from Mother Nature's attack.

As Duke continued walking up the incline, Joe grumbled, "I thought it was still summer. Did I lose a few months when I was asleep last night?"

Ten minutes later, he reached the summit and couldn't see the wagons but wasn't surprised. His visibility was so restricted that it seemed as if he was riding in a cloud. The downslope simply disappeared after about a hundred yards.

After starting down from the top of the pass, Joe began taking short peeks at the trail ahead and hoped that the sudden late summer storm would end as quickly as it had arrived. He wasn't sure what time it was as Duke slowly made his way to level ground.

He knew he was getting close to the bottom of the pass when the biting ice pellets became the ice-cold drops of rain he'd expected. The fierce wind was abating, so Joe was able to look ahead again. When he felt the back of his slicker cease behaving like a cape, he pulled both corners of the front end free.

The wind was less violent, yet still strong enough to push the cold rain into his face. But it was a definite improvement. He now had almost a thousand yards of visibility but still couldn't find the wagons. He had no trouble seeing the ruts, so he picked up Duke's pace.

Ninety minutes later, the wind and rain had begun to diminish, so he was still able to see almost a mile in front of him now. He was surprised that he hadn't spotted the wagons yet and tried to understand how that was even possible.

He was close to imagining that everyone in the entire wagon train had decided to make a dash for the gold fields around Idaho City or they'd been swallowed by a giant sink hole when the back of a covered wagon appeared out of the mist. Joe laughed at himself but didn't pick up the pace. He estimated that he should reach them in another ten minutes at his current speed.

As the last wagon grew in size, he began to see other wagons but no walkers. If Mary's wagon, now Will and Mary's wagon, was the trailing wagon, he would have seen Faith by now. But the Lilleys now occupied the last position, and the Boones' wagon was fourth in line. It had taken Joe three days to adjust to the new order and sometimes wished he hadn't made the suggestion to Bo in the first place. But just seeing the wagons was a relief.

Joe continued to gain on the slow-moving wagons and smiled when he recalled how difficult it had been to arrange the horses after Will and Mary were married. They finally decided that Will would trail Noah and Cloud on one side and Faith would tie Duchess and Bernie on the other. Betty, Bessie and Nellie were now all trailing behind the Witherspoons' wagon.

Before he reached the Lilleys' wagon, Joe heard Nora ring the bell and watched as the dozens of wagon wheels slowed then stopped turning. Just as the folks began to unharness their teams, Mother Nature decided to be kind and turned off the spigot and stopped passing wind. She even generously added a few degrees to the chilly air.

Joe was about a hundred feet from the ruts when he waved to Theo Lilley. He had shifted his approach more to the left after Bo had moved Mary's wagon closer to the front, so he would be able to greet Faith properly.

Faith wished she had been able to ride with Joe but knew she'd only make him worry if he'd allowed her to join him. She really was tired, but at least she knew the reason. It was also why she hadn't argued more forcefully. Even before they reached Fort Bridger, Faith was sure she was carrying their baby.

But when the storm arrived just after the noon break, she began worrying about Joe. As the wind began buffeting the canvas walls and the rain began to hammer the wagon, Mary huddled with William and Alfred while Faith hugged John and Laddie sat on her other side. She was looking out the back of the wagon hoping that Joe would return early, but knew he was probably struggling to cross the pass. If she had known how much worse the weather Joe had experienced, she might have bundled up then mounted Duchess to find him.

She noticed that the wind had stopped rocking the wagon and the rain was now just a light drizzle, so she looked at Mary and said, "I was hoping Joe would have returned by now."

Mary smiled as she replied, "He's probably soaked to the skin, but other than that, I'm sure he's fine."

"I guess his slicker wouldn't help much with that much wind, would it?"

"Probably not. But I imagine that you can help him dry off and get warm, too."

IDAHO CITY

Faith smiled and said, "I'll do my best."

When she turned her eyes back to the outside world, she laughed when she saw Joe riding slowly towards her. As soon as her blue eyes caught sight of him, Joe pulled off his soggy hat and waved it three times over his heat. Faith was still smiling as she excitedly waved back.

Then John waved and exclaimed, "Uncle Joe is back!"

Joe slowed Duke just before he reached the back of the wagon then pulled up behind the tailgate.

Faith slid closer and asked, "Are you going to dismount, Mister Beck?"

"Not yet, ma'am. I need to head over to the Witherspoons and retrieve our mares so I can set up the tent."

"Okay. Are you all right, Joe? I was worried when that storm seemed to come out of nowhere."

"I'm fine. Did you get any ice pellets down here, or was it all rain?"

"You had ice pellets?"

"Yup. I reckon it was because I was another thousand feet higher. Those mountains made the wind whip around like crazy, too. I felt like I was riding between a pair of twisters."

"Go and get our things and I'll stay here until you come to get me."

Joe grinned and said, "I always told you how smart you were," then rode away to collect the mares.

After he'd gone, Faith said, "I didn't know that the weather could be so different just a few miles away. I'm sure that Joe was right when he said it was because of the higher altitude."

Mary said, "That and those tall mountains on either side of the pass."

John looked up at Faith and said, "I'm happy the wind didn't blow his horse down."

Mary nodded but felt her stomach twist in a knot when she realized what might have happened to Joe if Duke had broken an ankle or been spooked and tossed Joe from the saddle again. Tonight, she'd strongly recommend he start bringing Bessie along.

———

After Joe tied Bessie's reins to his saddle, he rode to the front of the line to talk to Bo. He didn't have anything to report but wanted to ask about the extent and strength of the gold rush fever.

Before he reached the lead wagon, he made two brief stops to pass a few words with Herm and then Chuck. So, as he approached the front of the line, he knew he'd be able to have a private talk with Bo.

Bo waved when he spotted Joe and as he walked around the front of his team, Joe pulled up and dismounted.

Bo grinned and said, "I reckon the only ornery things you found back there were wind and rain, Joe."

"It was a lot worse up there, Bo. I was even besieged by ice pellets. I thought I must have overslept by a couple of months last night and wound up in late fall. Do you think that we'll lose anybody when we get close to Idaho City?"

Bo glanced at Nora before saying, "I reckon it's likely we might lose some of 'em. I think Chuck's got the gold fever pretty bad and Marigold is kinda excited, too."

"How about Herm? I heard he's leaning that way, but Becky isn't happy with the idea."

"I figure Herm is thinkin' about it 'cause Chuck is tryin' to convince him to partner up with him. I woulda thought he'd try and talk you into it first. After all, you ain't bein' paid and can go anywhere you want. Will is the same way, so I can't figure out why Chuck's workin' on Herm."

"I guess it's because he's been riding with Herm since we heard about the gold strike. I don't think I've talked with Chuck for more than a half an hour since we left Fort Bridger. And even then, he hasn't even said the word 'gold' to me. It's almost as if he's trying to avoid me."

"Do you want me to have Herm ride the back trail tomorrow, so you can talk to Chuck?"

Joe thought about it for a few seconds before shaking his head and replying, "It won't matter because I don't think he'd tell me his plans. He'd probably be worried that I might try to talk him out of it."

"I reckon that's so. Herm can be won over a lot easier than you can. Maybe I should send you out front with Herm, and you can talk to him."

"We won't reach that road that turns off to Idaho City for a few more days, is that right?"

"We'll reach the road that runs south into Utah in three days, then we'll stop at Fort Hall and find that fork to Idaho City three or four more days later. We should cross into Oregon a week after that."

"I'll ride trail tomorrow, but I'll ask Faith to talk to Becky about Herm while I'm gone. If I think I can get him to change his mind, then I'll let you know."

"Okay. It's kinda odd when you think about it. When we left Kansas City, I only had two scouts. Then after you started scoutin', we had three before we buried Mort. Then we had three again before I added Will. If we lose Chuck and Herm, we'll be back to just two again. And the ones we lost were the only ones gettin' paid."

Joe grinned as he asked, "How do you know that Will and I won't suddenly get infected with gold fever? Then you'd have no scouts at all."

Bo snickered then said, "At least we shouldn't be facin' any hostile Indians for the rest of the way."

"I reckon not. But now we'll have to be on the lookout for desperate white men heading to Idaho City to search for gold. They probably wouldn't try to hold up the wagon train, but if the stagecoach is still running from Salt Lake City, they could be waiting for it to show up and be more than happy to ambush our scouts while they're waiting."

"I know. After you set up your camp, come on back 'cause I want to talk to all of you about that. Maybe talkin' about those desperate men will make Chuck change his mind."

Joe didn't think it would affect Chuck's decision at all. Once a man's mind is filled with visions of immense wealth, there isn't any room for rational thought.

But he still nodded as he said, "I'll be back when we're finished."

Bo said, "See ya," then walked back to finish taking his team out of harness.

Joe mounted Duke then turned him around and headed back to Will and Mary's wagon. He didn't see Faith as he wound his way around the oxen and mules that were being led to a nearby creek but did spot Will returning to the wagon after securing their oxen.

Will waved, then after Joe pulled up, he asked, "How bad did the storm beat you up, Joe?"

"It could have been worse. I was just surprised it was cold enough to create ice pellets while it's still summer."

"At least it didn't last long."

While no one was nearby, Joe asked, "Have you heard much about folks leaving the wagon train to go to Idaho City?"

"I've heard a few fellers talking about it, but I don't know if their wives will let 'em go. Some of the older boys might skedaddle when we reach that cutoff, though."

"What about Chuck and Herm?"

Will did a quick scan for eavesdroppers before he stepped closer to Duke and said, "Chuck's got the gold fever really bad. I think Marigold wants to go, too. Herm is on the fence about joining him, but Becky isn't about to let her folks go to Oregon on their own. She wants them to be there when she has her baby."

IDAHO CITY

"That's what I thought, too. You don't have any urges to try your luck at prospecting, do you?"

"Not a bit. I already found my treasure when I met Mary."

Joe smiled before he said, "I'm glad to hear that, Will. I have no intention of leaving Bo in the lurch either. He wants me to try to convince Herm that it's a bad idea, and I told him I'd have Faith talk to Becky first to find out how close Herm was to following Chuck."

Will nodded then said, "Good luck. Are you and Faith gonna join us for supper?"

"I'll ask Faith in case she has other plans."

Will chuckled before saying, "You ain't got reservations at some fancy restaurant, do ya?"

Joe grinned, said, "You never know," then walked Duke to the back of the wagon.

When he turned the corner, Joe saw Faith sitting on the tailgate with Laddie and John.

She said, "I heard you talking to Herm, so I knew you'd be here shortly."

Joe dismounted, removed his slicker and as he began rolling it up he said, "Herm wanted to know if we were going to share supper with him, Mary and the boys. I told him I'd check with you first."

"That's fine, but where can we set up our camp that's not too muddy?"

Joe pointed to the north and said, "On that small rise. Most of the rain would have drained to lower ground. You can stay with Mary until I get back."

"Thank you, kind sir."

When Joe stepped closer to the tailgate, Faith leaned down and kissed him before he untied Duchess and led their equine entourage away.

The rise he'd chose for their campsite was a little higher than he'd expected, but that made it an even better choice. The only downside of using the rise was that there weren't any trees or bushes to secure the hitch rope. So, before he began unsaddling the horses and Bernie, he removed two of his bayonets from one of Nellie's packs and stuck them into the ground. He pushed them as deeply as he could before stepping on each one until only two inches of steel was showing. He took the trail rope from Betty and tied it to one bayonet and wrapped around the second then gave it a hard tug before laying it on the ground.

After tying their reins to the hitching rope, Joe began unsaddling Duke. When all of the horses and Bernie were free of their saddles and packs, he started erecting the tent and twenty minutes later, the camp was ready. He decided not to build a firepit because they wouldn't be cooking. But he had filled the kerosene lantern and placed it inside the tent more for the heat it produced than the light.

As he started down the rise, he saw Faith talking to Mary while Will dug a firepit. Laddie was besieged by the three boys but didn't seem to mind their attention.

Faith must have either sensed his approach or had been periodically peeking at their campsite because as soon as he reached level ground, she smiled and waved. Joe was just fifty feet away but still pulled off his waterlogged hat and waved it over his head. As he pulled it back on, he saw her whole face smile.

When he arrived, Faith said, "It looks as if you never even wore your slicker. Aren't you cold?"

Joe grinned as he replied, "I'm not toasty warm, but I'm all right. I was wearing my slicker before the rain started, but even after I tucked the front corners under my saddle, the wind still blew a lot of the rain onto my coat."

"When we get to the tent, you need to get out of those wet clothes."

"Yes, ma'am."

Faith was surprised that Joe hadn't taken verbal advantage of her request to take off his wet clothes. She didn't think it was because Mary or John could hear him, either.

Mary said, "Will just told me that you were concerned about Chuck and Herm leaving the wagon train to hunt for gold near Idaho City."

"Bo thinks that Chuck is determined to go but believes that Herm is unsure about it. What do you think?"

"I believe that Becky will put her foot down. I'm just not sure if that's enough to keep him with the wagons. Will said that Bo asked you to talk to him."

"He did. But I was going to ask Faith to have chat with Becky tomorrow to find out if it would do any good."

Faith said, "I was going to talk to her about something else anyway, so I'll ask her what she thinks Herm will do."

As he lit the cooking fire, Will said, "I figured that Becky wouldn't leave her folks, but I don't know them as well as everyone else does."

Faith said, "That might not be an issue. I think Marigold might pressure Becky to come along, too. If she can convince Becky, then I'm sure that Mr. and Mrs. Witherspoon would join them."

Joe nodded then said, "When you talk to her tomorrow, if it sounds as if she's wavering, remind her that the town has dozens of saloons and a lot of lonely, desperate men."

Faith replied, "She already heard those stories but didn't seem concerned."

IDAHO CITY

Joe sighed before he said, "Well, I guess they're all adults and whatever they do is up to them."

Faith said, "I'll still talk to her tomorrow."

As Joe nodded, Mary said, "I can live with whatever they decide or whoever else leaves, as long as you and Faith don't abandon us. Now let's make use of the fire before it burns out."

———

About an hour later, Joe and Faith left the Boones and headed to their camp with Laddie trotting alongside.

When they reached the tent, Joe waited for Faith to enter but she just stared at him as she said, "Get in there and start taking off those wet clothes."

Joe nodded, said, "Yes, ma'am," then ducked and stepped into the tent.

Again, Faith was puzzled that Joe hadn't replied as she'd expected but entered the tent without commenting.

Joe set his hat on the right side where he'd laid a spare slicker that already being used to keep his guns dry then began unbuttoning his coat.

As Faith undid her own coat's buttons, she asked, "Are you all right, Joe?"

Joe laid his coat on the top of the slicker then replied, "I'm fine. Why are you asking?"

Faith pulled off her coat and replied, "I don't know. You just seem to be out of sorts. Is it because you're worried about Chuck and Herm?"

Joe set his gunbelt onto his coat and said, "Not really. I guess I'm just worn out."

Faith wasn't sure if that was the real reason but let it go.

After Joe wedged his wet shirt and britches between the tent supports and the canvas to let them dry, he slid under the blankets then turned to face Faith.

After Joe joined her, she rolled onto her side and said, "I know you said I would get tired, but I didn't expect to get this tired. Is it because I don't have enough fat?"

Joe smiled as he replied, "I don't think so, but you've got to start eating a lot more. Our baby is a hungry little girl and she's eating more than you would expect."

Faith quietly asked, "But what if I eat so much that I get used to it? Then I could keep eating after she's born and get fat?"

Joe kissed her forehead and said, "You won't get fat, sweetheart."

Faith stammered, "But what…what if I get fat…and…and you don't like me anymore?"

IDAHO CITY

Before Joe could formulate a reply, Faith covered her face with her hands and began sobbing.

Joe wrapped his wife in his arms before saying, "Then I guess I'd just have to look elsewhere for female companionship. Do you think Duke would get jealous if I started wooing Duchess?"

Faith pulled her hands from her eyes, then after a short delay, began laughing. Tears still flowed from her eyes and dripped onto the bed, but Joe was pleased with his answer.

When Faith stopped laughing, she wiped her cheeks and said, "I'm sorry, Joe. That was a foolish thing for me to ask."

"No, it wasn't foolish, Faith. It was normal behavior for a lady in your condition. Remember I told you that pregnant women go from happy to sad in a heartbeat for no reason?"

"I guess that I forgot about that. I was too excited after you explained why my breasts were so sore. Will this go away like Marigold's morning sickness?"

"I'm not sure, but I don't think you should worry about it."

"How come Becky and Marigold don't seem to be so moody?"

"You haven't been around them very much lately, and I imagine they're like that when they're alone with their husbands. You can ask Becky about it tomorrow."

"Do Chuck and Herm say anything about it?"

"Chuck complained about it a couple of times when we used to ride together, but Herm didn't. I don't think he'd ever say anything bad about Becky."

"He really loves and respects her, doesn't he?"

"He does, but not as much as I love and respect you, sweetheart."

Faith smiled and asked, "Even if I do get fatter?"

"Always. But I expect you'll be adding a few pounds even if you weren't pregnant because you were already on that path before you conceived. I did mention it if you recall."

Faith giggled then said, "I remember what you said and what inspired you to say it."

Joe kissed her then said, "Just remember that I'll always love you, Faith. Never doubt that. Now get some sleep and in the morning, I'll fix you a big breakfast before I leave."

"Alright. But are you sure you're feeling well? You must have been freezing for hours."

"I'm fine. Goodnight, my love."

Faith kissed him and said, "Goodnight, Joe."

Joe smiled then looked past her and said, "Goodnight to you too, Laddie," and rolled onto his back.

IDAHO CITY

Faith turned to face her constant companion and whispered, "Goodnight, Laddie," before she closed her eyes.

Before Faith awakened, Joe had built a fire outside their tent, filled the coffeepot and made a mix of rice, cooked venison, molasses and corn meal. He sprinkled in some salt after it had begun to bubble and tasted the concoction before adding another pinch. It wasn't great, but it was nourishing, He knew he needed to do some hunting soon because their meat supply was getting low. While there wouldn't be much game in the vast lava beds they'd soon be crossing, the trail followed the contour of the mountains, so the forests that were trying to reclaim the flatlands should provide the necessary meat.

When Faith left the tent, she smiled at Joe before she hurried to the other side of the rise. While she was out of sight, Laddie sat next to Joe and stared at the pot.

Joe rubbed his head and said "I don't think you'd like it, Laddie. But here's a big piece of jerky to keep you busy for a few seconds."

After Laddie snatched the dry beef from his hand, Joe slid the pot from the fire then dumped some coffee into the coffee pot and pulled it away from the flames.

By the time Faith reappeared, he'd filled two bowls with stew and set them on the ground before pouring steaming coffee into two tin cups.

Faith sat close to him, picked up her coffee and held it with both hands as she said, "It's pretty chilly already, isn't it?"

"Yes, ma'am. But it's not too bad. I didn't even need to light the lantern last night. I thought I'd need the heat to dry out my clothes, but I guess between you, me and Laddie, we kept it warm enough."

Faith nodded then took a sip of coffee before setting the cup down and picking up her bowl of stew and a spoon.

Joe watched her take her first bite and when she didn't grimace, he began eating.

Faith was surprised when she ate all of the stew and then partially refilled her bowl. But at the same time, she was pleased that Joe really did want her to eat more and wasn't concerned that she might gain too much weight.

———

Forty minutes later, Faith kissed Joe then walked down the rise and headed for Mary's wagon with Laddie trotting beside her. After she'd gone, Joe began saddling the horses. When Faith had suggested he bring Bessie along, he'd explained that having a packhorse would only slow him down and now that they were on level ground, he wouldn't be out of sight anyway.

When the horses and Bernie were ready, Joe mounted Duke and led the rest down the rise. Ten minutes later, the wagons began moving while Joe sat on Duke just watching them roll away. As he sat in his saddle, he studied his surroundings, including the sky. He didn't see any dark clouds on the horizon, so he didn't expect a repeat of Mother Nature's shenanigans. The flatlands here were more like the Laramie Plains, but that would change before the wagons stopped for the night. But it was the mountainous terrain to his left that he found interesting. He planned to pay a visit to the forests along the foothills to do some hunting. He'd increased his mobile armory by sliding the shotgun into his bedroll and hoped to find some quail or turkeys.

When the wagons were almost out of sight, Joe set Duke to a faster pace and angled toward the trees. The forest was more than two miles away, but he was still gaining on the slow-moving train. Even though the threat of attack by hostile Indians was much lower, Joe still scanned the horizons. The mountains behind them blocked the sun, so he was able to see clearly. He saw nothing moving to the north and only spotted some eagles soaring in the mountain updrafts behind him.

He kept monitoring the wagons' progress as he drew closer to the forests. When he was less than a thousand yards from the tree line, he turned Duke to follow a parallel course with the distant ruts even though he couldn't see them any longer. He rode for another half an hour until the last wagon was on his right side then shifted Duke closer to the pines. With the wind coming from the north, he wouldn't be able to get downwind of his prey, but they wouldn't be downwind of him, either.

Joe walked Duke into the trees and continued heading south listening to the sounds of the forest: the birds chirping and squawking, a woodpecker hammering, a small furry critter yapping, and all with the background hush of the wind blowing through the branches. As his stallion wound its way around the thick trunks and Joe bowed and twisted to avoid the branches, Joe heard some nearby clucks and pulled Duke to a stop. He reached back, pulled the shotgun from his bedroll, cocked one hammer then waited.

A few seconds later, he heard the clucking again and pinpointed its location. He figured the big tom turkey was about fifty feet away at his four o'clock position. It must not have spotted him in the shadows and was still on his perch high off the ground. If he had seen him, he would have run or flown as far away as possible.

Joe turned Duke ninety degrees to his right before he nudged him into a slow walk. While he had an idea of where the turkey was, that didn't mean it would be easy to find. Their dark feathers blended into the shadows making him almost invisible. Joe was hoping he'd start clucking again when the turkey must have finally noticed him and dropped from his branch before spreading his massive wings.

Joe was momentarily startled, but quickly cocked one hammer and pulled his shotgun to his shoulder. As the big tom began his rolling turn to fly away from the threat, Joe fired. The turkey's momentum carried him another ten feet before he plowed into the forest floor.

IDAHO CITY

Joe slid the shotgun back into his bedroll then walked Duke to the tree, dismounted then tied his reins to the closest branch before he walked to retrieve the turkey. When he lifted it from the ground, he estimated it must have weighed more than twenty pounds.

———

Ten minutes later, as he left the forest, he spotted the distant wagons then angled Duke to the northwest. He hadn't returned for the noon break since leaving Fort Bridger but wanted to deliver the turkey and talk to Faith. He hoped she had a chance to meet Becky and ask her about Herm.

———

Just twenty minutes after the wagons began moving, Faith had walked to the Witherspoons' wagon to find Becky, but her mother said she was riding on Bo's flatbed wagon with Marigold. After thanking Mrs. Witherspoon, Faith thought about just returning to Mary's wagon. Then she changed her mind when she saw it as an opportunity to learn just how serious Marigold and Chuck were about going to Idaho City.

Before she reached the wagon, she saw Marigold and Becky laughing but couldn't hear what triggered their laughter. Just as she passed the tailgate, Becky caught sight of her out of the corner of her eye and waved.

As Faith climbed onto the driver's seat beside Becky, Marigold said, "We were just talking about you, Faith. We were wondering why we haven't seen you around."

Faith said, "I've been helping Mary. How have you been?"

Becky replied, "I'm tired a lot and probably eat too much, too."

Marigold said, "I have the added joy of morning sickness, but at least it gives me a day off more often now."

Faith hadn't told them that she was pregnant yet because she didn't want to sound as if she was just pretending.

So, she said, "Pretty soon we'll reach a real road and might start seeing stagecoaches and freighters heading to Idaho City."

Marigold smiled then said, "I don't care about them. But I can't wait to see Idaho City."

Faith was surprised that Marigold was so open about their decision to leave the wagon train and said, "I didn't think we'd see Idaho City. I thought it was out of our way."

Marigold replied, "It's not on our route, but Chuck wants to go there, and so do I."

Faith tilted her head before asking, "Why would you want to go there? I heard it was a rough town."

Marigold laughed then asked, "Haven't you heard about the gold strikes, Faith?"

"Of course, I have. But I imagine that for every miner who finds gold, there are ten who don't find any and another ten who want to steal it from him."

Marigold snapped, "I'm not afraid and neither is Chuck! And we're not going alone, either. Herm and Becky are coming with us and so will the Witherspoons, the Smiths and Arv Vardakas and the Carlisles. You should come with us, Faith. We could be richer than you could ever imagine."

Faith looked at Becky who didn't seem nearly as thrilled as Marigold and quietly asked, "Is that true, Becky? Does Herm really want to take you and your parents to Idaho City in the hope of finding gold?"

There was a short pause before Becky replied, "Herm first asked me three days ago, and I wasn't sure. But it seems that he's determined to go, so I finally agreed. My parents tried to convince us to stay with them, but Herm wouldn't change his mind. So, I guess we'll be going. I just wish you and Joe would come with us, Faith."

Faith had no doubt that Becky wanted to stay with the wagons but knew that there was no point in arguing in front of Marigold. It would be up to Joe to convince Herm that he was making a mistake and was confident he'd be successful.

Faith smiled at Becky and said, "I hope Chuck and Herm strike it rich. Then you and Marigold can buy big houses to raise your children."

Becky just nodded while Marigold grinned and said, "And I'll buy everything I ever wanted, too."

Faith didn't want to make it appear as if her visit was just to learn about their intentions, so she began talking about Laddie and Mary's boys just to continue the conversation

After an hour of idle chatter, Faith left the flatbed to return to Mary's wagon.

When she reached the Witherspoons' wagon, she turned and began walking alongside the driver's seat and asked, "How are you, Mrs. Witherspoon?"

Doris smiled down at her and replied, "We're fine, Faith. Come to check on your horses?"

"Yes, ma'am. I just talked to Becky, and she told me that you're planning to leave the wagon train to go to Idaho City."

Doris took a deep breath, exhaled then said, "Herm seems determined to find gold, and we're not about to leave Becky."

Abe then leaned past his wife and said, "I tried to tell Herm he was making a mistake, but I figure Chuck got him too excited for him to listen."

"It sounds like you're not happy about it, Mister Witherspoon."

"I'm not and neither is Doris. I wish there was some way to pound sense into Herm."

"I think Joe could get him to change his mind."

Doris quickly asked, "Do you really think so, Faith?"

Faith nodded as she replied, "I do. I'll ask him to talk to Herm when he returns."

"If he could do that, it would be more important to us than stopping those Shoshone."

Faith smiled as she said, "I understand," then waved and headed to Mary's wagon.

She hoped Joe would return for the noon break so she could tell him what she'd learned. It would be an interesting conversation.

―――

Just forty minutes after leaving the forest with his feathered bounty, Joe heard Nora ring the bell. He was less than a half a mile away when he angled toward Mary's wagon. He didn't expect that Faith would be watching for him but when her blonde head appeared from the wagon's shadows, he quickly yanked off his hat and waved it three times.

Faith had been hoping Joe would return for the noon break, so she was pleasantly surprised when she spotted him. After she returned his wave, she hurried down from the tailgate, but commanded Laddie to stay before she began walking towards him. She'd just taken four steps when she noticed feathers fluttering in the wind on the back of his saddle. For a few moments, she thought he'd brought his headdress along but soon realized they belonged to a large turkey.

Joe soon pulled up, dismounted and dropped his reins before wrapping Faith in his arms and saying, "I brought you something to keep you busy this afternoon and satisfy your appetite."

Faith smiled as she said, "I don't mind the work, and I'm sure there will be more than enough meat to fill my demanding stomach. That is a big turkey, Joe."

"I'll go get him."

Faith followed Joe as he stepped beside Duke, untied the cord that had kept the turkey from flying away, then slid the enormous bird from his saddle before pulling the shotgun from his bedroll.

She stared at the turkey and asked, "How much does he weigh?"

"I'm sure it's more than twenty pounds but could be almost thirty. He tried to fly off, but I had the shotgun ready to fire, so he didn't get far."

Faith took the turkey and said, "I've never seen one this big before. I'll save the feathers after I pluck him."

Before they started walking back to Mary's wagon, Faith said, "I talked to Becky and Marigold this morning. Marigold made it clear that she and Chuck would be going to Idaho City, and was convinced that Herm and Becky, the Witherspoons, the Smiths and Arv and the Carlisles would be coming with them."

Joe's eyebrows shot up as he asked, "All of them?"

"That's what she said. But when I asked Becky, she seemed unhappy with the idea but only agreed because Chuck had made Herm enthusiastic about it. After I finished talking to them, I stopped on the way back and asked Mr. and Mrs. Witherspoon how they felt. They told me that they weren't happy about it and only agreed to go because they didn't want to leave Becky."

Joe nodded as he said, "I reckon Arv is just going to start a new store, but the others must be infected with gold fever. I'll ask Bo to have Chuck ride the trail position tomorrow and I'll try to learn how serious Herm is about leaving."

"I told the Witherspoons that I would ask you to try and convince him to change his mind. I think you're the only one who could, Joe."

"I think Becky could if she put her foot down, but I think she's afraid that she might lose Herm if she did."

"I think you're right. Let's take your prize turkey to Mary's wagon and impress her and Will."

Before they walked ten feet, Will hopped down from the driver's seat and exclaimed, "That's one helluva turkey, Joe!"

"And tonight, you and Mary can share the meat."

Will grinned and said, "I was kinda hoping you'd let us have some. I haven't had turkey in more than a year."

After sharing a short but pleasant lunch, Joe mounted Duke and headed east, then after ten minutes, he made a U-turn. The wagons were less than a mile away, but he kept Duke walking. There were no signs of any threats and there was no reason for him to be so far back.

As he watched the wagons, he began to think about how to convince Herm not to go to Idaho City. He couldn't use the 'it's dangerous' argument because Herm already knew about the town's reputation, whether it was deserved or not. For all he knew, it could be a pleasant, peaceful place filled with law abiding citizens. He had to find a different angle.

Joe worked on the problem for hours and finally decided that he'd wait until he and Herm were out front tomorrow. He'd ask some vague, probing questions to get a sense of Herm's commitment and go from there. By the time he settled on procrastination as a solution, Duke was just less than four hundred yards behind the wagons. He twisted around to check the eastern horizons one last time before he decided to call it a day.

He angled Duke to the southwest so he could see Faith then turned west after a minute or so. It wasn't long before he pulled his hat from his head and made his triple-wave greeting. After Faith had returned his wave, he pulled his signal hat back on and shifted Duke to the northwest. Shortly after his head was covered, Nora rang the bell, and the wagons began lurching to a stop.

As he drew closer, he glanced to the front of the wagons and spotted Bo climbing down from his wagon, so he decided to tell him that he wanted to ride out front tomorrow before Chuck and Herm returned. Then he realized they should have returned already and assumed they were already with their wives. He shifted his eyes to the flatbed and saw Marigold stepping down then found Becky talking to her mother as Abe began unharnessing his team.

When he looked for Bo again, he saw the wagon master beckoning to him. Joe shifted Duke toward the front of the line then looked at Faith and signed that he had to talk to Bo.

He hadn't even dismounted when Bo said, "Chuck and Herm ain't back yet, and I can't see 'em comin'. Can you go find 'em?"

"Sure. When was the last time you did see them?"

"About two hours ago. They were ridin' close together, too. I reckon they were talkin' about what they were gonna do when they got rich."

Joe nodded then said, "Can you tell Faith that I'll be late? Tell her to save some turkey for me."

Bo didn't waste any time to ask about the turkey, so he just said, "I'll let her know."

Joe said, "Thanks, Bo," then started riding into the low sun at a medium trot.

As he headed west, Joe wondered what could have kept Chuck and Herm from returning. He knew they wouldn't have kept riding to Idaho City. It would still be a four-or-five-day ride and they'd need supplies. He didn't think either of them had enough money to buy a claim, either. Maybe their heads were so filled with their imaginary piles of gold that they failed to notice that the sun was almost touching the horizon. While he couldn't imagine that they would lose track of time, it was still likely they weren't focused on their job. While the wagons wouldn't reach the stagecoach road for another day, Joe wondered if Chuck and Joe had run into some bad sorts on their way to Idaho City.

Joe pushed Duke into a faster trot as he slid into his enhanced mode and looked for any signs of Chuck and Herm. He'd been following Cheese and Willy's hoofprints since he left but after riding for twenty minutes, he hadn't seen any signs of them or their horses. He hadn't heard any gunfire, either. He checked his backtrail and the wagons were already out of sight, so he slowed Duke to get a better look at their trail. Joe began shifting his focus from the ground to the landscape ahead, and just a few minutes later, he pulled up. He stared at the disturbed soil and could almost visualize what had happened. There were four sets of new hoofprints, and Cheese and Willy's tracks were all over the place. But what was most alarming was the splash of dark blood near some of Cheese's scuffled hoofprints. He didn't follow the trail left by the six horses but turned Duke south to follow four sets of footprints. There were two other sets that were heading back to the ruts, but he was sure they didn't belong to Chuck or Herm. He was convinced that the two in the middle belonged to Chuck and Herm, and after Duke had walked twenty feet, Joe knew it was Herm who had been shot. *But where were they?*

Joe looked ahead and even in his enhanced mode he couldn't see them. He followed their tracks for another fifty yards when he saw a small gully and just a heartbeat later, he spotted Chuck and Herm laying on the bottom of the gully bound and gagged.

He dismounted and led Duke to the wall of the gully, then dropped his reins and slid down the side. Chuck and Herm had their eyes closed, but Joe knew they were alive.

He took a knee next to Herm and saw the bullet wound in his left upper arm. His shirt sleeve was soaked in blood, but there wasn't a large pool on the ground, so the shirt must have stopped the bleeding which meant it wasn't too bad.

Joe reached across and pulled the gag from Chuck's mouth before he yanked down Herm's gag.

Then he laid his hand on his shoulder and loudly said, "Herm! Wake up! It's Joe. What happened?"

Chuck's eyes popped open immediately and Herm drowsily opened his own eyes before Chuck exclaimed, "Joe! I thought you were those bastards comin' back to finish us off!"

Joe ripped open Herm's shirt and asked, "What happened?"

Chuck snapped, *"Can't you cut these damned ropes first, Joe?"*

"Just a second. I need to look at Herm's wound."

After spreading the bloody cloth away from his arm, the wound began to ooze blood again, but it wasn't too bad. The bullet had passed through the back edge of his bicep but would need to be cleaned and sutured.

Joe stood and said, "I'll be right back," then clambered up the five-foot-high wall and pulled a towel from his left saddlebag then grabbed his canteen.

When he returned, he set the towel on Herm's stomach and left the canteen on the ground before pulling his knife. He sliced Chuck's bonds first and as he sat and began rubbing his wrists, Joe cut the ropes tied around Herm's ankles and wrists. He then used the knife to slice Herm's left shirt sleeve before he slid the blade back into its sheath.

As Joe slid the sleeve from Herm's arm, Chuck growled, "We didn't even see those bastards! They were hidin' behind those boulders up yonder and when we were close, all four of 'em opened fire with their pistols. Herm was hit and fell outta his saddle, and I had to get to the ground myself. I didn't have time to draw my pistol before they had us surrounded. I figgered they were gonna just kill us and two of 'em wanted to do it, too. But the tall feller said that they had what they wanted and to just tie us up. The last one just giggled like a girl but never said a word. The fellers who wanted to shoot us weren't happy about it, but I reckon they were afraid of the big guy. After they walked us to the gully and tied us up and gagged us, one of 'em said that if we died, it wasn't their fault."

Joe wrapped the towel around Herm's wound and asked, "How long ago did they head off?"

"About an hour or so."

Joe nodded then used some of the cut rope to keep the towel in place before asking, "Can you walk, Herm?"

Herm slowly sat up and after a few seconds, he replied, "I reckon so. I just ain't sure how long I can keep goin'."

"That's alright. Chuck, I'll let you have my pistol. When you start back, as soon as you see the wagons, fire a few shots and I'm sure Bo will send somebody to help you."

Chuck sharply asked, "You ain't gonna go after them, are ya? The sun's gonna set before you could catch up to 'em and you'll lose their trail."

"Maybe. But when you get back, have somebody tell Faith that I'll keep my promise."

"What promise?"

Joe smiled as he said, "She'll know. Now let's get you out of this gully."

After Chuck and Herm were slowly walking east along the ruts, Joe began following the trail left by the four horse thieves. They soon crossed the ruts and must have picked up a pack animal before they headed northwest into the open ground. After they'd traveled for about a half a mile, they turned west. Joe wasn't worried about losing their trail after sunset, so after they kept their westward path for more than a mile, he focused most of his attention on the western horizon. He didn't expect to see them silhouetted against the red sky but wanted to study the lay of the land ahead. While he suspected that they didn't expect to be followed yet, he wasn't about to be ambushed. He had a promise to keep.

His only real concern was that they might hear the gunshots when Chuck fired his pistol. He was less concerned when just a few minutes later, he heard the faint echo of three gunshots. Even in the hushed silence of the night, by the time those sounds traveled another mile, they'd be nothing more than a whisper.

―――

Bo was standing a few yards in front of his wagon looking into the late evening sky. Becky and Marigold were standing beside him peering into the growing darkness when they saw three distant flashes then a couple of seconds later, the subdued reports reached their ears.

Becky quickly asked, "Is that them?"

Bo replied, "I'm sure it is, Becky. I don't think they're ridin', though. They might need some help, so let's ride out there."

Marigold said, "Why didn't Joe let them ride back with him?"

As they headed back to the wagons, Bo said, "I ain't got a clue, Marigold."

Bo had saddled Ranger and Becky and Marigold hadn't unsaddled their mules, so just five minutes after hearing the gunshots, they rode away to meet Chuck and Herm.

Faith and Mary were roasting the turkey after cutting it into smaller pieces. They had also dumped the chopped gizzards into a pot and added rice water and salt before setting it on the fire.

After Bo had told her that Joe had gone to look for Chuck and Herm, Faith hoped that he'd be back before long. Unlike Joe, she suspected that Chuck had convinced Herm to ride all the way to Idaho City. But after ninety minutes without seeing Joe, she changed her mind. And even though Bo had told her that Joe said he would keep his promise, she was still worried.

Just a few minutes later, she heard the distant gunshots and looked west before she asked, "Who do you think took those shots, Will?"

Will was looking in that direction as well as he replied, "I ain't sure. But Bo, Marigold and Becky were waiting out front, so I'll go find out what they saw."

"I'll come with you."

Will nodded before he and Faith hurried toward the front of the line. Just before they reached the flatbed, they saw Bo untying Ranger while Marigold and Becky were mounting their mules.

Bo mounted then spotted them and said, "I think Chuck and Herm are on foot and need some help. We're ridin' out to meet 'em."

Will quickly asked, "Do you want me to come along?"

"No. I need you to take charge until I get back."

Will nodded before Bo, Marigold and Becky rode off.

Faith watched them disappear into the growing darkness before she asked, "Why do you think they're on foot, Will?"

"I reckon we'll have to wait until they get back to find out. Do you want to wait here or go back and help Mary?"

"You stay and wait, but I'll go tell Mary what we know so far."

IDAHO CITY

Will said, "Okay," before Faith hurried away.

As he stared into the dark, Will suspected that Chuck and Herm had been ambushed by men who were heading to Idaho City's gold fields. He hoped that neither of them had been shot but was surprised that Joe wasn't with them. He couldn't imagine that Joe would try to chase them down in the dark even knowing that he'd rescued Mary much later in the night. But back then, he'd only had to deal with one distracted deserter but now would probably face four or more desperate men. He wished Joe had returned and asked him to join him, but it was too late now. He hoped Joe gave up the chase and returned, then he and Joe could hunt them down tomorrow.

Herm was sitting on the ground when Chuck exclaimed, "Here they come!"

Herm raised his eyes and saw three riders in the dim light of the crescent moon. He smiled when he noticed that two of them were wearing dresses then slowly got to his feet. He checked the towel bandage and found that the dark blood stain hadn't gotten any larger than it had been the last time he checked. He still felt the effects of his blood loss and hoped he didn't fall on his face when Becky arrived.

Just before they pulled up, Becky saw the towel wrapped around Herm's arm and knew he'd been shot. As soon as her mule stopped, she hurriedly dismounted and rushed to Herm.

When Bo and Marigold stepped down, Bo asked, "What happened, Chuck?"

As Chuck explained how they'd been ambushed, Becky took her husband's hands and asked, "How bad is it, Herm?"

"Joe said it wasn't too bad before he washed it and wrapped it up."

"Can you get onto my mule?"

"I think so."

Becky didn't bother listening to Chuck's explanation as she guided Herm to her mule and helped him into the saddle. Once he was sitting, she pulled his boot from her left stirrup, then awkwardly mounted behind him. She waited for Chuck and Marigold to mount then after Bo stepped into his saddle, they started back to the wagons at a slow pace.

Now that they were moving, Becky asked, "Can you tell me what happened now, Herm?"

Herm replied, "Okay. I guess it's our own fault 'cause we were talkin' and not payin' attention. We were surprised by four men who…"

―――

The sun was gone, and the moon wasn't providing much light, but Joe still hadn't seen any sign of the four men and was beginning to wonder if he'd lost them. He pulled up and dismounted but held onto Duke's reins because he didn't want to be left afoot again. He headed south and after he'd walked a hundred and fifty-four steps, he spotted their tracks. They had changed direction to the southwest, and he would never have found them if he'd continued following their earlier trail.

He mounted Duke and started him at a medium trot heading back toward the ruts. He rode for another thirty minutes before he spotted a distant light that had to be their campfire. He estimated it was a couple of miles ahead, so when he began his approach, he had Duke moving at a slower pace.

As he drew closer to the fire, he shifted more to the west and soon understood why they felt secure enough to build a campfire. Their camp was next to a stream that cut between two low hills. Even If someone left the wagon train in the night to hunt for them, they wouldn't see the fire until it was too late. The wind was blowing from the northwest, so any searchers wouldn't smell the smoke either. He wouldn't have seen the fire either if he'd missed their turn. It was just a matter of good luck that he'd caught it, but it would be bad luck for them.

He kept his focus on the fire as Duke carried him closer. He didn't want to shoot them but planned on taking back Cheese and Willy as well as two of their horses. They hadn't seemed to care that Chuck and Herm might have died, so he wouldn't feel bad about making them ride double. He'd have to approach them on foot, so their horses wouldn't alert them to Duke's presence. To avoid that risk, he shifted Duke further to the east. After he rode for another five minutes, the campfire suddenly disappeared. He knew that they hadn't extinguished it that quickly, so the eastern hill must have blocked his view.

He slowed Duke to a walk until he spotted a stubby pine and pulled up. He dismounted, tied Duke's reins tightly to the small tree and pulled his Henry from its scabbard. After patting Duke on his neck, Joe levered in a live round then started walking towards the hill. It was less than thirty feet above the level ground but if he was able to get to the top without being spotted, he'd be looking down at them from about fifty yards. With any luck, they'd already be snoring in their bedrolls. But that late change in direction which was obviously designed to lose any pursuers meant that they weren't stupid. They were shrewd thieves and probably set up a watch.

Before he reached the hill, he heard a deep voice say something followed by loud laughter. After his recent positive appraisal of their skills, he was surprised that they were so relaxed. It sounded as if they were having a small party. The celebration continued as Joe began slowly climbing the hill. He didn't think they'd notice if he knocked a rock loose but didn't want to take the risk.

As he ascended, he heard one of them exclaim, "I don't believe we got two Henrys and two Spencers from those boys!"

A high-pitch voice giggled then said, "I can't wait to try my Spencer."

Then a third man growled, "We shoulda killed 'em, Hack."

IDAHO CITY

Hack quickly snapped, "I told ya, Rat. If we murdered 'em, they'd all come after us."

"They're probably gonna die anyway, Hack. They ain't got any water and one of 'em is gonna bleed out even if they do find 'em."

Hack replied, "If they do, it ain't gonna be by our hands. It'll be their fault for not findin' em."

Rat said, "We still shoulda cleaned up our tracks after we tied 'em up. A blind man could follow our footprints to that gully."

Joe was close to the top of the hill when a new voice said, "I agree with Rat, Hack. I reckon those folks will find 'em and come after us even if they're both still alive."

Hack's frustration was obvious when he exclaimed, "Shut up, Lou! I reckon they ain't gonna send anybody after us even if they're madder'n hell. We took those two with just our pistols, but now we got four repeaters."

Joe couldn't hear anyone argue with Hack, but imagined they were at least grumbling. When he reached the crest, he removed his hat and set it down before he dropped to his knees and began crawling. When he saw the six horses and a pack mule tied to a hitch rope about thirty yards to his left, he noticed that they were all saddled, and the pack mule was still loaded down. Seconds later, he spotted the first two men sitting on the west side of the campfire. He kept crawling until the other two appeared then moved slowly forward until he had a clear line of fire and laid on his belly.

Each of them was sitting and quietly admiring his new repeater. He remembered that Chuck had said the tall one seemed to be in charge, so he assumed the biggest man was Hack. He had a Henry, so he assigned the second Henry to Rat. The unnamed giggler had a Spencer, so he figured Lou had the second. It probably didn't matter who they were, but Joe wanted to give names to the men he may have to kill.

There were four bedrolls already stretched out behind each of them, so Joe decided to wait until they were asleep. He hoped they'd slide the rifles into their scabbards on their horses before they made use of their bedrolls. Once they were asleep, he'd just sneak around the back of the hill, untie their hitch rope and lead all six horses out of their camp. He'd release two of them after he returned to Duke.

That was how Joe wanted it to happen but realized it was just wishful thinking when he heard Hack say, "Pete, you take first watch. Wake up Lou when the moon gets to the top of the sky."

In his girlish voice, Pete replied, "Okay, Hack," then began to stand.

Joe couldn't afford to let Pete out of his sight, so he shouted, "Hold it right there!"

All of them quickly turned to look at the hill as Joe yelled, "I have my Henry cocked and ready to fire! I won't shoot unless

IDAHO CITY

you go for your guns! Just set your rifles on the ground and stand up!"

None of them even twitched before Hack shouted, "Who are you and why are you tryin' to rob us?"

Joe yelled back, "I'm not trying to rob you. My name's Joe Beck and I'm another scout from the wagon train. I found my two friends you ambushed and sent them back. Now, I'm willing to forget that you shot one of my friends if you just leave their guns on the ground then mount your own horses and ride away."

Hack loudly replied, "I don't know what you're talkin' about, mister. We're just on our way to Idaho City to do some prospectin'."

"I'm sure you're telling the truth about your intentions, but you were less than honest when you said you didn't know what I'm talking about. I heard you talking about what you did, and I'll give you some credit for keeping Rat from killing my friends. If I'd found them dead, we wouldn't be having this conversation. Now set the rifles on the ground and before you leave, I want each of you one at a time to pop off all of the percussion caps on your pistol."

Rat glanced at Hack and winked before Hack shouted, "Okay. I'll go first."

Joe was surprised that they'd given in but said, "Alright. Go ahead."

Hack shot a quick glance to Rat and barely nodded before he slowly removed his pistol.

Joe had seen Rat's glance but not the wink, but he noticed Hack's hat dip slightly when he'd taken that brief look at Rat. As Hack began to remove his pistol, Joe set his sights on the big man's chest. He was about Joe's height but probably outweighed him by forty pounds.

Hack fully cocked his hammer knowing that the scout wouldn't notice the difference between its firing position and the half-cocked position that released the cylinder. He turned the pistol on its side as if he was removing the first percussion cap when he suddenly sidestepped to his right, pointed his muzzle at the top of the hill and fired.

Joe heard the bullet ricochet off some rocks to his left as he swung his Henry's sights a couple of inches to his left and squeezed the trigger. He was levering in a new round when Hack collapsed, and the others began grabbing their repeaters.

Joe knew each of them would have to work the lever, but the two Spencer shooters would have to cock the hammer manually, so he moved his sights to Rat who was bringing a live round into the Henry's chamber. Just as Rat prepared to shoot, Joe fired.

By the time Rat fell onto his back, the other two had their Spencers ready and giggling Pete quickly fired. Joe knew he wasn't even close when he'd seen the Spencer pointing to his left, so he picked Lou as his next target even as Pete's .56 caliber missile passed overhead. Lou was more patient and had been waiting for Joe to fire at Pete, so he could shoot at the scout's muzzle flash. But when Pete began working his Spencer's lever, Lou realized that Pete wasn't the scout's next target. That revelation was his last thought before he saw the muzzle flash and felt Joe's .44 slam into his chest. The bullet only cracked one rib before it punctured his aortic arch, filling his chest cavity with blood. As his blood pressure dropped to zero, Lou fell to his knees and slowly tilted forward until his nose rammed into the ground.

Pete was about to cock his hammer for the second time when he saw Lou fall. He looked to the top of the hill before he tossed the Spencer away, threw his hands into the air and shouted, "Don't shoot! I give up!"

Joe yelled, "Take out your pistol and drop it onto your friend's back!"

Pete slowly lowered his right hand, lifted his Colt from its holster and gingerly let it fall onto Rat's back before he raised it back over his head.

Joe stood, lowered his Henry's muzzle then bent at the knees and snatched his hat from the ground. After pulling it on, he began to slowly descend the hill. He closely watched Pete as he stepped down but glanced at the other three just in case that any of them were playing possum. He didn't think Lou would fall onto his face unless he was dead and was reasonably sure he'd hit the other two in the chest, but he still kept them in sight.

By the time he reached level ground, Pete had his eyes closed and Joe hoped he didn't pee his pants, so he said, "You can open your eyes and lower your hands. I'm not going to shoot you, Pete."

Pete's eyelids opened just a crack until he saw Joe then lowered his hands.

After he fully opened his eyes, he asked, "How'd you know my name?"

"I told you that I heard you talking. I've got to get back to the wagons, so which of those horses is yours?"

Pete pointed to a dark brown gelding and said, "The bay. Are you gonna let me go?"

"I'll let you leave with your horse and the pack mule, but I'm taking Hack and Rat's horses as payment for what they did to my friends. You can take the other horse, too. So, let's head over there and I'll get them tied to a trail line."

"Okay. But, um, what are you gonna do with the bodies?"

As they began walking to the horses, Joe replied, "They're your friends, so you can bury them or leave them for the scavengers. It's up to you."

"But I ain't got a shovel."

"Then it would be hard to prospect for gold when you got to Idaho City, wouldn't it?"

"We were gonna…never mind."

Joe suspected that they planned to sell Cheese and Willy then buy what they needed but didn't say anything. He glanced at the pack mule and was surprised that it didn't have any tools whatsoever strapped to the packs.

When they reached the horses, Joe asked, "Which one belonged to Lou?"

"The black mare. Rat has the sorrel gelding and Hack rides the gray gelding."

Joe nodded then as he released Cheese, he asked, "Why did you boys come east? I imagine there would be more pickings on the road used by the stagecoach and freight wagons."

"We were out there and were gonna rob three freighters, but they all had shotguns and we were lucky to get out of there alive. One of 'em had a rifle and began takin' shots at us, so we kept ridin' 'til we figgered we were outta range. Then we kept goin' and set up camp when we were sure we were safe. We waited all mornin' because we didn't want those freighters to see us again when we spotted two riders comin' from the east, and Hack said it was our lucky day."

"I reckon so, but it wasn't a lucky night for him, was it?"

"I guess not."

Joe set up a trail rope for Cheese, attached the black mare, then added Willy and the sorrel before he and Pete headed back to the campfire.

He slid Hack's unfired Henry and a Spencer into Herm's scabbard and the other Henry and Spencer into Chuck's before he asked, "Where are my friends' pistols?"

"They're in their saddlebags. You can check if you've got a mind to."

"That's alright. You can have the rest. Maybe you can sell everything and buy a claim for yourself. But if I get back and those two gunbelts aren't there, then I'll come back to find you."

"I reckon you can do it, too. How old are you anyway?"

"I'll turn seventeen in February."

Pete's eyed grew wide as he exclaimed, "You're just a kid!"

Joe nodded then said, "Yup," before he led the four horses around the bodies leaving Pete to decide what to do with them.

He still held his Henry in his right hand as he headed for Duke. He wasn't surprised that Hack had decided to shoot it out rather than give up his horse and maybe he shouldn't have made the demand. But one of them had shot Herm, and Rat and Lou wanted to kill both of them, so Joe didn't feel guilty for what happened. He didn't believe that Pete was the one who'd shot Herm but didn't want to know.

When he reached Duke, he slid his Henry into his scabbard, secured the trail rope to his saddle, then untied his reins and mounted his stallion.

Once underway, he angled to the southeast to find the ruts. He knew it was around midnight but expected to return within three hours. It might be much sooner as he wouldn't be taking the same looping path that he'd used when he was following the bushwhackers.

He hoped that Chuck and Herm had been picked up and Becky was already nursing Herm's wound. He assumed that Mrs. Witherspoon would do the suturing as she had been a midwife for years.

He soon found the ruts and picked up the pace. After stopping at a stream to water the horses, he kept riding next to the ruts.

Becky asked, "Do you think it's going to get infected, Mama?"

Doris smiled at her daughter as she replied, "I don't think so, sweetheart. Joe washed it before he bandaged it and I doused it with moonshine before I closed the wound. It's still possible, but not likely. The bullet passed right through the back of his bicep, so there won't be any cloth inside."

Becky sighed then looked at her sleeping husband before she said, "This will keep him from riding with Chuck when he takes that road to Idaho City, won't it?"

"I'm sure it will. Are you going to try to convince him not to go?"

"Maybe. But I think Joe would have a better chance, especially after he just saved them both."

Doris nodded then quietly said, "I wonder if Joe caught up with those four evil men. If he did, I hope he didn't get shot trying to take back their horses."

Becky smiled as she said, "He promised Faith that he would always return to her and would do his best to avoid being shot again."

"Those are two promises I hope he keeps. Now let's get some sleep. It's well after midnight and you need to rest more than I do."

"Okay, Mama."

―――

When Joe spotted the boulders that had served as the ambush site, he knew he was just about an hour from the wagons. For the first time since they'd been married, Joe wished that he didn't see Faith waiting for him and hoped she was asleep.

IDAHO CITY

As tired as he was, he knew that Duke was close to exhaustion. He'd been moving almost constantly for more than twenty hours, so Joe kept him at a walk. When he went out again, he'd ride Bessie and let Bernie carry her packs now that Laddie rode in Mary's wagon or walked when Faith did.

It seemed like just a few minutes had passed when he first saw the wagons but suspected that he'd just lost track of time. He was relieved when he didn't see Faith waiting in front of Bo's wagon. He'd drop off the horses then unsaddle Duke and try to get some sleep before sunrise.

Before he reached the wagons, he pulled up, dismounted, then led the five horses to Bo's wagon. After he passed the driver's seat, he walked to Willy and detached him and the gray gelding and tied their reins to the wagon's front right wheel. Then he led Duke, Cheese and the black mare to the Witherspoons' wagon and untied Cheese and knotted his reins to their wagon's right front wheel.

He stopped at the back of the wagon, patted Bessie on her shoulder and whispered, "I'll give you some exercise in the morning, ma'am," then led Duke to the back of the line.

He was going to leave Duke behind Mary's wagon but thought he might disturb Faith. So, he continued to the last wagon then led Duke around the other side and headed north for thirty steps before turning to walk parallel to the wagons until he reached the Boones' wagon. He tied Duke's reins to a scraggly bush then began unsaddling the stallion. By the time he finished, Joe was close to exhaustion. He untied his bedroll and spread it on the ground before taking off his hat and lying down. Sleep overtook him just seconds later.

CHAPTER 2

Joe felt the earth shake and thought he was experiencing his first earthquake until his brain returned to the conscious world and he heard, "Joe! Wake up, Joe!"

He slowly opened his eyes and blinked before he saw Bo standing over him and mumbled, "I'm awake, I'm awake," then slowly sat up.

He yawned and looked up as Bo asked, "What happened? When did you get back?"

Joe replied, "Give me a minute," then pushed himself to his feet and looked at the wagons before turning around and unbuttoning his britches.

After watering the prairie grass, he fastened his buttons then turned to face Bo and said, "I caught up with them late last night. They had set up their camp between two low hills, so I climbed one of them. Before I even reached the top, I heard them talking about their new repeaters and arguing about what they should have done. Two of them had wanted to kill Chuck and Herm, but their boss didn't. Anyway, I got into position with my Henry and shouted a warning then told them that I just wanted to retrieve what they'd stolen.

"Then I made a mistake. I didn't want to take their pistols, so I told them to remove all of their percussion caps. I knew their leader was named Hack and his number two man was called Rat. When Hack pulled his pistol, he and Rat glanced at each other and I realized they weren't going to give up, so I aimed at Hack. He had his pistol pointed in my direction and pretended to be removing the first percussion cap when he sidestepped and fired. His shot was a lot closer than I expected, but I fired before he could take his second. Then the other three grabbed Chuck and Herm's repeaters. They got off some shots, but I put two of them down when the last one, a guy named Pete, dropped his Spencer and threw up his hands.

"After that, I gathered Cheese and Willy, took two more of their horses for what they did to Chuck and Herm, then I picked up their Henrys and Spencers. I let Pete decide what to do with their bodies, but if he left them there, I'll see the buzzards later this morning. The two hills were about a half a mile north of the ruts, but I don't think the wagons will get there until tomorrow."

Bo asked, "Why did they ambush Chuck and Herm?"

"They were heading for Idaho City and tried to rob three freight wagons but were scared off when the freighters opened up with their shotguns. They headed east and were staying put until they were sure the freighters were gone when they spotted Chuck and Herm then set up behind some boulders."

"I reckon Chuck and Herm were too busy talkin' to be lookin' for an ambush."

"That's what they told me before I left. I reckon Chuck told you where I found them."

"Yup. He said that if you didn't show up when you did, it was likely that Herm mighta died."

"I don't think he would have bled out. His bleeding was just a leaking ooze when I patched him up. How is he doing?"

"Doris Witherspoon sewed him up, but I haven't checked on him this mornin'. We waited 'til midnight then I ordered Faith to get some sleep before she collapsed, so I reckon she's anxious to see ya."

Joe nodded as he said, "I'll head over to Mary's wagon in a minute. Herm's going to be laid up for a while and Chuck is probably sore, so I'll ride out front today. I'll probably reach those hills before noon, so I'll bring my shovel along just in case."

Bo grimaced before saying, "I really hate to do this to ya, Joe. You gotta be pretty tired yourself."

Joe grinned then said, "I'm still a kid, Bo. We don't get tired."

Then he swatted Bo on his shoulder, snatched his hat from the ground and trotted to Mary's wagon. The sun hadn't appeared yet, so he wasn't sure Faith was awake. But he hoped that either Will or Mary was up and moving.

Before he reached the wagon, Will emerged from the front of the wagon and stepped onto the driver's seat. When he spotted Joe, he waved him over then turned and took something from the wagon.

Joe angled to the front of the wagon and watched Will climb down.

When Joe stopped before him, Will said, "Faith is still sleeping, and Mary told me to be quiet."

"That's alright. Faith needs her sleep."

Will handed Joe the oddly shaped cloth-wrapped item and said, "When Faith returned last night, she wrapped this and planned to give it to you when she woke up."

Joe unfolded the cloth and smiled when he found a turkey drumstick.

He took the drumstick then gave the cloth back to Will and said, "I'm pretty hungry, so I'll have my breakfast while I walk to the Witherspoons' wagon to check on Herm and pick up Bessie."

Before Joe could take his first bite, Will asked, "Who is gonna ride out front this morning?"

"I am. I'll be back in a little while, but don't wake up Faith."

Will seemed as if he was about to ask another question but after a brief hesitation, he simply said, "I won't."

IDAHO CITY

Joe nodded, sank his teeth into the turkey leg then began walking and chewing at the same time.

When Abe Witherspoon saw Joe heading towards him, he set his teams' reins on the ground then stepped a few feet away from the wagon before he stopped.

Joe's drumstick was half-naked when he reached Abe and asked, "How's Herm doing, Mister Witherspoon?"

"Doris sewed his wound last night and said you did a good job cleaning it before you bandaged it with that towel. She thinks he'll be all right in a few weeks. When I left the wagon, I noticed that Cheese had a mare tied to his saddle. Why did you leave her here?"

"I had to shoot three of the four bushwhackers. One surrendered, so I let him have his horse, one of the others and their pack mule. I took two horses from the men who ambushed Herm and Chuck because I felt they were owed some form of compensation for what those bushwhackers did. I gave a gray gelding to Chuck, but I thought Herm would like to give the mare to Becky. She's a pretty gal and looks a lot like Faith's Duchess."

Abe smiled as he said, "I'm sure Herm will want Becky to have her. Thank you for the mare and even more for rescuing Herm. Will you be able to talk to him about Idaho City when you get a chance?"

"I'll be riding out front today, so I'll visit him after I return."

"I hope you can talk some sense into him, Joe. We'd prefer to stay with the wagon train but don't want to leave Becky, either. We thought we'd never be grandparents and want to meet our grandchild."

Joe nodded then said, "I need to take Bessie with me because Duke had a long day. I'll be as quiet as possible because I know how tired Becky and your wife must be."

"Do you need any help, Joe?"

Joe replied, "No, sir. But thanks for the offer," then turned and walked to the back of the wagon.

He stopped when he was next to Bessie then held the drumstick with his teeth as he untied her from the wagon's handhold. After she was free, he tied Betty to the handhold then led Bessie to the front of the line.

When he reached Bo's flatbed, he temporarily tied Bessie to the rear wheel then quickly stripped the remaining meat from the drumstick. He was still chewing when he tossed the bone into the grass then began removing her packs and setting them on the wagon's bed.

He had moved three of the four packs when Bo stepped close, handed him his pistol, and said, "Chuck said to give this back to you."

As Joe holstered his Colt, Bo asked, "Is Herm awake yet?"

IDAHO CITY

Joe was releasing the pack saddle's cinches when he replied, "Nope. Neither are Becky or Mrs. Witherspoon. I talked to Mister Witherspoon, and he told me that his wife thinks Herm will be back to normal in a month or so."

"That's a relief. Are you gonna leave those packs here until you get back?"

"If that's alright with you."

"I got room for 'em now. I hope to fill it up when we get to Fort Hall. It's been providin' supplies to settlers for a long time. And now it's the last stop for all those folks headin' to Idaho City, so it should have everything we need to get to Oregon."

Joe pulled the pack saddle from Bessie then set it on the flatbed before he said, "I wonder how many will keep going to Oregon after we pass that turnoff to Idaho City."

"Your guess is as good as mine. We could lose as many as six or seven families. And that doesn't include Chuck and Marigold. Maybe gettin' shot will keep Herm from leavin'."

"Maybe. I guess all we can do is see what happens when we reach that intersection."

"That's the truth."

Joe slid Bessie's saddle blanket from her back, rolled it up and set it next to the pack saddle. He untied her reins then nodded to Bo and after stopping to take the shovel from Nellie, he led the first horse he'd ever owned back to Mary's wagon.

The sun drenched the landscape with light before he reached Mary's wagon, but he still didn't see Faith. He wasn't about to disturb her much-needed sleep, so he angled towards Duke. After tying Bessie's reins to the same bush, Joe tossed his saddle blanket over her back then lifted his saddle from the ground and set it in place. He had just hung the Spencer on his saddle when he saw Faith slide down from the Boones' tailgate. He smiled, pulled off his hat and waved it three times before yanking it back on.

Faith smiled and waved back as she hurried through the tall, dry prairie grass.

Joe stopped preparing Bessie and took two steps towards Faith, and as soon as she reached him, he scooped her into his arms and kissed her.

After he set her down, Faith asked, "Why didn't you wake me when you returned?"

"It must have been around three o'clock in the morning when I got back, and you needed the sleep."

She glanced at Bessie before asking, "Are you going out today after just three hours' sleep?"

"Herm is laid up and Chuck is still recovering from being bound and gagged. I'll be fine."

IDAHO CITY

"At least you didn't get shot. What happened after you found Chuck and Herm?"

"I followed their trail for a while, then I..."

Faith listened intently as Joe told the story for the second time that morning and tried to visualize each scene as he spoke.

When he finished, she said, "I'm glad that you gave Becky a mare that looks like Duchess, but I think you should have given both of the horses to Herm. If Chuck hadn't been so busy trying to sell Idaho City to Herm, they probably wouldn't have been ambushed. Chuck should have been the one who had been wounded, not Herm."

"I agree that it was mainly Chuck's fault for the inattention that let them get ambushed. But Herm could have ignored Chuck, so he wasn't blameless. If I'd given both horses to Herm, then Herm would probably feel bad. Chuck would be mad at me too, and it would only make the situation worse."

Faith sighed then said, "I suppose so."

Joe smiled as he said, "Thank you for the drumstick. It was a very nice breakfast."

"I saved you the wings too, so I'll pack them with one of your pickles for your lunch."

"That'll be even better. How did you cook that big bird? It must have taken hours."

"Mary and I cut it into pieces first. I made a turkey and rice stew with some of it, and we roasted the big pieces. Laddie was very happy when I gave him his share."

Joe glanced at Mary's wagon then asked, "Where is Laddie?"

"I told him to stay, but I'm not sure if it was necessary. If he'd tried to follow me, he would have had to shake John and Alfred loose first."

Joe grinned as he said, "I'll finish saddling Bessie then I'll bring her and Duke to the wagon and tie Duke next to Duchess. He needs an easy day."

"So, do you, Mister Beck."

"Maybe I do, but I won't get one for a while."

"I'll wait while you finish getting Bessie ready."

He hung the Henry on the saddle then secured the shovel on top of his bedroll before untying the two horses' reins.

As they started back to Mary's wagons, Faith said, "Please come back before sunset this time, Joe."

Joe smiled as he replied, "I promise."

When they reached Mary's wagon, Faith said, "Wait until I get your lunch."

IDAHO CITY

Joe was tying Duke's reins to the wagon as he replied, "Yes, ma'am."

Mary materialized from the back of the wagon, handed Faith a leather pouch then said, "Good morning, Joe."

"Good morning, Mary. How are the boys this morning?"

"They're all happy because Laddie didn't leave with Faith. I was surprised that Bo asked you to ride out front after you got back so late."

"It should be a boring day, so maybe I'll saddle nap."

Faith slid the pouch into Joe's left saddlebag before saying, "If you start dozing off, you'd better pull up, so you don't fall out of the saddle."

Joe was grinning as he mounted and said, "Duke might not care if I toppled over, but Bessie is a good girl and wouldn't let that happen, Faith."

Laddie stepped to the tailgate and barked making Faith laugh before she rubbed his head then turned and said, "I guess he's scolding me for abandoning him for a male of my own species."

Joe smiled as he said, "I hope he doesn't get so jealous that he marks my face while I'm sleeping," then he waved and walked Bessie behind Duke and Duchess before turning west.

As he passed the wagons, he saw Marigold talking to Bo, but neither looked at him, so he picked up Bessie's pace and soon left them behind. It felt odd to be riding Bessie again after becoming accustomed to Duke. He knew she was only four inches shorter than Duke, but it felt much lower. Bessie did have a smoother gait, and he could trust her not to run off when he really needed her.

With the sun at his back, he had a good view and knew that soon, the northern horizon would lose its grass and be replaced with volcanic soil and lava beds. The ruts would hug the mountains where there was water, grass and trees until they reached Fort Hall and crossed the Snake River. Then they would spend three days crossing the barren land before they reached more mountains, and two days later, they'd arrive at the junction with the road that led to Idaho City.

After Faith told him who Marigold believed were going to take that road, he wondered how accurate that information was. Bo seemed to think that as many as six or seven families would make the turn north, so maybe Marigold was right. He could understand Arv's decision to head to the growing town, and the Smiths would want to stay with Marigold. The Carlisles would join them because Beth Carlisle had married Russ Smith, and if the Stanburys left, he suspected that the Dooleys would probably join them rather than leave Jenny. The links between the families which had been forged on the long journey meant that Bo might have underestimated the number of wagons that would head north rather than continue west to Oregon.

Joe imagined that over the next few days, there would be a lot of meetings and discussions among the families and some of them would invariably become arguments that might lead to serious fights. But it would be up to Bo to keep the peace if things became ugly.

As Bessie carried him westward, Joe shifted his train of thought to the job that he might have to do in another couple of hours. He didn't see any circling buzzards yet, so maybe Pete had at least covered his friends' bodies. The other possibility was that some large predators had arrived from the forests near the mountains and dragged the carcasses away. But that wasn't likely. If bears, cougars, wolves or coyotes arrived, they wouldn't waste time by moving the bodies before having a feast.

Less than hour later, Joe saw the buzzards circling in the distance. He didn't blame Pete for not burying the bodies as he probably wanted to get as far away as possible as quickly as he could. He wasn't going to dig a deep hole but just one that was big enough to hide all three bodies.

But before he even dismounted, he'd ride around the western hill to be sure that Pete had run away and hadn't decided to ambush him. He knew it was highly unlikely as none of them had been carrying a rifle, which he thought was odd. If Pete wanted to ambush him from the top of the hill with a pistol, it would be an almost impossible shot. But Joe wasn't about to follow Chuck and Herm's example.

Shortly after spotting the vultures, the first hill rose above the horizon. He still scanned in all directions, including his backtrail but focused mainly on the hills. When the hills were fully revealed, he didn't see any large predators but suspected they might already be having breakfast. He wouldn't reach the first hill for another twenty minutes but pulled his Henry and reminded himself that it still needed to be cleaned.

A few minutes later, he angled to the northwest towards the hills then spotted a pair of coyotes as they backed out from the narrow valley between the hills. They didn't notice him yet as they stared at whatever larger scavenger had forced them out.

Joe slowed Bessie when they were about a thousand yards out and just seconds later, his mare tossed her head and whickered.

Joe returned his Henry to its scabbard then patted Bessie on her neck and softly said, "It's alright, Bessie," then pulled out his Spencer.

If some critter had been fearsome enough to scare away the coyotes, Joe might need the Spencer's heavier and more powerful round.

With the wind still blowing from the northwest, Joe approached the southern side of first hill to stay downwind of whatever scavengers he might find. He'd give the coyotes a fair amount of space, too.

The pair of coyotes finally realized he was there when he was around four hundred yards away but didn't run off. Instead, one bared his teeth and snarled while the other yapped.

Bessie twitched but didn't slow or change direction as Joe focused on the coyotes. As more of the valley came into view, he spotted a large black bear staring at the coyotes while its front paws pressed down on Hack's body. Then he saw a second, smaller bear still ripping apart Rat's body. Lou's carcass had been partly scavenged but was currently unoccupied. A few seconds later, he saw some buzzards strutting a few yards away from Lou's body patiently waiting for the four-footed scavengers to leave.

Bessie continued carrying him closer but was becoming more agitated, so Joe let her slide further to the left which seemed to calm her down somewhat. When he was about two hundred yards away from the coyotes, he cocked the Spencer's hammer and pulled Bessie to a stop. He hoped that he would be able to frighten all of the scavengers away as he set his sights on the ground just in front of the snarling coyote and squeezed the trigger.

Just a fraction of a second later, the loud report echoed across the ground and the .56 caliber slug of lead slammed into the soil spraying the coyotes with dirt. As Joe worked the Spencer's lever to bring a live round into the chamber, the coyotes sprinted away, heading south to the protection of the distant trees. Both black bears rose to their hind legs for a few seconds before dropping down and roaring in an attempt to frighten the new challenger.

Joe waited until the coyotes were almost a half a mile away before nudging Bessie into a walk again. He didn't cock the Spencer's hammer yet as he watched the two bears continue to growl and expose their array of sharp teeth. He knew that they couldn't be scared off so easily but hoped the sow would leave after he killed her enormous mate.

The bears' warning growls and roars grew louder as he continued to approach them, and Joe began to worry that Bessie might bolt, so he pulled her to a stop again and cocked his hammer. The large bear was over a hundred yards away, and he wasn't sure that the Spencer had enough power to stop the bear at that range with just one shot. He should have enough time to take a second or even a third if the wounded bear or his mate charged, but Bessie might be terrified at the sight, so Joe decided to dismount.

He kept his eyes on the bears as he slowly stepped down. He let the reins drop and wasn't surprised when Bessie trotted away. He had six more shots and the five in his Colt if things got that bad.

As he began walking toward the bears, the smell of the exposed flesh made his stomach flip, but he was able to keep his drumstick breakfast where it belonged. It should all be digested by now anyway.

The bears stood again and spread their paws wide as they bellowed, but Joe continued his slow approach. He had just stopped and brought the Spencer into a firing position when the male dropped to all fours and charged. Joe quickly aimed at his large head then steadied the sights for just a second before he fired.

The bullet missed the bear's head because of its loping charge and passed below his chin before it punched into his massive chest. The boar stumbled but soon regained his footing as Joe levered in a fresh round and cocked the Spencer's hammer. The bear was just twenty yards away when Joe fired his second shot. This time, the heavy slug slammed into the back of the bear's open mouth and severed his spinal cord where it attached to the brain. The five-hundred-pound monster collapsed to the ground and slid another six feet before coming to a stop.

Joe quickly worked the lever then cocked the hammer again when he saw the sow leave Rat's body and race towards him. She wasn't moving as fast as the boar but was already less than fifty yards away. He steadied the sights on her mouth, but this time he made allowances for her head-bobbing attack.

She had almost reached her fallen mate when Joe fired, and the sow crumbled to the ground just two seconds later. When she stopped moving, her nose was just inches from the boar's back feet.

Joe noticed that the vultures had all risen to join their circling friends before he quickly checked behind him to make sure the coyotes hadn't returned. Then he spotted Bessie standing about two hundred yards away staring back at him. When he began walking towards her, he was pleasantly surprised when the mare started trotting to meet him.

After man and horse were reunited, Joe took her reins, slid the Spencer into its scabbard then rubbed Bessie's nose as he said, "It's alright, Bessie. I understand. At least you didn't run back to the wagons like Duke might have."

He climbed into his saddle and walked Bessie around the western hill to make sure Pete wasn't there, then headed back to the valley with the dead bears and human remains. Before he reached the small valley, he dismounted, tied the reins to a large sage bush then removed the shovel.

After he entered the valley, he searched for someplace to bury the three bodies, or what was left of them. Now that he was upwind of the remains, the stench wasn't as overpowering, but the sight was still nauseating. He walked to the edge of the western hill and found a slight depression that would save him some time. He took off his shirt, tossed it to the ground then removed his hat and set it on top of the shirt before he began to work.

He dug for more than a half an hour before he'd deepened the depression enough to provide room for the three bodies. Now came the disgusting part of the job.

As he walked to Lou's body, he noticed that his pistol was still in his holster then checked the other two. Rat was still wearing his gun, and Hack's Colt was lying on the ground near his body. He wasn't sure if Pete was in so much of a hurry to leave that he hadn't bothered taking them or simply didn't want to go near the bodies. Whatever his reason, Joe wasn't about to bury them with their guns.

He held his breath as he unbuckled Lou's gunbelt then pulled it from his body and set it aside. He grabbed Lou's corpse by the ankles and dragged it quickly to the hole and rolled it inside. He stepped back, took a deep breath then headed to Rat's body. After removing his gunbelt, he towed it to the hole and dumped it on top of Lou's.

When he reached Hack, he still removed his gunbelt but left the pistol where it lay before sliding his gored body to the half-filled hole. After adding his remains to those of his partners, Joe grabbed his shovel and quickly began scooping the dirt back where it came from.

He was sweating profusely when he finished and while the stench was still pervasive, at least the gruesome sight was gone. He left the shovel on the ground then returned to gather their gunbelts and pistols.

Joe inspected each of the weapons before returning it to its holster. They were all Colt New Army models and in good condition. He hung the three gunbelts over his left shoulder then returned to the grave. As he stood next to the burial site, he opened Hack's ammunition pouch and pulled out two of his paper-wrapped ball and powder rounds. Then he ripped them open and scattered the black powder across the fresh dirt in the hope that it would keep the scavengers at bay. After tossing the lead balls onto the gravesite, Joe grabbed his shovel, snatched his hat from his shirt and pulled it on before picking up his shirt.

When he reached Bessie, he set the shovel down, hung the gunbelts from his saddle horn then donned his shirt. After taking down his canteen and quenching his thirst, Joe decided to have his lunch before heading back. He opened his saddlebag, pulled out the pouch Faith had given him and opened the flap. He smiled when he pulled out the sour pickle and took a big bite. The vinegary taste and smell were almost sweet after having worked with the powerful odor of death hanging over him.

He finished the pickle then went to work on the first of the two turkey wings. It didn't take long before he had cleaned the first one down to the bone and started ripping the meat off the second.

After his much-appreciated lunch, Joe moved the gunbelts into his saddlebags, strapped the shovel onto his bedroll, then mounted Bessie and walked her into the valley. He wouldn't be able to harvest the bear meat, but didn't want it to go to waste, either. So, he decided to just guard the bears until he spotted the wagons. They should be about an hour behind him by now, so he shouldn't have to wait long. Then he removed the shovel again and laid it on the boar's furry back. He'd probably need it later after they removed all the meat and fat.

After he left the small valley, Joe dismounted and tied Bessie's reins to a different bush then removed his two repeaters.

He spread his slicker on the ground then took the three gunbelts and his gun cleaning kit from his saddlebags. After laying them on the slicker, he sat down and looked at the guns.

Joe cleaned Hack's Colt first because he knew it had been fired. After checking the other two pistols, he set them aside and picked up his Henry.

Before he began cleaning the carbine, he said, "Sorry it took me so long to remove your residue, Henry."

When the Henry was finished and reloaded, he picked up the Spencer and cleared it of its remaining cartridges then pulled the magazine tube out of the stock. He was about to start cleaning the heavier carbine when he saw the two coyotes emerge from the distant forest, but they weren't alone. Six more coyotes soon left the shadows to join them. He continued cleaning the Spencer but frequently glanced at the coyotes. Joe figured that they'd be wary as they should have already picked up the powerful scent of the cleaning fluid. The new and strange odor obviously made them cautious as they were taking a slow, winding approach.

He quickly finished cleaning the Spencer, returned the cartridges to the magazine tube then inserted it into the stock and locked it in place. Then he levered a cartridge into the firing chamber and set it down beside the Henry.

The coyotes had separated into two group of four but were still snaking their way towards him. He didn't want to reclean any of the guns he'd just finished, so he picked up Lou's Colt then quickly stood to face the coyotes. His sudden move made them jump back a few feet before they stopped. Then the biggest male began to growl before the others added their vocal threats or just bared their teeth.

They were still more than a hundred yards away when they resumed their cautious stalking. Joe cocked the pistol before he bent at the knees and picked up Rat's Colt and pulled back its hammer. He glanced at Bessie who was anxiously shifting her hooves as she stared at the pack of coyotes, so he began walking towards the eight animals.

When they were sixty yards away, Joe shouted, "Get out of here!"

The startled coyotes jumped back a few feet for the second time but didn't run away.

Joe didn't want to shoot them but pointed both pistols at a small pile of dry horse dung twenty yards away and pulled both triggers.

When the .44 caliber balls exploded into the dirt and the sharp stereo sound produced by the twin Colts reached their ears, the coyotes scattered. Joe used his thumbs to cock the pistols and hoped they were spooked enough to return to the trees.

After their shocked reaction, the coyotes suddenly turned and raced away in an almost choreographed display. He didn't release the Colts' hammers until they were more than halfway to the forest.

He finally lowered the triggers then checked on Bessie before he returned to his slicker. After he sat down, he set Lou's pistol down then started cleaning Rat's Colt while monitoring the departure of the coyotes. He'd finished cleaning the revolver before they disappeared into the distant trees then started on Lou's.

He returned the gunbelts with their clean pistols to his saddlebags with his cleaning kit then returned his repeaters to his scabbards. After he rolled up his slicker and stored it behind his saddle seat, he decided to climb the hill to see if he could spot the wagons.

Before he had reached halfway to the summit, Joe smiled when he saw the wagons rolling from the east. He turned then trotted back to level ground, untied Bessie's reins and mounted. When he started Bessie moving, he headed southwest to reach the ruts but continued to check the trees in case the coyotes tried to take advantage of his departure.

Now that his gruesome task was done, Joe started thinking about the future of the wagon train. *If ten families chose to leave for Idaho City. would the others join the flood?* For the first time since he asked Bo if he could follow the wagons with his tent-cart, Joe realized that one way or the other, his and Faith's journey would soon end. It had always been a distant, almost imaginary event, but now the reality hammered into his mind. He had no real skills that mattered, and his youth would pose a serious obstacle if he wanted to pursue his dream of becoming a lawman. *How could he support Faith and their baby if he didn't have a job?*

Joe stared at the oncoming wagons and tried to control his burgeoning worries that were approaching panic. He closed his eyes, took in and released a deep breath then opened them again and patted Bessie's neck.

"Everybody keeps telling me how I look much older and sound like a man twice my age, but now I'm acting like I'm a thirteen-year-old boy, Bessie. I've got to stop worrying then come up with a way to make a good home for Faith and Kathleen Maureen and provide them with whatever they need to be happy."

He smiled and set Bessie to a fast trot in order to reach the wagons sooner. Then he recalled where he was a year ago which pushed his concerns aside. If he could get this far in just a few months, then he should be able to do even more before he turned seventeen. Joe's faith in their future was strengthened as his self-confidence was restored, and his deep love for Faith reinforced his determination.

IDAHO CITY

When he saw Joe coming back less than two hours after the noon break, Bo hoped that Joe hadn't run into trouble.

Almost as if she had read his mind, Nora asked, "Why is Joe coming back so early?"

"I don't know. I thought I heard some gunfire a little while ago, but I wasn't sure."

"I wish Faith was sitting with us."

Bo looked at her and asked, "Why?"

"Because Joe would see her and if everything was alright, he'd wave his hat over his head three times, and we'd know that there was no trouble ahead."

Bo grinned as he said, "You're right. It's kinda like those signal flags the army uses, but he only does it for Faith. He'll be here in another few minutes, so we'll find out why he headed back early."

Joe had created a fifty-yard gap between Bessie and the ruts in the hope of seeing Faith but couldn't find her. He figured that she must be inside Mary's wagon with Laddie and the boys.

When he was close, he slowed Bessie and angled toward Bo's wagon. As it passed, he made a wide U-turn then pulled up beside the driver's seat.

Bo asked, "What brings you back so soon, Joe?"

"I was going to bury those three bushwhackers, but when I got there, they were being scavenged by two black bears. I tried to scare them off, but the big boar charged, so I shot him. Then the sow charged, and I had to shoot her, too. After I buried what was left of the three bodies, I decided to wait until I saw the wagons before harvesting the bear meat. I imagine after dressing we'll have over four hundred pounds of meat and fat. I was cleaning my guns when a pack of coyotes showed up and was able to scare them off. I'm going to head back there to keep the scavengers away, but can you send some help and your flatbed?"

"I'll send 'em along as soon as I can."

Joe nodded then said, "I'm going to talk to Faith before I head back."

"I'm kinda surprised you talked to me first."

Joe grinned, tipped his hat to Nora, then wheeled Bessie around and headed to Mary's wagon. As soon as he did, he saw Faith sitting next to Will and immediately pulled off his hat and waved it over his head the required three times. He had barely tugged it back on when he had to turn Bessie around again then match the wagon's speed.

IDAHO CITY

Faith had been smiling since Will told her that Joe was back and had stopped to talk to Bo, so she'd joined him on the driver's seat knowing that Joe would soon pay her a visit.

When he pulled up beside her, she asked, "What happened, Joe?"

Joe quickly told her about the bears before saying, "I'm going back there to protect them from the coyotes and buzzards, but the wagons should be there soon."

"Okay. You can tell me the rest of the story when I see you again."

"There isn't much left to tell, but I'm glad I rode Bessie today. I think if I'd ridden Duke, I'd be walking back. Oh, and thank you for adding the pickle. I almost swallowed it whole."

Faith laughed then waved as Joe rode away.

———

After Joe returned to the valley, he had to drive off the buzzards that had just landed but didn't find any coyotes. He dismounted, tied Bessie's reins to the shrub and walked into the valley. He noticed that the gravesite hadn't been disturbed yet, and after they butchered the bears, there would be enough blood on the ground to distract the scavengers.

He inspected the bears to see where they'd been hit but could only see his second shot on the boar, so the first bullet must be buried in his chest. As he began walking the perimeter of the narrow valley to keep the buzzards at bay, he wondered why the male bear was called a boar and the female a sow. Bears weren't related to hogs, so it didn't make any sense.

What was even stranger was the names given to coyotes. Males were boars, like bears and hogs, but the females were bitches, like domesticated dogs and some humans. Then there was the deer mystery. Male deer were bucks and females were does, but their bigger cousins, elks and moose were called bulls and cows, as if they were related to cattle. He wondered if the men who gave the different animal sexes their names were busy downing a few bottles of whiskey at the time.

He was about to enter the avian world of nomenclature when he figured he'd make better use of the time by digging a hole for the guts. So, he stepped to the boar, picked up his shovel and began digging. It didn't need to be nearly as big as the one he'd dug earlier, so he didn't bother taking off his shirt. He finished the job in five minutes then laid the shovel on the pile of loose dirt.

When he walked out of the valley to get his canteen, he spotted the flatbed and two riders approaching. Before he reached Bessie, he identified Chuck and Russ Smith as the ones on horseback, and Bo was driving the wagon with Homer Newbury sitting next to him.

He continued watching them as he emptied his first canteen and was curious why Fester Newbury's son had come along

IDAHO CITY

with Bo. He didn't know much about Homer because he was a quiet man and spent most of his time with his wife, Alice and their one-year-old son, George.

He hung the empty canteen on Bessie's crowded saddle then waved to Bo. Bo waved back but kept the flatbed rolling along the ruts until the ground was better. Chuck then turned Willy away from the wagon and Russ Smith soon joined him on Grant, the black gelding Joe had given to him.

As they approached him, Joe wished that Russell had stayed with the wagon, so he could talk to Chuck about his decision to leave the wagon train. If Chuck did head to Idaho City, Joe wondered if Bo would give him all of the money that Chuck had been promised for scouting the wagons to Oregon. He figured it wouldn't be that much less anyway as Oregon was just another hundred and fifty miles from the turnoff to Idaho City.

Just before Chuck and Russ arrived, Joe waved for them to follow then began walking to the bears. When he reached the boar, he turned and noticed that Bo's wagon was bouncing along the uneven ground behind Chuck and Russ.

Chuck was grinning when he pulled up, dismounted, then said, "That's one mighty big black bear, Joe."

Joe nodded as he replied, "It took two shots from my Spencer at a range of less than fifty yards to bring him down. The sow only needed one bullet to stop her."

"Sow? I thought lady bears were cows."

Russ stepped down and said, "Nope. Joe's right, Chuck. Female bears are called sows, just like hogs."

Chuck mumbled, "That's just plain stupid."

Joe smiled and said, "I thought so, too. And don't get me started on coyotes."

Russ stared at the two bears as he said, "There's a lotta meat in those bears, Joe."

"I reckon we should be able to get about four hundred pounds of meat and fat. The days are getting shorter and colder, so they'll have more fat than they would have had a couple of months ago."

Then he looked at the approaching wagon and asked, "Why did Homer Newbury come along?"

Chuck replied, "He's a butcher. Didn't you know that?"

"Nope. I probably spend less time with the folks than anyone else and haven't talked to him much. How are you doing, Chuck?"

"I'm okay."

Russell asked, "Why did you come back here, Joe?"

"I needed to bury those three bushwhackers. I was the one who killed them, so I was the one who should put them in the ground."

Russ quietly asked, "Was it scary, Joe?"

Joe replied by asking, "Do you mean burying them or shooting them?"

"I meant the gunfight. Were you afraid of dying?"

"No. I was too busy and, to be honest, I wished they'd just done as I asked rather than opening fire. But shooting them wasn't nearly as hard as burying them. The scavengers had already done a lot of damage, so it was a horrible sight, and the stench was overpowering."

Russ pointed as he asked, "Is that their grave over there?"

"Yes, it is. I sprinkled some black powder over the dirt to keep scavengers away, but I don't know if it works. After we harvest the meat and fat, there should be enough blood and scraps to keep their attention away from the grave."

Then Russ brought up the subject he'd hoped to discuss with Chuck when he asked, "Are you and Faith gonna go to Idaho City too, Joe?"

Joe glanced at Chuck before he replied, "Nope. I promised Bo that I'd help him get the folks to Oregon and I always keep my promises."

Chuck snapped, "You ain't even gettin' paid, Joe! I figgered you'd head up there to hunt for gold even if nobody else did."

Joe shrugged but before the conversation continued, Bo pulled up with the flatbed.

When Bo and Homer climbed down, Bo looked at the bears then said, "We got a lot of work ahead of us, so let's get goin'."

The job of butchering the two large carnivores took more than an hour. When they finished, they piled the large mass of meat and fat onto the bearskins then folded them into large sacks and tied them off with heavy rope before lugging them onto the flatbed. Joe had cut four thick steaks and one small roast for Laddie then stored them in the pouch that had been emptied of its turkey wings and pickle.

As they washed the blood from their hands, Joe said, "You really know how to get the most meat out of them, Homer. I wish I knew you were a butcher when I shot all of those other large critters."

Homer just smiled as he removed his butcher's apron.

Joe looked down at his bloody britches and knew that he'd have more work to do when he returned. They'd been using Mary's washtub since she became the new Mary, and he would put it to good use before sunset.

The wagons were close when Bo and Homer boarded the flatbed, and the three riders mounted their horses.

IDAHO CITY

Russ was riding between Joe and Chuck, so Joe wasn't able to resume the brief, interrupted conversation about Idaho City. But Chuck's single, sharp statement which made it appear as if Chuck expected him and Faith to join him had taken him by surprise. Now he wished he'd used Russ' question as a springboard to ask Chuck what he planned to do, and who were going to join him. He also noticed that Chuck hadn't expressed his gratitude for giving him the gray gelding and tack.

But he pushed thoughts of Chuck and Idaho City aside when he spotted Faith sitting beside Will. He yanked his hat from his head, waved it overhead and as he pulled it back on, he heard Chuck mumble something that included the word 'stupid'. He just let it go and didn't even glance at Chuck but wondered if Chuck had heard that the Witherspoons had asked him to talk to Herm and now considered him an obstacle. But Joe didn't care if he had been told and was determined to still have the conversation with Herm.

He kept his eyes focused on Faith as he loudly said, "Goodbye, gentlemen," then set Bessie to a fast trot.

Will grinned as he said, "It looks like Joe is anxious to see you, Faith."

"I'm anxious to see him, too. I still get a tingle down my spine when I see him wave his hat over his head."

"From what Joe told you, I reckon we'll all be eating bear for the next couple of days."

"I'm so hungry these days, I think I could eat a whole bear."

Mary laughed from inside the wagon and said, "I'm not surprised, Faith. I'm just jealous because you don't suffer from morning sickness."

Will turned to Faith and quickly asked, "You're pregnant?"

Faith smiled as she nodded and replied, "Yes, but I haven't told anyone yet."

Will grinned and said, "Except for Joe."

"No, I didn't need to tell Joe. He told me. He even told me we'd have a daughter and name her Kathleen Maureen."

Will's eyebrows shot up and his eyes popped wide as he asked, "How did he know before you did?"

"When I asked him how he knew, he told me that he was just trying to calm my nerves but later confessed to the real reason he believed I had conceived. That's when I knew that I was carrying our baby."

Mary said, "I'm not nearly as surprised as Will is, Faith. Once I stopped being a witch and started talking to Joe, I realized how intelligent and mature he is. He said he wasn't a preacher, but I'm beginning to wonder if he's prescient."

Faith twisted to look back at Mary before she said, "I thought the same thing after he figured out the Blackfeet plans. But long before he set that prairie fire, I realized that it was because he was able to figure things out very quickly. He's the smartest person I ever met."

"I'm still in awe of your sixteen-year-old husband. And I'm also impressed with his fifteen-year-old wife."

Faith smiled as she said, "I'll be sixteen next month."

Mary laughed and said, "I guess that means you're ready for a rocking chair."

"I'd rather have a home that doesn't move."

Mary nodded then said, "So, do I."

Faith smiled then turned back to watch Joe as he drew closer.

When Joe slipped Bessie into position near the driver's seat, Faith asked, "Did Bo say how long we'll keep going?"

"For at least another hour. There will be a lot of sharp-toothed critters visiting that valley between the hills, so we need to put some space between us and the valley before we stop for the night. Then I need to do the laundry, too. Either that or throw out my britches."

"Joe, I can still do the laundry. Ask Mary. Oscar goes through a lot of diapers."

"I'll still wash my britches. Oh, and I cut four thick bear steaks and have them in my lunch pouch. I added a small roast for your canine companion, too."

Faith smiled as she said, "I'm sure he'll appreciate it. Are all the steaks for me?"

Joe laughed then turned and pulled the sack of succulent steaks from his saddlebag as he replied, "I'll give you mine if you believe you'll be able to eat them both."

Joe handed the pouch to Faith and said, "I'm going to check on Herm. I didn't see him on the driver's seat, but he should be awake."

Then he waved to Faith, Will and Mary before he rode away.

Faith set the pouch in the footwell rather than tempting Laddie as Will said, "I wonder if he talked to Chuck about Idaho City. Chuck seems to be the leader of the revolt."

Faith was still watching Joe when she replied, "I'm sure he'll tell me later."

"Maybe he'll tell us all when we're eating those bear steaks."

Faith smiled as she said, "He probably will, Will."

———

IDAHO CITY

When Joe pulled up next to the Witherspoons' wagon, Abe grinned and said, "Howdy, Joe. I heard that you shot a couple of bears."

"Yes, sir. A large boar and a sow. How's your patient?"

Doris leaned in front of her husband and replied, "He's doing fine. If we weren't still rolling, you could ask him yourself."

Joe said, "We'll be moving for another hour, so I'll just tie off Bessie with her sisters then pay him a visit."

Abe nodded, then Joe pulled Bessie to a stop, dismounted and took her reins just as Becky's new black mare walked past. He walked next to Nellie and tied Bessie's reins to her pack saddle before he hopped onto the tailgate and crawled inside.

Becky smiled as she said, "Thank you for the horse, Joe. She's a lot prettier than my mule, and I gave him to my father, so he can use him for plowing when we end our journey."

"You're welcome, Becky."

Then he looked at Herm and asked, "How are you holding up, Herm?"

Herm seemed uncomfortable as he replied, "I'm okay. But I feel so damned useless just lyin' here."

"Quit complaining, Herm. Just enjoy the time off when you can get it."

Herm shrugged then said, "Thanks for findin' Cheese and shootin' those bastards, Joe. I probably wouldn't even be here if you didn't find us. I really owe you, Joe."

"You would have done the same for me if I was the one who was ambushed."

"You wouldn't be as stupid as me and Chuck."

"You forget that Mort put a slug into me, and I didn't even know he was there."

"But that was different, Joe."

Joe grinned as he said, "I was just lucky that I was bending over when he fired. By the way, did you know that none of those boys had rifles? All they had were Colt New Army pistols. I let the one who surrendered leave, and I guess he was worried I might change my mind, so he left all of their guns behind. I've got them in my saddlebags if you want one."

"No, thanks. I don't want anything to remind me of how I got this hole in my arm."

"I understand, but don't even think about taking Becky's new horse away from her."

Herm grinned, looked at Becky and said, "I'd never do anything to make you unhappy."

Joe saw the opportunity to bring up Idaho City and said, "When Chuck showed up with the others to harvest the meat from the bears, he never mentioned the gray gelding I left for Marigold. Then Russ Smith asked me if Faith and I were going to be going to Idaho City. When I told him we weren't, Chuck almost snapped my head off and said that he assumed we'd be going even if nobody else did. I was startled but never got a chance to explain why we would stay with the wagon train."

Herm just looked at him, but Becky asked, "Why wouldn't you leave? You aren't being paid and neither you nor Faith have any family here."

Joe said, "I promised Bo that I'd help the folks get to Oregon and I never break my promises. But from what I've heard about Idaho City, it's not the kind of place a man brings his wife, especially now that she's expecting."

Becky exclaimed, *"Faith's pregnant?"*

Joe grinned as he replied, "Yes, ma'am. She hasn't told anyone yet, but I wouldn't be surprised if Mary hasn't figured it out because Faith is staying in her wagon."

"That's wonderful news, Joe!"

"We're both really happy about it. That's the best reason for not taking her to Idaho City. Most towns that are built to cater to treasure seekers are wild places. I heard that they have dozens of saloons already. Anyone wearing a badge would have his hands full, and I imagine their jail is packed with lawbreakers."

Herm said, "It sounds like you're afraid of the place, Joe."

"I'm not afraid of Idaho City, Herm. I just want Faith to be safe and happy. I couldn't bear to see her hurt. She's just too precious to me. I'm sure you feel the same way about Becky."

Herm smiled at Becky and nodded as he said, "I sure do."

Then he stared at Joe and said, "Maybe it's not as bad as you figure. You'll be out front, so when you reach the road to Idaho City, why don't you ride up there and take a look for yourself?"

Joe believed he wouldn't be able to get Herm to change his mind on hearsay, so he replied, "Maybe I'll do that, but I'll talk to Faith first. We can learn more when we stop at Fort Hall in a few days, too."

Herm said, "I know you won't lie about it, but maybe I can ride with you by then. I can't use my left arm much, but I should be able to ride as long as I don't have to saddle Cheese or Corky."

Joe smiled as he said, "We'll see. I'm going to head back to Faith and take all of our four-footed ladies with me, so the back of your wagon won't be so crowded."

Becky smiled back at him as she said, "Thank you for everything, Joe."

Joe tipped his hat, replied, "You're welcome, Becky," then back crawled until he reached the tailgate and dropped to the ground.

IDAHO CITY

He untied Betty's reins from the wagon, then quickly led the three mares to the side before the Smiths' wagon passed. He waved to Marigold's parents then waited for Mary's wagon to reach him.

After Will waved, Joe began moving the horses closer to the wagons then quickly walked them next to Duchess and tied Betty's reins to the same handhold. Then he wound his way around the herd and patted Duke on his flank before hopping onto the tailgate.

Faith was sitting next to Mary with John on her lap and Laddie sitting on her other side while he managed to find a small space to sit down.

As soon as he was settled, Faith asked, "How is Herm?"

"As you might expect, he's frustrated by being out of commission. And after he thanked me for giving Becky the horse, we had an interesting conversation."

"Did he say anything about going to Idaho City?"

"Not until Becky gave me an opening and I told her about the unusual, but short exchange I had with Chuck on the subject."

"What did Chuck say?"

"Russ asked me if we were going to Idaho City, when I told him we weren't, Chuck seemed surprised and a bit angry. He seemed to believe that we would go even if no one else did.

Then Bo arrived with the flatbed which ended the conversation before it really began."

"So, what did Herm say when you told him?"

"I kind of put him into a bind when I told him that I didn't want to take you into a town with that kind of reputation because I love you too much. He said he loved Becky, too but pointed out that I didn't know what the town was really like. He suggested that I ride up there to check it out when I reached the road to Idaho City with Chuck."

He expected Faith to be surprised and immediately voice her objection, but she did neither.

Instead, she just calmly asked, "Are you going to go?"

"I wanted to hear what you think of the notion first."

Faith chewed on her lower lip for a few seconds before saying, "If you did go, then when you returned, you might be able to convince everyone to stay with the wagon train."

"Only if it was as lawless as the rumors made it out to be. And if I went alone, I'm not sure that the folks would believe what I reported. But Herm wanted to come along, so if he is able to confirm what I say, that would probably dissuade at least some of them. I'm sure that Chuck will want to take a look, too. But I have a feeling that unless the town is hell on earth, he'll make it sound like the Garden of Eden."

IDAHO CITY

"I still think you should go and not wait until the wagons reach the intersection, either. You'll need more time to do your evaluation."

Joe focused on her blue eyes as he asked, "Are you sure you won't worry if I'm gone for more than a day?"

"Of course, I'll worry. But it won't be nearly as much as it was last night because I'll know where you are."

"Okay. Then I'll plan to visit Idaho City two days before the wagons reach the turnoff."

Faith smiled as she said, "When you get there, don't spend all your time in one of the dozens of saloons."

Joe leaned in front of Laddie and kissed her before saying, "I think if I even entered one, they'd toss me out on my ear because I'm not old enough to have a beer."

"I don't think they'd throw John out if he snuck inside and ordered a whiskey as long as he showed them a dollar."

Joe laughed then said, "You're probably right."

Just a couple of hundred feet away, Chuck was having a less pleasant conversation with Marigold.

She glared at him as she sharply asked, "What difference does it make if Joe and Faith don't want to go?"

Chuck quickly replied, "I don't care if they come or not, but he might get Herm to change his mind. He might make the others stay, too."

"So what? I don't care if we are the only ones to leave. My family will still come with us, too."

Chuck was still fuming as he snapped, "What if the Carlisles change their minds? Then Beth will wanna stay with her folks, and Russell ain't gonna leave her. Then your folks will have to choose between you and him."

Marigold sighed then said, "Listen, Chuck. We have at least another week before we ever reach the road to Idaho City. You'll be out front with Joe tomorrow, so you can talk to him."

A few seconds passed before Chuck said, "Alright. He said he was only stayin' 'cause he promised Bo that he would, so maybe I can tell him Bo probably doesn't care that much anyway. If I can't get him to come along, I'll find out if he's gonna try to convince the other folks to stay. I can even start off by thankin' him for givin' us the gray gelding."

Marigold rolled her eyes before asking, "You didn't thank him when you first saw him?"

"I kinda forgot when I saw those bears."

Marigold glanced at the horse before she asked, "Bo told me that Joe said the horse was for me. So, can I have him?"

IDAHO CITY

"Sure. I haven't checked the saddlebags yet, so I'll take a look when we pull up for the day."

Marigold smiled and said, "Maybe they already found some gold and there are sacks of dust in there."

Chuck grinned then said, "I don't reckon those boys ever made it to Idaho City, but after we get there, it won't be long before I fill 'em with gold. Then you can buy anything you want."

Marigold giggled as she clutched Chuck's forearm then said, "And you can buy anything you want, too."

The wagons were almost two miles past the hills when Nora rang the bell.

As the menfolk began unharnessing their teams of oxen and mules, Joe and Faith, accompanied by Laddie, led their horses and Bernie away from Mary's wagon and headed north. Just a few minutes later, they stopped beside the bank of a good-sized pond. While Faith led them to the water, Joe unraveled the hitch rope and tied one end to an arroyo willow tree. After securing all of their horses and Bernie to the rope, he and Faith began stripping them of their tack and loads.

When they finished, Joe began digging a large fire pit while Faith walked to the pond to fill the coffeepot and their canteens. By the time she returned to the campsite, Joe had the firepit filled with wood and the cooking grate in place.

She set the canteens near their saddles then placed the coffeepot next to the firepit when she noticed Laddie standing next to Joe staring at him.

"How did you steal Laddie's affection?"

Joe's answer was to lift the bear-meat-filled pouch and hand it to her. When Laddie left Joe's side and trotted close, Faith laughed then ruffled his fur.

"After you left to talk to Herm, I looked inside the pouch. Those are thick steaks, Joe. I don't care how hungry I am, I'd never be able to eat two of them. I'll probably have trouble finishing one."

"Whatever you don't finish can be your breakfast. The Boone family will be here soon, so I'll get this fire going."

"I'll get the pans and skillet."

Joe watched Faith for a few seconds before he lit the kindling. He was still unsure about going to Idaho City two days before the wagons arrived at the road. He wasn't worried about Faith but was beginning to feel uneasy about Chuck. When he told Russ that he and Faith weren't going, Chuck seemed more than just angry. There was a look of distrust in his eyes.

He and Chuck would be riding together for a few days and was hopeful that their friendship was strong enough to overcome the tension. But if Chuck was still angry or just distant tomorrow, Joe knew he'd have to avoid even talking about

Idaho City. Maybe he could smooth things by offering him a gift. He'd already planned to wear one of the Colts in his saddlebags. He'd turn the holster backwards, so he could draw the pistol on his left side with his right hand. So, when he met Chuck in the morning, he'd be wearing two Colts and ask him if he'd like to have one of the gunbelts. It couldn't hurt unless Chuck took the pistol and shot him.

The thought made Joe snicker before he used a bayonet to move a piece of maple onto the flames and was still grinning when Faith returned with the cookware.

Faith cut a large piece of her bear steak and had just put it into her mouth when Mary asked, "Are you going to go to Idaho City alone, Joe?"

Joe replied, "If Chuck finds out I was going there early, I'd be surprised if he let me visit the town on my own. He'd still come along even if Marigold expected him to return."

Faith swallowed before saying, "If she gets worried, I'm sure she'll ask me about it. If she does, I'll tell her the truth."

Mary asked, "Did she talk to you again about their decision to leave?"

Faith shook her head then said, "Not a word. I don't want to ask Becky about it because it gets her upset."

Will said, "I reckon if I talked to Chuck, he wouldn't tell me anything. Maybe I can talk to Herm tomorrow during the noon break. I haven't seen him since he was shot, so I should pay him a visit."

Mary smiled at her husband and said, "I'm sure he'll be glad to see you, Will. Just don't push the issue."

"I won't."

Joe asked, "Will, do you want another pistol? I have three extra Colts and gunbelts. I was thinking of wearing two and giving one to Chuck."

Will grinned as he replied, "I'd appreciate it. I ain't very good with my left hand, so I'd probably just wear it with the butt forward."

"That's what I was going to do."

"I know you're a true marksman with your rifles. Are you as good with your pistol?"

Joe shrugged then replied, "Nope. I don't do much target shooting with my Colt. How about you?"

"I'm better with a rifle, but I'm still pretty good with a pistol."

Joe set his almost empty plate down, then stood and walked to his saddlebags and pulled out two gunbelts. When he returned, he handed one to Will then sat down.

IDAHO CITY

As Will inspected his new revolver, Faith said, "You're almost as bad as Joe, Will."

Will slid the Colt back into its holster then said, "I might be worse, Faith. I just never had so many nice guns before."

Faith looked at Joe as she said, "Not counting my Henry or Colt, Joe has seven guns. He has his Mississippi rifle, the Sharps breech loader, the Spencer, the Henry, a shotgun and the two Colt New Army pistols. That's assuming he gives one to Chuck."

Will grinned and said, "I guess I was wrong about liking guns more than Joe."

Faith then said, "And his weapon collection isn't limited to guns, either. He's got two knives and still has those eight Confederate bayonets and the eight Arapahoe knives. If his bow hadn't snapped when he tried to start the grassfire, he'd have the trifecta of weaponry. At least he still kept four of the Crow arrows to give to our children."

Will said, "I saw the ones he gave to Mary," then looked at Joe and asked, "Are you thinking of starting your own army, Joe?"

Joe had removed the holster and ammunition pouch from the gunbelt and was sliding the holster on to make it face backward when it was on his left side when he replied, "If I did, then I'd ask you to be the general."

"I'd rather be a sergeant, if it's all the same."

After the Boones had gone back to their wagon, Joe set up the tent while Faith washed the plates and cookware. There was no sign of rain, but the nights were getting chilly bordering on seriously cold.

When Joe and Faith slipped beneath the blankets, Faith asked, "You don't think Chuck will cause you any trouble, do you?"

"No, I don't. He might be sullen or indifferent, but he won't turn into another Mort. I just wish he wasn't so stricken with gold fever. But when I see Idaho City, maybe it won't be nearly as bad as it those rumors make it out to be. Then I won't feel bad if any of the other folks leave. They were going to start a new life somewhere, so if the town is decent, it's as good a place as any."

"That depends on the land being suitable for farming. And that's only if they don't all decide to prospect for gold."

Joe nodded then pulled her close, kissed her and said, "Enough about Idaho City. Let's put our buffalo bed to good use."

CHAPTER 3

Joe waved to Faith before he rode Duke to the front of the line to meet Chuck. He was only wearing one pistol but had his left-handed gunbelt in his left saddlebag and the Colt he'd give to Chuck was in the other. When Joe spotted Chuck sitting on Willy, he waved, and Chuck returned his silent greeting.

After Joe reached him, Chuck said, "We might reach Fort Hall this afternoon, Joe."

"Then we can see how big that sutler's store is."

Chuck nodded before he and Joe rode past Bo's wagon without seeing Bo.

They rode side-by-side for almost five minutes before Joe asked, "Do you want another pistol, Chuck?"

Chuck looked at him and asked, "Are you gonna give me yours?"

"Nope. The last bushwhacker rode off and left the guns with the bodies. I gave one to Will last night and was wondering if you wanted one."

"What kind is it?"

Joe twisted in his saddle, pulled the gunbelt out of his right-hand saddlebag, then showed it to Chuck as he said, "They were all Colt New Army models in excellent condition. I cleaned and reloaded all of them, too."

After Chuck accepted the gunbelt, he let his reins drop then pulled the pistol out of its holster.

As he examined the pistol, Chuck said, "This is better than mine. I wonder if this was the one that they used to shoot Herm."

"I don't think we'll ever know. It's not important anyway. They're still nice guns."

Chuck jammed the Colt back into the holster then spent almost a minute strapping the gunbelt on with the buckle at his back.

When he finished, he said, "I reckon I gotta fix this later."

"I already moved the holster on mine."

"How come you ain't wearin' it?"

Joe shrugged then replied, "I just didn't think about it when I was getting ready to leave."

Chuck didn't reply but just took his reins in his left hand then began to practice cross drawing the pistol.

As he watched Chuck work to improve his draw, Joe decided not to wear the second pistol after all. He'd just leave it in his saddlebag as a backup. When Chuck had donned the second gunbelt, it made him look almost like an outlaw, even with the oddity of having the buckle at his back. But even after he'd been given the pistol, Chuck hadn't mellowed. He hadn't thanked him for the gun and had yet to smile.

Ten minutes after giving Chuck the pistol, Joe was studying the landscape when Chuck loudly asked, "Why did you let that one bastard run off, Joe?"

Joe didn't look at Chuck as he replied, "After he saw the last one of his partners get hit, he dropped his pistol then surrendered. He had his eyes closed when I reached him and was so afraid that I thought he was going to pee on himself. He wasn't a threat, and I wasn't about to shoot an unarmed man."

"Then why didn't you bring him back with ya?"

"He wasn't a hard man like the others. He even giggled like a girl. I think killing three of them was more than sufficient punishment for what they did."

After a short pause, Chuck asked, "How did you know his name?"

When Joe finally looked at Chuck, he saw the anger in his eyes and came close to telling him he didn't know his name.

But he quickly realized that Bo might tell him otherwise, so he replied, "The one I let go was named Pete. They called their leader Hack, and the ones who wanted to kill you and Herm were Lou and some guy who called himself Rat."

"You don't know Pete's last name?"

"Nope. I only knew their Christian names because I heard them talking to each other before I even saw them."

Chuck huffed then growled, "Pete better hope that I never catch sight of him or hear his girlish voice."

Joe didn't ask what he planned to do to Pete if he did meet him but believed there was almost no chance that it would ever happen.

After riding for fifteen more minutes without passing a word, Chuck suddenly and loudly said, "You ain't gonna talk me outta goin' to Idaho City, Joe."

"I wasn't going to even try to do that, Chuck. What you do is your decision."

"I already made up my mind and Marigold is pretty excited, too."

Joe grinned as he said, "I can tell," then asked, "Did Marigold like the gelding?"

"Yeah, she liked the horse. I forgot to say thanks for givin' it to us."

IDAHO CITY

"That's alright. I figured you were still tired after what happened."

Chuck nodded then said, "We should reach that road from Salt Lake City pretty soon."

"Yup. Then this afternoon we'll see Fort Hall. I wonder how many soldiers deserted after they found gold all over the place just a few days ride north."

"Probably more'n they lost when the rebels left to change uniforms."

"We haven't heard any news since we left Julesburg, so when we get to Fort Hall, we can find out how the war's going. The Union wasn't doing very well back in June. Maybe Mister Lincoln got rid of those incompetent generals and the new ones can get the job done."

Chuck looked at him then asked, "Since when did you start to worry about the war?"

"I don't worry about it. I just hope the Confederates don't keep winning battles. I grew up in Missouri, so I know a lot of summer of '62. Now it looks like it's going to drag on for another two years if we're lucky."

"That war ain't bein' fought out here, Joe. So, it ain't important to me who wins."

"It should be important to all of us because if the Confederates keep winning, the war could last a lot longer. They'll never defeat the Union army because they don't have the industry or the manpower that the North does. The only way they can win is to keep fighting long enough for the folks up North to get sick of war. Then they'll elect Democrats to Congress and start demanding that Mister Lincoln sign a peace treaty and let the rebel states keep the South as a separate country."

Chuck asked, "So what if they did have their own country? It won't change anything out West."

"I figure even if they set up borders, it wouldn't be long before they started another war."

Chuck shook his head before saying, "You got some mighty peculiar notions, Joe. Especially for a kid who ain't even had any schoolin'."

"I know. Things just pop into my head sometimes and I don't even know how they got there."

Chuck snickered then said, "Maybe they came from your nether regions."

Joe laughed before saying, "Maybe so."

Now that the tension was gone, Joe wasn't about to let it return by talking about Idaho City, so he said, "I need to check out my new Colt, so do you want to do some plinking?"

"Sure. I haven't used my pistol for a few weeks."

Joe grinned and said, "You probably fired mine almost as much as I have. I don't think I've fired a pistol ten times in my life."

Chuck looked at him in disbelief before saying, "You're kiddin'. Why's that?"

"I used my father's Mississippi since I was eight. Even after accumulating all these guns, I've only needed to use my rifles. I figure I'll only need to use a pistol as a last resort, and it'll be at close range."

"You oughta practice more 'cause you might need to use it if your stallion runs off with your rifles again."

Joe smiled as he nodded, then turned, opened his left saddlebag and removed the Colt New Army but not the gunbelt.

Chuck drew his left-hand pistol then pulled Willy to a stop.

When Joe halted Duke, Chuck pointed at a small sage bush about thirty yards away and said, "We'll use that bush for a target."

"That's about the size of a horse's head, Chuck."

Chuck grinned then said, "Worried about embarrassin' yourself, Joe?"

"Nope. I'd be surprised if I put a bullet within five feet of that lump of sage."

"How about we make a small bet, say for a dollar? We'll each take three shots. If you don't even hit the bush, I have to hit it with at least two shots to win the bet. If you hit it once, then I gotta hit it with all of mine. If you hit it twice, then you win."

"That isn't fair, Chuck. I'll take the bet, but the winner only has to have more hits."

"Okay. If that's the way you want it, Joe. You ain't been joshin' me about how good you are with your pistol, are ya?"

"Nope. I haven't fired it very often, but I was pleased with my accuracy when I did. That's why I wanted a fair contest. I didn't want you to think I was cheating."

Chuck nodded then looked at the sage bush and said, "I'll go first."

Joe watched as Chuck aimed, then cocked his hammer and fired. The slug punched into the dirt a couple of feet in front of the bush and about a foot to the left.

Chuck looked at Joe and said, "It pulls to the left a bit."

Joe nodded before he pointed his muzzle at the bush, cocked his hammer and visualized the bullet's path before he slowly squeezed his trigger. The Colt bucked in his hand and the bush fluttered as the lead projectile passed through its green stalks.

Chuck huffed before he aimed his pistol for his second shot and fired. His next attempt was closer as the bullet ricocheted off a rock just a few inches to the right of the bush which didn't move.

He didn't make any excuses for his second miss as Joe prepared to take his next shot. Joe thought about intentionally missing but decided it would be dishonest.

When his second shot made pieces of the bush fly into the air, Joe said, "This one doesn't pull like yours. It looks like I chose the better pistol. Do you want to switch?"

"Maybe. Let me see if I can figure this one out."

Chuck's third shot ruffled the bush, so he smiled and said, "Okay. Now I got it figgered out. Take your third shot."

Joe nodded then said, "If I get a hit, you can take two more now that you zeroed in your sights. It's only fair."

"Okay."

Joe's last shot was another hit, so Chuck carefully aimed his next shot and after putting it on target, he grinned at Joe before aiming his pistol.

When the innocent sage bush suffered another wound, Chuck said, "I'll keep this one, Joe. I reckon we'll just call it a draw."

Joe returned his Colt to his saddlebag then said, "Fair enough."

After Chuck holstered his pistol, they continued riding west, and ten minutes later, they reached the road that connected Salt Lake City to Oregon. Joe was relieved that Chuck was able to make his last two shots. If Chuck had to pay off the bet, he probably wouldn't have said another word for the rest of the day.

For the next two hours, they carried on a fairly normal conversation without a single mention of Idaho City.

When it was close to noon, Chuck asked, "Do you wanna head back?"

"I told Faith that I'd probably stay out front."

"Okay. Then let's take a break when we reach a creek."

Twenty minutes later, they dismounted and let their horses drink at a small, shallow creek. After they tied them off, Chuck took a leather pouch from his saddlebag while Joe just walked to Duke and removed his saddlebags.

Chuck sat down, reached into the pouch and grabbed a biscuit. Joe then set his saddlebags down before sitting next to him before pulling the gunbelt and his gun-cleaning pouch from his saddlebag.

IDAHO CITY

When he removed a small rag and the flask, which was filled with kerosene rather than proper cleaning fluid, Chuck asked, "Ain't you gonna have lunch?"

Joe grinned then pulled a piece of jerky from his jacket pocket and ripped off a piece.

Chuck snickered as Joe began removing the used percussion caps from his Colt.

After he'd finished cleaning and reloading his pistol, Joe stood, hung his saddlebags, then took down his canteen and took a few swallows.

Chuck was still reloading his Colt when Joe asked, "How much farther is Fort Hall?"

"I reckon we'll see it in about an hour or so."

Joe looked west and said, "I hope their telegraph line is still up, so I can find out about the war."

Chuck snickered then said, "It sounds like you're hopin' it's over before you turn eighteen and get conscripted."

"If I was eighteen when I was living with the Quimbys, I would have walked to Iowa to enlist in the Union army."

Chuck glanced at Joe then just shook his head.

Ten minutes later they were riding west along the road, and Joe tried to imagine what his life would be like if he had been old enough to join the army. He wouldn't have headed west with Newt then found Bernie. It was almost terrifying when he thought of having never met Faith. He shuddered before he settled his mind and focused on the western horizon.

It was just a few minutes later when he spotted a distant ribbon of water and asked, "Is that the Snake River?"

Chuck stood in his stirrups before he replied, "Yup. It sure is. That means we'll spot Fort Hall pretty soon."

After Chuck returned to his saddle, Joe studied the river. It flowed from the north and as he followed the river's path, he knew it had to curve to the west before it reached the mountains to the south. He knew it continued gathering water from smaller creeks and rivers until it reached the Columbia River which emptied into the Pacific Ocean.

He tried to recall the maps he'd studied at the library in Warrensburg but couldn't recall the exact path the Snake River followed. He did know that the Columbia River formed Oregon's northern border, so after the Snake turned west, it had to curve back to the north to reach the Columbia. The Snake River was the largest river he'd seen since the mighty Missouri, but he doubted if the Snake would be as peaceful as the Missouri.

Joe was focused on the point where the river was hidden by the mountains when Fort Hall appeared on the horizon.

Chuck noticed it at the same time and exclaimed, "There's Fort Hall, Joe!"

Joe replied, "It's a lot bigger than Fort Sanders. They've got a large Indian camp outside, too."

"You can see that from here?"

"Yes, sir. They have some soldiers in those watch towers, but there are some large buildings outside the walls, too. I imagine one of them is the sutler's store."

Chuck said, "I thought I had good eyes, but you got eagle eyes in your head, Joe."

"They didn't help me see Mort before he shot me."

"You're lucky he missed."

"He may not have missed, but I was really fortunate when I fell into that creek, and he didn't bother searching for me."

"I never did get to see that wound he gave ya. Is it as ugly as Faith said it was?"

Joe unbuttoned his jacket, folded it back then pulled up his shirt.

When Chuck saw the large patch of rugged, miscolored skin, he grimaced and said, "That musta hurt like hell when you stuck that red-hot bayonet onto the hole."

Joe tucked his shirt in, let his coat drop then said, "It gave me a hint of what it would feel like if I was condemned to hell. Now it's just ugly."

"Did Faith faint when she saw you do it?"

"She helped me set it up and didn't even flinch when I pressed the bayonet to the raw flesh. The sizzling sound and smell of roasting meat didn't affect her, either. I was already impressed that she'd come looking for me and was even prouder when she helped me stop the bleeding. She's a strong woman."

"I reckon so."

When they reached the outskirts of the fort twenty minutes later, they pulled up when three soldiers approached them.

The corporal asked, "Who are you and where are you boys headed?"

Chuck replied, "My name's Chuck Lynch and my young partner is Joe Beck. We're scouts for a wagon train a few miles back."

Corporal Oxnard glanced at the empty roadway before he said, "You can step down."

After they dismounted, Chuck said, "You boys seem kinda jumpy. Are you havin' trouble with the Indians?"

"Nope. The Shoshone are peaceable enough. The colonel wants us to make sure no strangers start trouble. Ever since they found gold up north, troublemakers of all sorts started showing up. One pair tried to rob the sutler's store and killed one of our men who tried to stop 'em."

"We ran into four bushwhackers a couple of days ago."

"Did you kill 'em all?"

"Nope. We only got three of 'em. The last feller got away."

Joe remained silent as the corporal said, "Well, three outta four ain't bad."

"We'll just pay a visit to the sutler's store if it's alright."

"We'll come with ya."

Chuck nodded, then Joe asked, "We haven't heard any news about the war since June. How are things going back East?"

Corporal Oxnard grinned as he replied, "Lee took his army into Pennsylvania and got his butt whipped at a town called Gettysburg. But Meade didn't chase after him and what was left of his army escaped across the Potomac into Virginia. On that same weekend, Grant took Vicksburg, so the Mississippi River is in control of the Union now. Before he took Vicksburg, he defeated another rebel army in Corinth, Mississippi, too."

Joe smiled and said, "That's great news. Maybe Grant should run all of the Union armies."

"I figure if he was in charge at Gettysburg, Bobby Lee wouldn't even have an army anymore."

Chuck rolled his eyes before he led Willy to the sutler's store with two of the soldiers behind him.

When Joe started walking, the corporal said, "My name's Oxnard, and I'm a Joe, too. Where are you from?"

"I grew up in western Missouri."

"How come you didn't join the rebels?"

"If I was old enough to enlist, I would have signed up with the Union army."

"You aren't old enough? How old are you?"

"I'll turn seventeen in February."

As Joe tied Duke at the hitchrail beside Willy, Joe Oxnard shook his head and said, "I don't mean to call you a liar, Joe. But you sure look a lot older. I woulda figured you to be around twenty or so."

"If I was that old, I wouldn't be here. And I wouldn't have met my wife, either. She's with the wagons."

"Then I reckon you're lucky you're still sixteen."

As they entered the store, the corporal asked, "When you were in Missouri, did you see any battles? Some of us out here feel kinda left out."

"I witnessed a battle outside of a town called Lone Jack. That's where I got this pistol and the Henry hanging on my horse."

As they walked down the first aisle, Corporal Oxnard asked, "How did that happen?"

Joe picked up a twenty-five-pound sack of wheat flour, tossed it over his shoulder and replied, "I was living on my own in a shelter nearby while the two armies had it out within eyesight. I saw a Yankee company try to flank the rebels when they were cut off by the Confederates. Their captain had been out front and thought his men were still behind him but soon realized he was alone. The rebels had cut him off and a dozen of them chased him towards me. He took a hit in the right arm just before he reached the slope where I was watching. He had a Henry but couldn't even use his pistol.

"The rebels were still coming, so I asked him to give me the Henry. He wasn't sure what I was going to do with it but didn't have a choice. I shot eight of the Confederate soldiers and the others ran away. When I was sure they were gone, I set the Henry down and began tending to his wound. Some of the captain's men arrived and thought I was trying to kill him. One of them fired his musket at point blank range, but another one had already butted me in the head with his rifle. When I woke up, everyone was gone. I scavenged what I could from the dead rebel soldiers then stored them in my shelter.

"The captain sent some of his men to find me the next day, and we talked for a while then I returned to my shelter. The next morning, the armies were gone, and I found a heavy duffle bag hanging from a branch. It had the Henry, the Colt I'm wearing, and a few other things Captain Chalmers thought I might need. He included his home address, too."

The corporal stared wide-eyed at him as he asked, "You shot eight of 'em?"

"They were only sixty yards out and were standing like statues."

"They weren't shooting at you?"

"Some of them were, but they should have dropped to their bellies to make themselves smaller targets."

Before Corporal Oxnard could ask more questions, Joe picked up a five-pound bag of salt, a tin of baking powder then snatched a can of black peppercorns from the shelf. He didn't add a pepper grinder to his purchases, but if Faith wanted one, they could buy one when the wagons arrived.

As he carried his selections to the large counter, Corporal Oxnard stayed glued to his left shoulder.

When Joe set everything on the counter, the sutler asked, "Are you paying in Yankee dollars, son?"

"Yes, sir."

The sutler nodded then after scanning the items, said, "That'll run you four dollars and twenty-two cents. That tin of peppercorns cost more than the sack of flour."

Joe nodded, then slid his wallet from his jacket's inner pocket, found a five-dollar note and handed it to the proprietor.

The sutler examined the bill closely before opening his cash drawer, counted out his change and handed the silver to Joe before bagging the salt, baking powder and pepper.

Joe put the coins into his pants pocket, then showed the wallet to Corporal Oxnard and said, "Captain Chalmers gave me this. It was filled with enough money so I could start my journey, too."

As Joe returned it to his jacket pocket, the corporal said, "I reckon the captain probably thought it wasn't enough."

Joe smiled as he said, "I don't think he did, either. When I finally find a permanent home, I'll write another letter to him and hope he replies."

Chuck stepped to the counter, so Joe hefted his bag of flour onto his shoulder, grabbed the cloth sack, then said, "I'm going to get these loaded."

Chuck set his few selections on the counter and said, "I'll be out shortly."

Joe and Corporal Oxnard headed for the door and once outside, Joe set the bag on the ground next to Duke before he laid the sack of flour over his saddlebags.

Joe looked at the nearby Snake River and asked, "How is that ford?"

"We use it all the time, and none of those heavy freight wagons have had any problems crossing."

Joe nodded then started to secure the flour with cord when he asked, "Have you been to Idaho City?"

"Nope. But we talk to the freighters who visit the place. It used to be called Bannock, by the way. Are you thinking of going there?"

"I'm supposed to take a look at the town for my boss. Is it as bad as I've heard?"

"It ain't that bad. They got a lot of saloons and dance halls, but they got six churches and a school, too. They got all sorts of businesses, including a sawmill, two grain mills, a tannery, two general stores, a chemist, and three hotels. The place is growing really fast, too."

"Is there a lot of trouble?"

"I reckon there's enough to keep their sheriff and his deputy busy, but it's not as bad as some of the towns I've seen. I figure it's because the men who actually find some gold settle down."

IDAHO CITY

"A county with that many people only has two lawmen?"

"Yup. They had two more deputies, but I heard they didn't last long. I don't know what happened to them, though."

Before Joe could ask another question, Chuck exited the store followed by the two privates.

Joe hung his bag from his saddle horn, then shook Corporal Oxnard's hand and said, "Thanks for your help, Joe."

The corporal snickered then replied, "You're welcome, Joe."

Joe Beck smiled, untied Duke then mounted while Chuck hung his bag from his saddle horn and released Willy's reins.

When Chuck stepped into his saddle, Corporal Oxnard looked up at Joe and said, "Look me up when your wagons get here, Joe."

Joe grinned and replied, "Sure thing, Joe."

Chuck said, "We gotta get movin' if we wanna get back before sunset, Joe," then turned Willy and rode off.

Joe waved to Corporal Oxnard then followed Chuck.

After Duke came abreast of Willy, Joe said, "Corporal Oxnard said the ford across the Snake River is pretty good. Even the freighters don't have any problems crossing."

"That's what the sutler told me when I asked. He said he was surprised we didn't see any freight wagons after we reached the road to Salt Lake City 'cause he's expectin' a large shipment. I asked him about Idaho City, and he said it was a busy town but not as bad as all those rumors made it out to be."

"Maybe I should check it out after we cross those barren flatlands."

Chuck looked at Joe in surprise and asked, "Are you thinkin' of huntin' for gold yourself all of a sudden?"

"Nope. I was just curious about the place."

"Maybe you'll get bitten by the gold bug when you get there."

Joe smiled as he said, "Maybe. Who knows?"

Chuck was obviously pleased with Joe's apparent shift towards staying in Idaho City and asked, "How about if we both just go up there before the wagons even reach the turnoff?"

"Sounds like a good idea. I'll need to tell Faith, and we have to clear it with Bo, too."

"Bo already knows about it. I told him that I might go on ahead, and Marigold wants me to go there early so I can tell her about it."

Joe nodded and wondered why Bo hadn't told him that Chuck was planning to do an early reconnaissance of the town. Maybe Chuck really hadn't told him yet and was hoping that saying Bo already knew about it would keep him from mentioning it to the wagon master.

On the way back, they passed six heavily loaded freight wagons heading west to Fort Hall. The drivers were noticeably leery as Joe and Chuck passed, even after Joe greeted them with a smile. He could understand their suspicions especially after they'd noticed how heavily armed he and Chuck were. Chuck still wore both gunbelts, so Joe wouldn't have been surprised if the triggers on the shotguns and rifles had been cocked.

―――

The wagons had already pulled up for the night when Joe and Chuck returned. After they reported to Bo, Joe walked Duke to Mary's wagon. When he spotted Faith, he quickly yanked his hat from his head and waved it overhead then barely had enough time to put it back on before he pulled up and dismounted.

Faith stepped closer, smiled and said, "It looks like you've been doing some shopping."

Joe kissed her then replied, "Yes, ma'am. I suppose I could have waited until the wagons reach Fort Hall tomorrow, but I wanted to make sure I could buy the flour."

"What else did you find?"

"Salt, baking powder, and a can of peppercorns."

Faith excitedly asked, "You bought peppercorns? That's a wonderful surprise. I imagine that they cost a pretty penny."

"More than that big sack of flour, but I think it was worth it. I didn't buy a grinder, but if you want one, you can pick it up when you visit the store. Let's gather Duchess, her sisters and Bernie then we'll set up our camp."

"Okay. Then you can tell me about your day with Chuck."

Joe nodded but before he could retrieve their horses from the Witherspoons' wagon, Will arrived and asked, "How were things at Fort Hall?"

"We didn't go into the fort. We just stopped at the sutler's store. But I did talk to a corporal for a little while."

"What did he tell you?"

"I asked him about the war, and he told me that the Army of the Potomac met Lee's army at a town called Gettysburg in Pennsylvania on the first weekend in July. The Confederates lost the battle, but General Meade didn't chase after him, so he was able to escape into Virginia. The other news was even more impressive, especially for the folks out West. General Grant took Vicksburg that same weekend. He even defeated one rebel army in Corinth, Mississippi before capturing Vicksburg."

Will whooped, slapped his right thigh and exclaimed, "About time we kicked some rebel butt! I bet that if Grant had been at

Gettysburg, Lee's army never would have reached the Potomac River, either. Lincoln oughta have U.S. Grant run the whole Union army!"

Joe grinned as he said, "That's what I told Corporal Oxnard."

"Those Eastern generals are all too worried about looking bad. They need more Western generals like Grant and Sherman who know how to fight."

"You're preaching to the choir, but I've got to get to work."

"Sorry for holding you up, Joe."

"That's alright. Stop by later and I'll tell you about Chuck."

"Anything bad?"

"No, sir. But it was interesting."

Joe waved to Mary then led Duke to the Witherspoons wagon to collect the ladies.

———

Ten minutes later, as Joe and Faith led their herd away from the wagons, Faith asked, "So, how was Chuck?"

"He was quiet for a while. Then I gave him one of the spare pistols and he asked me why I let the last bushwhacker leave. After I told him, he said something that made it sound as if he'd shoot the guy if he ever saw him again."

"Do you think he would?"

"I don't know, but it's not likely to happen, so I just let it go. Then he was quiet for a while before he suddenly told me that he was going to Idaho City, and I couldn't change his mind. It was odd because I never even mentioned the town."

"What did you say?"

"I just told him that it was his decision, not mine. Then he said that Marigold was excited about it, but he didn't tell me not to try to convince anyone else to stay with the wagons."

"I guess that's something, anyway."

As Joe tied off the hitch rope, he said, "Then we took some target practice, and after that, we were able to have a normal conversation."

"Did you learn anything about Idaho City when you stopped at Fort Hall?"

"Yes, ma'am. I'll tell you while we're stripping the horses and Bernie."

———

Thirty minutes later, all of their equine companions were devoid of saddles and packs, and the campsite was almost finished. Joe had passed along everything that Corporal Oxnard had told him about Idaho City and included what he'd learned about the war.

IDAHO CITY

Joe was setting up the tent, and Faith was preparing supper when she asked, "How long before you go to Idaho City?"

"I figure we'll start crossing those flatlands the day after tomorrow. It'll take five or six days to reach the turnoff, so I think I'll head there four days after we cross the Snake River."

"And you're sure that Chuck isn't going to give you any trouble along the way?"

"I'm sure. After I told him I was going to the town a day before the wagons reached the turnoff, he was enormously pleased about it. He thinks that once I see the place, I'll be bitten by the gold bug. I didn't deny the possibility because I wanted to keep him in a good mood."

"You aren't going to come back and tell me you want to become a prospector, are you?"

Joe smiled as he replied, "No, ma'am."

Joe finished putting up the tent and made their buffalo bed before joining Faith for supper. Laddie was intently watching them, so Faith gave him a piece of her leftover bear steak.

When they began eating, Faith said, "While you were gone, Marigold paid me a visit. She didn't mention Idaho City directly, but she did ask me if you decided what you would do when we left the wagon train."

Joe swallowed then asked, "And what was your answer?"

"I told her that you wanted to be a lawman but knew you'd have to wait until you were older. She looked at me as if I was joking then giggled before she said that you should figure out what to do for the next few years."

"She giggled? I thought she already knew what I wanted to do."

"I never told her, so maybe she didn't. But now that she knows, don't be surprised if Chuck tries to convince you to spend those next few years digging for gold."

"I'd rather shovel manure in a livery than be a prospector. It would be boring, but I could improve my skills and learn more about the law until I was older."

Faith smiled as she said, "I think you already have the skills and knowledge to be a good lawman. You're also the most honest man I've ever met."

"That's because you haven't met many, Mrs. Beck. Now let's finish supper because I think we're going to have visitors soon. Will wants me to tell him about my day with Chuck. I wonder if Chuck had asked him to go to Idaho City with him."

"He hasn't. If he did, Will didn't tell Mary about it."

Joe nodded before they hurried to finish their supper.

Twenty minutes later, Will entered their camp and sat on one of the pack saddles, so Joe sat on his and Faith pulled Duchess' saddle closer and took a seat.

Will said, "Mary was tired, so after we put the boys to sleep, I told her it'd be okay if she stayed to get some rest while I paid you and Faith a visit."

Joe nodded then said, "I'll tell you about my day with Chuck in a minute. But while it's still on my mind, has Chuck asked you to accompany him to Idaho City?"

"Nope. I reckon he hasn't spoken more than fifty words to me this week. Why'd you ask?"

"Just out of curiosity. Anyway, after we left this morning…"

Faith rubbed Laddie's neck as she listened to Joe. She soon noticed new details in his story, including the target practice bet, and Chuck's decision to wear both pistols. She understood why Joe decided to keep his second gunbelt in his saddlebag before he even explained it to Will.

It only took Joe five minutes to finish speaking, and after he answered two questions about Fort Hall, Will stood, said goodnight and walked back to Mary's wagon.

Ten minutes later, Faith and Joe were snuggling together beneath their blankets and Faith asked, "Joe, how much money do you have left?"

"We have about eighty dollars in our bank. Why did you ask?"

"I didn't want to spend too much at the sutler's store."

"Is there something that you want?"

"I could use some more clothes."

"Then buy whatever you need."

"But we'll reach Oregon in three more weeks, won't we?"

"I think so. You're worried about how I'll be able to support you when we're on our own, aren't you?"

Faith sighed then whispered, "I suppose I am…just a little. But I wouldn't be if I wasn't carrying our baby, Joe."

Joe kissed her softly then said, "I understand, sweetheart. So, I'll make you a promise right now that I'll always provide for you and our children. We'll have our own home even if I have to build it myself."

Faith smiled as she said, "Thank you, Joe," then closed her eyes.

Joe let her roll onto her back but stayed on his side as he studied her peaceful face. He understood her concerns because he had the same crushing realization that the future was rapidly approaching. Now he wished he could feel as confident as he sounded and keep his promise to Faith.

IDAHO CITY

When he was sure that Faith was sleeping, he rolled onto his back and stared at the dark canvas roof. He closed his eyes and began to sing Kathleen Mavourneen in an almost silent whisper.

CHAPTER 4

Because the wagon train would reach Fort Hall just after noon, Joe and Chuck rode out later than usual and would keep within eyesight of the wagons. Chuck was wearing both Colts but had switched the holster so the buckle was in front.

Once underway, Chuck said, "I'm gettin' used to havin' that pistol on my left side already. After we got back, I practiced drawin' it with my right hand and was doin' pretty good, too. How come you're still wearin' just one?"

"I figured that if things ever became so bad that I needed another pistol, I'd have plenty of time to get it from my saddlebag."

"It just makes me feel better knowin' I got nine extra shots. Do you load the sixth chamber on your Colts?"

"Nope. For the same reason I don't keep a live round in my Henry's firing chamber. I do put the percussion caps on all of the nipples, though."

Chuck asked, "Why don't you have your Henry ready to fire?"

"Because it doesn't have a safety, it's more prone to accidental discharge. Having fifteen rounds in the magazine tube is more than enough. And because it doesn't have a forearm, you can't fire more than six or seven shots before the barrel gets too hot to handle."

"I ain't never taken more'n three in a row. How many have you fired without stoppin'?"

"I've fired eight rapid shots twice. I was concentrating on making the shots, so I didn't notice the heat until I stopped shooting. When I did, that scorching barrel made me finally figure out why they call it firing a gun. They need to redesign the gun and figure out a way to put a forearm under the barrel like a normal rifle.

"Besides the heat, they have to come up with a better way to load the cartridges, too. You have to be careful when you slide cartridges into the tube, or it might set off the primer. And that slot on the magazine tube lets dirt get mixed with the cartridges. Then there's the tab at the end of the spring that pushes the cartridges down the magazine tube. When it reaches your hand, you have to change your grip on the barrel, or the cartridges stop moving."

Chuck snickered then said, "Maybe you oughta go work for the Henry company and show 'em how to do it."

Joe grinned as he replied, "I'm not a gunsmith or a machinist, Chuck. All I could do was to tell them which wood looked nicer for the stocks."

Chuck then asked, "How much do you know about prospectin'?"

"Even less than I know about gunsmithing. I'm sure you know more than I do."

"I learned a few things already, so I guess I'll figure out the rest when I get to Idaho City."

Joe suspected that Chuck knew as little about hunting for gold as he did but didn't challenge the extent of his knowledge. When he met Corporal Oxnard again, he'd learn more about Idaho City and the other settlements in the area.

As they continued riding slowly westward, Chuck began practicing cross drawing his left-hand pistol with his right hand. He knew Chuck was distracted, and while it was unlikely that there was danger ahead, Joe still scanned the surrounding landscape for anything out of place.

When he checked their backtrail, he noticed they were getting too far ahead, so he said, "Chuck, we need to hold up to let the wagons get closer."

Chuck quickly looked back, said, "Okay," then pulled Willy to a stop and continued quick drawing his Colt.

Joe halted Duke then looked south at the nearby mountains and wondered what the view would be from the top of the highest peak. He envisioned seeing the Snake River coming from the distant northern mountains, then passing a tiny Fort Hall before it curved west. If the mountain was high enough, he might be able to see it swing back to the north and disappear into the mountains west of Idaho City. Maybe he'd even be able to spot the town nestled in the valleys.

The image was still in his mind when he spotted a bald eagle soaring on the mountains' updrafts and smiled. He may have been told he had eagle eyes, but his eyes would never see what was revealed to the majestic, high-flying eagle.

He was watching the eagle float on the air with its broad wings when Chuck said, "I reckon we can start movin' again."

Joe returned to earth, nodded then set Duke to a walk.

―――

It was just after noon when Joe and Chuck approached Fort Hall. Not surprisingly, Corporal Oxnard was already waiting when they pulled up.

As they dismounted, the corporal grinned at Joe and said, "I had our lookout let me know when he spotted your wagons."

Joe replied, "And here I was thinking that you just materialized out of the ether."

Corporal Oxnard chuckled then said, "Let's go have some of Bill Cox's coffee while we wait for your wagons to get here."

Chuck asked, "Who's Bill Cox?"

"He's the sutler. He's got a couple of tables in back and his missus always keeps a pot of coffee warming on their cookstove."

Joe tied off Duke's reins and said, "That sounds good, Joe."

Joe Oxnard snickered, then after Chuck looped Willy's reins over the hitchrail, they walked into the store. As he removed his hat, Joe noticed the restocked shelves and figured that the freighters must have paid Mister Cox a visit. But they hadn't seen the wagons heading back to Salt Lake City, so Joe thought they must have continued heading west to deliver the rest of their loads to the businesses in Idaho City.

Before they reached the counter, Corporal Oxnard waved to the proprietor and loudly said, "I hope Alice ain't let the coffee get cold, Bill."

Bill lifted his large porcelain mug from the counter and just as loudly replied, "I'm not drinkin' hot rum, Joe."

Joe Oxnard snickered then led the other Joe and Chuck past the counter and through an open door.

Once inside the back room, Alice Cox smiled at Corporal Oxnard as she said, "You know I wouldn't let my coffee cool off, Joe. And who are your new friends?"

The corporal grinned as he pointed to Joe and said, "This tall young feller was blessed by his folks when they christened him

IDAHO CITY

Joe. His family name is Beck. He's a scout for that wagon trail that's comin' down the road."

Then he looked at Chuck before saying, "His friend is another scout, but I can't seem to recall his name."

Chuck smiled at Alice and said, "I'm Chuck Lynch, ma'am."

Alice smiled back then said, "Why don't you have a seat and I'll fetch the coffee."

Joe Oxnard said, "Thank you, Alice," before Joe Beck added his thanks and Chuck expressed his gratitude.

After they took their seats, Joe Beck looked at the corporal and said, "We passed six freight wagons headed this way and I assume that's why the shelves are better stocked today. We didn't see them heading back to Salt Lake City, so did they leave for Idaho City this morning?"

"Yup. They headed out before dawn. I reckon they're already more than ten miles away by now. They used the old road 'cause they had to deliver some stuff to Bill. Most of them use the new, shorter route west of here."

Alice set four large mugs of steaming coffee on the table, then as she sat down, each of them thanked her again before Chuck asked, "How far is it to Idaho City?"

"I figure it's around a hundred miles or so, but the turnoff is around eighty miles away. Until you get start on the road to

Idaho City, the ground is pretty flat, and the road is still in good shape. The first thirty miles are barren, so your folks need to fill their water barrels after they cross the Snake River. After that dry stretch, there are creeks and pond every few miles. They just finished building a new Fort Boise at the junction with the road to Idaho City, too."

Joe asked, "How big is it?"

"It's supposed to be pretty big. They have three companies of infantry and one cavalry company. They even have a lumber mill and a kiln for masonry. I haven't seen it myself, but it's probably better than his one."

"I thought they stripped the western forts of a lot of men."

"They took most of 'em from the forts east of here. They moved troops from Washington to man Fort Boise. They even have a brigadier general in charge. I heard that a new town is growing nearby and they already named it Boise City."

Joe took a sip of his hot, strong coffee before he asked, "Why do they need so many soldiers?"

"After they shut down the old Fort Boise, the Shoshone began attacking the wagon trains heading to Oregon, so they decided to build the fort and send a large force to man it. The Shoshone settled down after they got there, but I figure that's mainly because they're heading east to join up with the Sioux and Cheyenne."

Chuck said, "We ran into a large Shoshone war party back east, but Joe set the prairie on fire, so they ran off to keep from gettin' roasted alive."

Corporal Oxnard looked at Joe and asked, "Did you set the fire on purpose?"

Joe nodded then quietly replied, "Yes, sir."

Chuck grinned then said, "But that ain't nothin' compared to what he did to stop an attack by the Crows. Joe blew up a ten-pound keg of powder to turn a buffalo stampede that the Crow were gonna use to crush our wagons. Then that big herd of scared critters crushed the Crow war party that was waitin' to attack us after they were supposed to crush our wagons."

Joe Oxnard stared at Joe with wide eyes as he exclaimed, *"How did you ignite that much powder without blowing yourself to bits?"*

Joe hesitated long enough for Chuck to answer, "Me and Joe walked with his donkey until we were more than two hundred yards away. Then he buried it and stuck a knife in the lid. When we got back, he set it off with one shot. I gotta tell ya, that was the biggest explosion I ever saw. I reckon the Injuns were so surprised that they didn't even notice all those buffalo headin' right at 'em until it was too late."

Joe squirmed and even blushed slightly while hearing the story, so he took a sip of coffee before Corporal Oxnard said,

"Hitting a knife blade at that range is an almost impossible shot, Joe. What rifle did you use?"

"I used a Remington Mississippi rifle but had my Sharps carbine ready in case I missed. I was kind of wondering if it would go off even if I hit the blade."

"Damn! That's mighty fine shooting, Joe!"

Joe shrugged and took another sip of coffee when Alice asked, "How old are you, Joe?"

"I'll turn seventeen in February, ma'am."

Alice's eyebrows rose slightly before she said, "I knew you were young, but I never would have guessed you were that young."

Chuck grinned as he said, "He's already married, too."

Alice surprised Chuck when she smiled and said, "I'm not surprised. What's she like, Joe?"

Joe was relieved by the change to the much more pleasant topic and smiled as he replied, "Her name is Faith, and she has blonde hair and blue eyes. She's tall and slim, but not as thin as she believes. She's pretty, but even more importantly, she's intelligent with strong character. She's decisive and firm without being overbearing. I'm always grateful for her help, too."

"When the wagons arrive, will you introduce her to me?"

"Yes, ma'am. I'm sure she'll be happy to meet you."

Chuck snickered then said, "And she's even younger than Joe."

Alice shot a malevolent glance at Chuck before saying, "I have a feeling that she behaves as if she's much older, doesn't she?"

Joe smiled as he nodded and replied, "Yes, ma'am. I told her that just a few days after we met."

Then Joe switched topics when he looked at the corporal and said, "Oh, by the way, Joe, when we left Fort Sanders, we were joined by an ex-sergeant named Will Boone. He was mustered out and due to unexpected circumstances, he now has two horses with US brands on their rumps. He won't get into any trouble for having them, will he?"

"I reckon he'll be okay. But if anybody raises a fuss, make sure he has his mustering out papers."

"I'll let him know. He's a good man and was going to be unfairly disciplined because he was following the orders of an idiot lieutenant who almost led his men to their deaths."

"Why did he get into trouble for following orders?"

"The lieutenant, who died in the action, was the commanding officer's nephew and the colonel preferred to punish the sergeant rather than tarnish his sister's oldest boy's reputation."

Corporal Oxnard snorted then said, "I've met officers like that and the best I could do was to stay out of sight."

They finished their coffee, then stood and carried the cups to the sink.

As they prepared to leave the back room, Alice said, "Don't forget to introduce me to Faith, Joe."

Joe smiled, said, "I'll remember, ma'am," then joined Chuck and Corporal Oxnard as they returned to the store.

When they stepped outside, the wagons were about a quarter of a mile away.

Joe pulled on his hat then stepped away from the store as Chuck hurried behind him leaving Corporal Oxnard alone.

As he walked closer to Bo's lead wagon, he spotted Faith walking beside Mary's wagon then ripped his hat from his head and waved it overhead three times.

Faith waved back and picked up her pace.

Less than a minute later, Chuck turned to join Marigold who was driving the flatbed.

When Joe and Faith met, he put his arm around her waist and said, "Let's buy you the clothes you need and remind me to introduce you to Alice Cox. She's the wife of the sutler."

Faith smiled up at him and asked, "And why does she want to meet me?"

"She made the mistake of asking me about you. After my very accurate description, I think she expects you to fly into the store on angel's wings."

Faith laughed before replying, "I hope she won't be disappointed when I arrive on foot."

"She won't be disappointed, especially when she sees you wearing your Colt."

"She won't think I'm dangerous, will she?"

"Of course not. She didn't even seem to care that Chuck was wearing two pistols."

"He's still wearing them?"

"Yup. He practiced drawing the left-hand pistol most of the morning, too."

"Did that bother you?"

"Not a bit. He can only fire one at a time, anyway."

Joe glanced behind them before asking, "Has John become Laddie's best friend now?"

"He may have changed his loyalty. I didn't even have to tell him to stay before I left the wagon."

Joe waved to Bo and Norma just before she rang the bell.

When they reached Corporal Oxnard, Joe said, "Corporal Joe Oxnard, I'd like to introduce you to my wife, Faith Hope Charity Virtue Goodchild Beck."

The corporal grinned, tipped his hat then said, "It's a pleasure meeting you, ma'am. Joe said a lot of nice things about you, and I can see that he wasn't exaggerating."

Faith smiled then took Joe's hand before saying, "I'm a very lucky lady. Joe's an amazing man."

"I kinda got that impression already. I reckon you gotta get your shopping done before the crowds arrive. I need to get back to work, but I hope we can talk later."

Joe nodded then he and Faith walked into the store while Corporal Oxnard headed for the fort's open gates.

After she selected two dresses, a pair of britches, some underthings and two pairs of socks, Joe escorted her to the counter just before the expected hoard began pouring through the doorway.

Alice was waiting behind the counter next to her husband, and when Faith set her selections on the counter, Alice smiled and said, "After your husband pays my husband, will you and Joe join me for coffee?"

Faith replied, "We'll be happy to," before Alice nodded then quickly entered the back room as Bill Cox checked the price tags on the clothes.

Joe had already calculated the total to be $5.75, so he was surprised when Bill said, "That'll run you four dollars and a quarter, Joe."

Joe didn't protest as he pulled out his wallet, handed him a five-dollar note then gave the Yankee currency to Bill.

After Bill scooped the money into his open cash drawer and handed him his change, Joe said, "I think your wife wants to talk to Faith."

Bill smiled as he said, "I reckon so. I'll bag these and bring them to the back room when I get a chance."

Joe glanced at the swarm searching the shelves before he said, "That might be a while."

As Bill chuckled, Joe and Faith walked around the counter and entered the back room.

When they entered, Alice was sitting at the small table, and as soon as she saw them, she smiled and said, "Please have a seat. Faith, you sit on my right. I added a little sugar and milk in your coffee."

Joe and Faith took their assigned seats, then Faith said, "Thank you, Mrs. Cox."

Before Joe could add his thanks, Alice said, "You're welcome, Faith. Please call me Alice," then she pointed to a basket and a burlap sack to her right and said, "When you leave, take the basket of eggs and the sack with you."

Faith glanced at the large burlap sack and basket then quickly said, "Mrs. Cox…"

Alice interrupted her by saying, "Alice."

Faith nodded then asked, "Alice, why are you giving us the eggs and whatever is in the bag? And unless I'm wrong, I think your husband discounted our purchases as well."

Alice smiled as she replied, "I suggested that my husband charge you our cost for whatever you chose."

"But why?"

"Because I joined the conversation between Corporal Oxnard, your husband, and the other scout. I believe his name was Chuck."

Joe may have been an active participant in that conversation, but he had no idea why Alice seemed to think of him so kindly.

Faith was equally befuddled as she waited for Alice to continue.

Alice noticed their confusion and her smile broadened before she said, "When your husband asked Corporal Oxnard about the Shoshone, Chuck told him how Joe started a prairie fire that drove a Shoshone war party away. So, Joe Oxnard asked him if he'd set it on purpose. Your husband seemed almost embarrassed when he answered, 'Yes, sir.'.

"Then Chuck told Corporal Oxnard how he and Joe buried a keg of powder to divert a herd of stampeding buffalo that prevented a Crow war party from attacking your wagon train. Your husband was obviously uncomfortable and seemed to wish that Chuck had never mentioned it. So, I decided to change the direction of the conversation and asked Joe how old he was.

"You can imagine my surprise when he told me he was only sixteen, but that didn't seem to embarrass him at all. Then Chuck seemed as if he was telling a joke when he said that Joe was married. So, I asked him about you and his face lit up as he described you. What impressed me was when he seemed prouder of your intelligence and character than what most young men find fascinating about women.

"Then Chuck took delight in telling me that you were even younger than Joe. I expected Joe to become angry after hearing Chuck's insulting tone, but he didn't even give Chuck a bad look. I was so impressed with your husband and his obvious love for you and his appreciation of your remarkable character, that I knew that I had to meet you. So, as soon as Joe left, I suggested to my husband that he charge you our costs for your items. Then I quickly gathered the eggs and other things but wasn't going to mention them until I met you. The moment I saw you wearing a pistol when you entered with Joe, I knew that he hadn't exaggerated in his description, so I decided to give you the basket and the sack."

Joe said, "Mrs. Cox…"

Alice stopped him when she quickly said, "Alice."

Joe smiled then continued, saying, "Alice, I appreciate your generosity, but we can pay you for the eggs and whatever is in the burlap bag."

"Oh, posh! You'll do no such thing! I have a coop full of chickens and those are just part of what I gathered this morning. And the potatoes came from my large garden. Now while we share our coffee, you can tell me about the prairie fire and the gunpowder bomb."

Joe hesitated before Faith smiled at her husband, took Joe's hand and said, "Before he stopped the Crows from massacring everyone on the wagon train, he prevented a potential fight with the Pawnee when he wasn't even a scout. Then he defeated eight Arapahoe renegades and convinced the Cheyenne to leave us alone. But the way he stopped the Crow attack was amazing. When the herd was still a mile away…"

Alice looked at Joe and noticed his cheeks shifting to a deep pink as Faith began describing the almost disastrous encounter with the Crows. But as he gazed at Faith, Alice could see his deep affection and respect for her in his eyes.

IDAHO CITY

Joe began to sip his coffee as Faith described the Crow attack in great detail. Then she began telling Alice about the blunted Blackfoot plan and how their war chief had even presented him with a war bonnet. He'd already finished his coffee when Faith eventually reached the prairie fire story.

When she finally stopped talking and began sipping her lukewarm coffee, Alice smiled at Joe and said, "You can stop blushing now, Joe. But would you and Faith please join us for supper?"

Joe looked at Faith and after she nodded, he replied, "We'd be honored, Alice."

"Good. Just come to the side door after we hang the closed sign on the front door."

"Yes, ma'am."

"And don't bring anything with you other than your appetites, either."

Faith said, "It seems that I always have an appetite these days."

Alice smiled as she said, "I'm not surprised."

Faith quickly finished her coffee then stood, took Joe's empty cup and carried them to the sink. Alice rose, walked to the wall and picked up the heavy burlap sack and said, "You can carry the eggs, Faith. We'll let your strong husband lug the bag."

Faith plucked the basket of eggs from the floor and as Joe accepted the weighty burlap sack, Alice asked, "Do you have a wagon, Joe?"

"No, ma'am. When I left Missouri, I was pulling a cart until I found an abandoned donkey. Now we each have a horse to ride and three more horses we primarily use as pack horses."

"You'll have to tell me and Bill how that all happened when you return."

Joe smiled, said, "Yes, ma'am," then he and Faith left the backroom.

Bill Cox was busy totaling the folks' selections as they walked to the counter. He nodded then pointed to Faith's bag, so she plucked it from the floor before they began winding their way through the crowded aisles and almost bumped into Bo and Nora.

Bo said, "I'm glad I found you, Joe. I noticed that the Snake River seems to be movin' faster than I expected, so I asked one of the soldiers about it. He said that it must be because there was a heavy rainstorm that drenched the mountains to the north. So, when we cross tomorrow mornin', can you stay in back to make sure everybody makes it across all right?"

"I'll do that, Bo. I hope I don't have to go for another swim, though. Is the water level much higher, too?"

"Not much. It's the speed of the current that might cause us some problems."

Joe nodded before he and Faith headed for the open doorway.

When they left the store, Joe pulled on his hat and said, "I'd prefer that you ride with Mary tomorrow when we cross the river. Okay?"

"I was going to ask you if I could. Are you curious what Alice put in the bag?"

Joe nodded then set it down, spread the top open and peered into the burlap sack. Before he told her what he found, he pulled out a glass jar which revealed its dark red contents.

He showed it to Faith and said, "I think this is strawberry preserves and those potatoes are the biggest ones I've ever seen. I guess the Idaho soil is ideal for growing potatoes. There's also a half slab of bacon inside as well as this."

Joe put the jar of preserves back into the burlap bag and extracted a smaller sack.

As soon as Faith saw it, her eyebrows popped and she exclaimed, "That's sugar!"

Joe grinned as he set it back inside then said, "Yes, ma'am. It's a five-pound bag of sugar. It's not the white granulated sugar they serve at fancy restaurants, but I prefer the dark brown sugar anyway."

Faith gushed, "I don't care what color it is. I just can't believe Alice gave us a bag of sugar."

"Maybe she was worried when she saw you wearing a gunbelt."

Faith laughed before Joe unhitched Duke, picked up the burlap bag and hung it over his shoulder before they headed to the wagons to release their hooved prisoners.

———

After they collected their four mares and one jack, they walked east for about a hundred yards where Joe set down the burlap sack then took down his rope from Duke's saddle and tied it to a sturdy pine tree. Faith lowered the basket to the ground next to the bag, then started stripping Bernie as Joe began tying off the horses.

When he had them all secured, he said, "It looks like Laddie won't be joining us."

Faith set Bernie's pack saddle on the ground then replied, "It's just as well. I don't think he'd be able to resist the bacon's siren call."

Joe laughed then began stripping Bessie.

As they worked, Faith asked, "Did you agree with Alice about Chuck being derisive?"

"I didn't think his comments about the prairie fire, or the Crow stampede were out pf line, but when he talked about you, he did sound somewhat demeaning."

"And you didn't get angry at all?"

"I didn't get angry, but I wasn't exactly pleased with his tone, either. When I glanced at him, I found him staring back at me and thought he was expecting me to react, so I decided to disappoint him. I just don't know why he used that tone when he talked about you."

"If you don't know why he did, then I doubt if I'll ever understand his motives either."

As Joe and Faith cleared the horses, they changed the direction of the conversation and began to talk about Bill and Alice Cox, tomorrow's river crossing and Idaho City.

When Joe was putting up the tent, Faith said, "Before we start rolling tomorrow, I'm going to make you a real breakfast with bacon, eggs and a lot of hot coffee."

Joe grinned as he said, "Just don't use all of the eggs or I'll explode."

Faith laughed before saying, "I may be eternally hungry, but I'm still not about to eat a half a dozen eggs."

The sun was low in the sky when Joe rapped on the store's side door.

Just a few seconds later, the door swung open, and Alice smiled at them as she said, "Please come inside."

Joe followed Faith into a surprisingly large and well-equipped kitchen.

As Joe took off his hat, Bill Cox stepped before him, shook his hand and said, "Alice told me some of the stories about you. She also seemed to think that there are even more she hasn't heard."

Joe smiled and said, "I reckon so," before he hung his hat on a coat rack.

Bill then guided Joe to the large table which already was set with porcelain dinnerware and silver utensils arranged on a linen tablecloth. There were even handsome glasses and folded napkins. He had never seen such an upscale setup and was sure that Faith hadn't either. For the first time since he left the Quimby farm, he felt out of place. He glanced at Faith who was helping Alice and wondered if she was as uneasy as he was.

Bill seemed to sense his discomfort and smiled as he said, "Just sit down, Joe. I've been living here for four years, and I'm still not used to it when Alice shows off her fine china. Her mother gave her the dinnerware and flatware for her hope chest, and I bought her the glasses and napkins on our first anniversary."

Joe slowly sat down in the chair that Bill indicated then smiled and said, "I don't know if I'll ever buy anything this nice for Faith. But if she asks, I'll do my best."

As Faith and Alice began carrying the food and a pot of coffee to the table, Bill said, "Faith told Alice that you weren't even a scout when you joined the wagon train. Where were you before that, and how did you become a scout?"

Joe knew it would be a long answer, so he began with that disastrous week in March of '57 when he lost his family. Before he even said the Quimby name, Alice and Faith took their seats, so he paused while Bill said grace.

Before he continued, Joe looked at the plate of roast chicken, mashed potatoes, a bowl of buttered sweet corn, a basket of biscuits, and even a full gravy boat before he said, "This is a feast, Alice."

Alice smiled as she replied, "I imagine you and Faith haven't had many full meals since you started your journey."

"We do the best we can, but I don't believe that President Lincoln has ever laid eyes on such a magnificent table."

Alice laughed then said, "I doubt that. Now continue your story while we load our plates and fill our cups with coffee."

As they moved the food from the large platters to their plates, Joe picked up his narrative with his arrival at the Quimby farm, mixing eating with telling his story. He realized that he'd be interrupted by their expected questions, so rather than spend all night talking, he skipped over the unnecessary events. But he knew that Faith would insert some of them he didn't want to mention, so he told them about Captain Chalmers and the battle outside of Lone Jack. Of course, that elicited a series of questions. Bill had lit two kerosene lamps by the time Joe told them about finding Bernie inside the half-burnt barn and creating the tent-cart.

He was able to return to simply eating after telling Bill and Alice how Faith had come to join the wagon train, which forced Faith to tell her story. Naturally, Bill, and especially Alice, were appalled when Faith explained how she'd stood near the wagons with a placard hanging from her neck announcing her selling price. She explained how she and Joe met before he took over the narrative again.

Faith and Alice were clearing the table when Joe finally told them about finding Chuck and Herm before he tracked down the four bushwhackers.

They were sharing the last of the coffee when Bill asked, "Why did you let the last one go?"

"I was planning to let them all go, but I made a mistake and asked them to remove their pistols' percussion caps rather than just having them drop them to the ground and stepping back.

When one of them fired at me, I shot him then the others picked up their rifles and began shooting. After two more were down, the last one dropped his rifle and threw his hands into the air. I couldn't shoot an unarmed man, Bill.

"I know that they had been close to shooting my friends, but the one who gave up seemed to be more of a timid follower. I had already punished the violent ones, so I decided not to bring him back with me. I reckon Chuck would have wanted to hang him if I did. So, I took two of their horses to give to Chuck and Herm, then let him take his horse, the last saddled horse and their pack mule. He was so anxious to leave that he didn't even pick up his friends' pistols."

"He didn't even bury them?"

"No, sir. I buried them the next day but had to scare off some coyotes and shoot two black bears first."

Alice shook her head before saying, "I can't believe that you're still not being paid."

Joe shrugged then replied, "Bo Ferguson keeps offering me the pay that he was going to give to the scout who tried to kill me. But when I first showed up, I told him that I'd do what I could to help and wouldn't ask for anything. I know it sounds illogical, but I believe that when I told him that, I was making a promise. And as Faith will tell you, I never break any promises."

Alice asked, "So, where are you and Faith going to settle down?"

Joe glanced at Faith before replying, "I don't have any idea where we'll make our home. I guess we'll have to figure that out pretty soon, though. The wagon train will reach the end of its journey before Faith turns sixteen in October."

Faith looked at Joe and even though he'd answered Alice's question calmly, she could see the concern in his eyes. Those same worries about their future had been bubbling in her mind since she heard that Chuck and Marigold were planning to leave. She'd been relieved when Joe promised her that he'd find them a home, but still wondered how he'd be able to fulfill that promise.

Alice smiled as she said, "I'm sure you'll provide a good home for Faith before your baby arrives. Finding a place to live is one obstacle that faces all of us, and you've already solved many more difficult problems, Joe."

Joe smiled and nodded before Faith said, "Thank you for a wonderful dinner and making this such a pleasant evening."

Alice replied, "Thank you and Joe for making it so interesting, Faith. But I'm sure that you need your rest because you'll be leaving in the morning. Just be careful crossing the Snake River. There must have been a heavy downpour up in the mountains to the north and it's running pretty fast."

Joe said, "Bo already mentioned it, so I'll be staying back to make sure none of the wagons have any problems when they ford the river."

Bill stood and said, "You be careful too, Joe."

As he and Faith rose to their feet, Joe looked at Faith before saying, "I promised Faith I'd always be careful."

Alice lightly laughed before saying, "And you never break your promises."

Joe shook Bill's hand before Alice kissed Faith on the cheek.

After they stepped out into the dark, chilly night, Joe took Faith's hand and said, "I feel as if have to waddle after eating so much."

Faith laughed before replying, "Strangely enough, my stomach doesn't even feel full."

―――

When they finally crawled into their tent and quickly buried themselves under the blankets, it was less than a minute before Faith drifted off to sleep.

Joe stayed awake for another half an hour as he thought about what Alice had told him. He knew that everyone faced the question about finding a home, but not many were his age with such a limited number of skills.

He was still pondering the question when sleep overtook him.

CHAPTER 5

The next morning, after a very satisfying breakfast of bacon and eggs, Joe and Faith saddled and loaded their horses and Bernie before leading them out of their campsite.

When they reached Mary's wagon, Laddie bounced down from the tailgate and approached Faith with his tail wagging.

Faith tied Duchess, Bessie, Betty, Nellie and Bernie to the wagon's left handhold and was petting Laddie when Will arrived.

Joe was holding Duke's reins as he said, "From what I hear, crossing the Snake River might be difficult."

Will nodded and replied, "It's moving pretty fast, but I think we'll be okay."

"Bo asked me to stay behind to make sure nobody decides to go for a swim."

"I heard you saved Lizzy Dooley from drowning before I got here."

Joe nodded before Mary looked out from the back of the wagon and said, "I hope you don't have to jump into the river this time, Joe. You'd probably wind up in Utah."

Joe grinned as he said, "Nope. If I get swept away, I'd eventually wind up in the Pacific Ocean after the Snake dumped me into the Columbia River."

"How does it get there from here?"

As Joe began explaining the looping path the Snake River followed, he was interrupted when Nora rang the bell.

He mounted Duke then said, "Trust me, Mary. It eventually heads north and after making a left turn, it empties into the Columbia River."

Faith was smiling as she climbed into the wagon and Laddie leapt in behind her.

Joe heard John and Albert's squeals of delight before he waved to Faith and turned Duke around to get into position.

When he reached the end of the line, he made a U-turn behind the Dooleys' wagon. After bringing Duke to a halt, Lizzy appeared at the back of the wagon. She smiled and waved at him, and Joe returned her wave and smile as the wagons began rolling.

After Ernie Dooley snapped his reins and his team lurched his wagon forward, Joe waited until there was a fifty-yard gap before he followed.

As he passed the front of the sutler's store, he spotted Bill and Alice at the doorway and waved. They were smiling when they waved back but seemed a bit sad.

Just twenty minutes later, Bo's wagon reached the crossing and slowly descended into the swift current. Joe slid Duke to his right so he could watch the water as it bubbled and churned into the side of the wagon. The water's level continued to rise until it was almost reaching the canvas, but the wagon wasn't pushed downstream enough for him to notice. He just hoped he'd waterproofed the packs well enough.

After Bo reached the opposite bank, Joe concentrated on Mary's wagon until it rolled onto dry ground. He was about to turn downstream to save anyone who needed rescuing when he glanced upstream.

He stared at the onrushing water, exclaimed, "Lord almighty!" then wheeled Duke to the north and charged along the riverbank.

Less than a mile upstream, the fast-moving river was carrying an entire tree, complete with his leaf-covered branches. It must have been pulled from the soil by the churning water because the dark roots flared into the air like Medusa's snakes. The drag of the leaves and branches were acting as a sea anchor and keeping the thick trunk pointed downstream. It would cause massive damage to at least one of the wagons when it arrived, so Joe had to find a way to keep that from happening with very little time to figure out how to do it.

IDAHO CITY

When he was about two hundred yards north of the wagons, he turned Duke left and let him descend the bank. As his stallion entered the water, Joe pulled the end of his rope from his saddle and extended it about three feet. He looped the end under the rope and tied a triple knot. He focused on the oncoming tree torpedo and when he thought he was almost in its path, he pulled Duke to a stop then turned him downstream.

He held his makeshift lasso in his right hand and was grateful when his enhanced state slowed the passage of time. He didn't have to shift Duke's position as he saw the base of the tree drawing closer. His timing had to be almost perfect, or Duke could be struck by the tree, and they'd both find themselves underwater.

He leaned far to his right and held out the lasso just before the tree arrived. Just as the spread of dark roots passed, Joe tossed the loop over the thickest root and jerked it back as if a large fish had just taken his hook. He yanked on his left rein and Duke was only too happy to turn away from the natural demon.

Some of the branches brushed Duke's hind quarters as the rope played out and Joe quickly wrapped the other end around his saddle horn.

Duke had almost reached the eastern shore when the rope snapped out of the water, and Joe felt his saddle shift as Duke stumbled. For one heartbeat, he thought Duke would collapse back into the river, but his powerful legs overcame the unexpected force. Duke regained his footing and slowly began moving toward the shoreline. Joe looked back and saw the tree beginning to swing and hoped his knots didn't come loose or the root didn't snap off.

Duke reached the river's edge and Joe urged him onto the dry ground as the tree exerted even more force when more of its branches were being pushed by the raging current.

As soon as Duke struggled onto the solid surface, Joe pulled him to a stop and watched the tree continue its counterclockwise rotation until the branches touched the shore. He wasn't going to ask Duke to tug the trunk out of the water but hoped to hold it against the shore until the Dooleys' wagon reached the far bank.

Duke was under less strain after the tree stabilized, so Joe changed his focus to the wagons. Just before the Dooleys' team climbed the bank, Joe carefully dismounted then walked to the tree with his hand sliding along the taut, dripping rope. Before he reached the river's edge, he pulled his knife and as soon as the last wagon left the water, he began slicing the rope. The blade only cut halfway into the thick hemp before the massive tension instantly separated the remaining strands. Joe barely had time to leap away before the rope whipped past him and Duke lurched away.

As he trotted to retrieve Duke, Joe muttered, "That was stupid. I should have backed Duke up before I cut the rope or just released it from the saddle horn."

Despite his mistake, Joe soon mounted Duke and began winding the rope. After he hung it on his saddle, he patted Duke on his neck then headed downstream. When he reached the ford, he turned his stallion right and as he entered the river, Joe was startled to see that the wagons had stopped rolling and now lined the western bank. He was even more surprised when he noticed the crowd beginning to gather. He had been so focused on the river then on collecting Duke and his rope that he hadn't paid any attention to the wagons. He hadn't heard the bell ring, either.

But as soon as he spotted Faith, he pulled off his hat and waved it three times overhead as the water rose above Duke's belly.

Faith shot her hand into the air and vigorously waved back to Joe as she watched him cross the Snake River. She'd left Mary's wagon after they reached flat ground and had witnessed each second of his attempt to keep the tree from smashing into the following wagons. She knew how dangerous it was but could only watch as he leaned over and tried to lasso the root. When the attached rope popped out of the water and almost pulled Duke into the river, she felt her heart skip a beat.

As she watched Duke carrying him across the fast-moving river, Faith was relieved and incredibly proud of her husband. She'd heard the bell ring but was surprised when she found herself surrounded. Before he reached the river's edge, she ran towards him leaving the crowd behind.

Duke stepped out of the river and the accumulated water was streaming onto the ground as Joe dismounted. He didn't care about the crowd or that his boots were still filled with water as he wrapped his arms around Faith, lifted her from the ground and kissed her.

After setting her down and releasing her, she breathlessly said, "I couldn't breathe when I was watching you trying to rope the tree. I thought you were going to be pulled down when the tree began to change direction. How close was it?"

"I'll admit that it was even closer than I expected, but Duke had enough strength to keep it moving. My biggest mistake was the way I released the rope. I should have at least backed Duke up."

"It doesn't matter now. You're safe and so are all the wagons."

Joe glanced upstream and was surprised to find that the tree was still hugging the bank. When he looked past Faith, he saw Bo approaching.

When he reached them, Bo said, "I didn't even see that damned tree, Joe. I reckon if you didn't stop it, we woulda lost the Lilleys and maybe the Dooleys, too."

Joe shrugged then asked, "Are you going to have everyone top off their water barrels now?"

"Yup. We'll start fillin' 'em now that you're on our side of the river."

Joe nodded then asked, "Did the Snake bite anybody?"

Bo snickered before he replied, "Nope. A couple of the wagons had their innards soaked, but that's all."

Joe looked at Faith and said, "I guess we need to fill all of our canteens, too."

Faith smiled as she said, "Yes, sir," before they walked to their horses to gather their canteens.

Joe was leading Duke as he and Faith passed the folks when Ernie Dooley patted Joe on the back and said, "You saved us again, Joe. And that doesn't even include savin' Lizzy."

Joe just smiled and tipped his hat before he and Faith wound their way through the crowd who began drifting back to their wagons to start filling their water barrels.

When they reached Mary's wagon, Will grinned and exclaimed, "Damn, Joe! *Why do these things keep happening to you?*"

When John giggled, Mary shot him a motherly warning glance before she said, "I sometimes wonder about that myself, Joe."

Joe smiled and said, "Faith once asked me if I was a trouble magnet, and now I'm beginning to believe she was right. We need to fill our canteens, but first I have to empty my boots."

Faith took Duke's reins and watched Joe sit on the ground then pull off his boots before she tied his stallion to Bessie's saddle.

As he dumped out the water, she said. "Take off your socks and I'll get you a dry pair," then handed Duke's reins to Will and walked to Nellie.

When she returned, Joe was wringing out his socks. After he finished, she exchanged the dry socks for his wet ones then walked to Bernie and hung the socks from one of the cords holding his packs in place. As she began taking down the extra canteens from Bessie, Joe arrived and took down the four from Duke and Duchess' saddles.

Before he and Faith left to fill them, Joe turned and asked, "Do you need help filling your water barrels, Will?"

"Nope. We'll take care of it."

Joe nodded then he and Faith headed to the river. As they approached the bank, the large cottonwood floated past.

Faith watched it bob downstream and said, "That's a lot bigger than I realized."

Joe grinned as he replied, "If it was a catfish, I'd tell everybody it was even bigger."

Faith laughed then as they dropped to their heels and set the canteens on the bank, she said, "You still haven't tried your feather fishing."

Joe was dipping one of the canteens into the cold water when he said, "I haven't seen one of those streams that Herm told me about back in Julesburg. Maybe I'll find one near Idaho City. It's surrounded by mountains, so if I spot one that's not crowded with prospectors, I'll give it a try."

"Can I come with you?"

"As long as you aren't overly inflated by then."

Faith glanced downstream, and after she didn't see anyone nearby, she asked, "Have you noticed any more changes, Joe?"

"Not really. What drove you to ask?"

Faith smiled then replied, "I was just testing you. If you told me that you'd perceived a change, I'd know you may have been exaggerating when you first told me you'd noticed some enhancements."

Joe grinned and shook his head as they continued filling the canteens. He was relieved that Faith hadn't noticed any significant changes. He believed anything new this early in her pregnancy wouldn't be good.

When all of their canteens were full, they headed back to Mary's wagon, passing lines of folks lugging full buckets and passing others carrying empty buckets to be refilled.

After hanging the canteens in place, Joe said, "I think it's time, Faith. I'm just debating about having some form of ceremony."

A puzzled Faith looked at him and asked, "What are you talking about, Joe? What kind of ceremony?"

"A funeral, or maybe just a wake. My mother said Irish wakes are closer to a party, so I guess I'll go that route."

Faith was even more confused as she asked, "Did someone die, and I hadn't noticed?"

Joe shook his head, replied, "Not yet. But I have to do this," then walked to Nellie and opened the flap to one of her packs.

His answer didn't solve Faith's confusion, but when he pulled out his sealed pickle pot, she smiled.

Joe set it on the ground, loosened the screw holding the lid in place, then slowly lowered the handle and removed the cover.

He reached into the vinegary reservoir, extracted his sole surviving sour snack and slowly stood.

Then he raised it in front of his eyes, and carefully intoned, "You are the last of your breed and I salute you, oh noble pickle. You have bravely withstood my many incursions into your domain, but for the last few days, you have suffered in loneliness. Soon, you will follow the path taken by your lost comrades and somewhere, in Idaho Territory, you will at last find peace. So, my dear friend, I now bid you a fond farewell."

As Faith held back her laughter, Joe elevated the pickle above his head then slowly lowered it, opened his mouth and chomped off a third of its tart, tangy torso.

Faith couldn't restrain herself any longer and began laughing as Joe gobbled up the rest of the pickle.

After he licked his fingers, he dumped the remaining pickle juice on the ground, picked up the lid and the pot and smiled at Faith.

"Arv already emptied his pickle barrel and when I saw him filling it with water, I knew it would come to this. We have two dry days ahead of us, and six critters to keep watered. I think we'll be okay with what we have in the canteens, but I'll still fill this with water."

Faith replied, "I'm sorry for your loss, Joe. Maybe you'll find more when you visit Idaho City."

Joe smiled, said, "Maybe," then carried his empty pot and lid to the river.

———

Forty minutes later, the wagons began crossing the dry flatlands. As Joe rode out front with Chuck, he thought they were crossing an almost alien landscape with its volcanic soil and sparse, scattered greenery. There were also larger patches of prairie grass that looked like tan and green ponds.

As they separated from the wagon, Chuck said, "This sure looks different, Joe."

"I imagine in another ten years or so, those colonies of prairie grass will make it look more like the Laramie Plains, but without the creeks and streams."

Chuck grinned and said, "As long as fellers like you don't burn 'em down."

"They won't need me or anyone else to do that, Chuck. Mother Nature has her own match when she sends bolts of lightning down from the storm clouds."

"She can do whatever she wants to this part of the territory. I'm just happy she put all that gold around Idaho City."

"I reckon there's not a lot of it that's easy to find. If it was, it wouldn't be worth much. That's the only reason gold demands a lot of money. It's not even useful like iron."

"That's ridiculous, Joe. Gold is made into coins and iron is only made into tools."

"It's only turned into money because it's rare. But if it was plentiful, it'd probably be worth less than iron. In ancient times, salt was worth more than gold."

"Now you're just makin' things up. Why would anybody think salt is worth more than gold?"

"Because salt was hard for many of those ancient civilizations to find and was critical to preserve meat. The Arabs would load caravans of camels with salt and carry them to Europe. The Romans used to pay their soldiers with salt. It's where we get the word salary."

"How do you know all that stuff?"

Joe shrugged and replied, "History books. I read every one I could find when I was a boy."

Chuck snickered then said, "You're still a boy, Joe."

"I reckon so. But let me ask you this. If you were dying of thirst in a desert, would you rather find a treasure chest full of gold or an oasis with a pool of water?"

"I ain't never gonna cross a desert, Joe."

Joe saw no advantage in clarifying the point, so he asked, "Where are you and Marigold going to live when you get there?"

"We'll figure it out when we see the town. I reckon we'll have enough money to hold us over 'til I start findin' gold."

"Is Bo going to give you all of your pay?"

"I ain't asked him yet. But if he doesn't, I figure he'll give me almost all of it 'cause we'd be just a couple of weeks from trail's end."

Joe was surprised that Chuck had answered the question rather than just angrily tell him that it was none of his business. But he felt as if he'd pushed Chuck as far as he could about Idaho City, so he ended the conversation.

They rode in silence for twenty minutes when Joe pointed to the northwest and said, "I wonder what attracted those buzzards' interest."

Chuck squinted in that direction then replied, "Maybe that Pete bastard got a taste of his own medicine and got bushwhacked. It'd be real justice if they killed him then took his horses."

Joe glanced at Chuck before turning his eyes back to the circling vultures. He'd been surprised that Chuck still held such deep hate for Pete but soon realized he shouldn't have been surprised at all.

A minute later, Joe said, "It looks like a dead coyote."

"How the hell can you see that from here?"

"I'm just guessing because of its size and coloring. I don't think a wolf or cougar would be hunting out here. But I am curious about what could have killed it."

"Maybe it just died of old age."

"That's possible, or maybe it was a youngster out on his own for the first time and thought a rattler would make a nice supper."

"Are you gonna go over there?"

"Nope. I don't want to disturb the buzzards. They need to eat, too."

Chuck muttered, "Too bad they ain't feastin' on Pete."

Joe didn't even glance at Chuck this time but continued looking at the dead critter as some buzzards landed and others took to the air.

They continued following the road and soon passed about a half a mile east of the vulture dining room.

Ten minutes later, Joe looked at the fresh ruts and said, "I wonder if we'll catch up to those freight wagons heading to Idaho City. If we don't see them, I'm sure we'll meet them on their way back."

"Maybe they'll be takin' some of that gold back to Utah."

"I think they'd probably put in a strongbox then load it onto a stagecoach that would be guarded by well-armed outriders."

"I reckon you're right, Joe. We might even see one of 'em before we get there."

"That's possible. I didn't ask Corporal Oxnard, but I imagine Idaho City has at least one assay office to ascertain the purity of the gold and two or three banks to pay the prospectors and store the gold in their safes."

Chuck grinned and said, "I'll bet they got a sheriff and a dozen deputies, too."

"He said the last time that he'd heard about it, the sheriff only had one deputy because it was hard to find men willing to take the job because of the gold."

"You told me you wanted to be a lawman, so maybe you oughta be a deputy."

"I'm only sixteen, Chuck."

Chuck snickered before he said, "You could tell the sheriff you're nineteen, Joe. If he's havin' a hard time findin' deputies, he'd just take your word for it."

"You know I wouldn't lie about my age or anything else, Chuck. Besides, I promised Bo that I'd help get the folks to Oregon."

"But you ain't even bein' paid, Joe!"

"And everyone keeps reminding me about it, but it's not important to me. I promised Bo and that's all that matters to me."

Chuck shook his head before saying, "I reckon you ain't as smart as I figgered."

Joe grinned and said, "I never claimed to be smart, Chuck. I just read a lot before I left the Quimbys."

"Too bad they didn't stay on that farm of theirs."

"I'm sure they left because they were about to be conscripted into the Confederate army and their older brother refused to pay the fee to keep them out of uniform."

"Didn't you even ask them why they took off?"

"Nope. I talked to them as little as possible, and they probably would have lied if I had asked why they left."

"At least you ain't gotta worry about any more of 'em showin' up."

"That's nearly impossible because John isn't about to sell the farm and head west."

Chuck just nodded as they continued riding north along the empty road.

It was late morning when Joe checked their backtrail and no longer saw the wagons even though they had kept their horses moving slowly because of the lack of available water.

Chuck then looked back as well before saying, "They're not movin' as fast as I figgered."

"Do you want to pull up until we spot them again?"

"Sure. I need to practice usin' a double draw anyway."

Joe had noticed that Chuck had changed his left-hand holster back to its original location so both Colts now had their butts facing backwards, but he didn't comment before he dismounted.

After Chuck stepped down, he tied Willy's reins to Joe's saddle horn then walked away and stopped after he'd gone about twenty feet. He spread his feet apart then began drawing both Colts at the same time.

Joe noticed that he was also cocking the hammer each time, which he hadn't done before. He closely watched Chuck's left hand on his second twin draw and thought it looked awkward. He was also cocking the hammer too early. If he wasn't careful, he might snag the Colt's front sight on the holster and could shoot himself. When Chuck did it two out of the three times, Joe thought about telling him, but figured Chuck wouldn't be grateful for the suggestion.

IDAHO CITY

After he'd drawn the Colts a dozen times, Chuck looked back at Joe and said, "It's gonna get noisy, so you might wanna hang onto Duke. He seems to get spooked easy."

As Chuck grinned and looked back to the west, Joe replied, "I've got a good grip, Chuck," then slid Duke and Willy a few feet to his left in case Chuck had an accidental discharge.

Joe couldn't see any possible targets within pistol range but didn't think it mattered to Chuck. He still focused on Chuck's left hand as he prepared to fire his first rounds.

A few seconds later, Chuck drew both pistols and cocked their hammers with his thumbs before the muzzles began to clear leather. When their barrels were almost level with the ground, he fired.

Joe saw the slugs slam into the dirt less than ten yards away and wondered if Chuck had intended to pull his triggers so early. He hadn't even paused to let his sights settle.

Nonetheless, when Chuck looked back at him, he still seemed pleased with his performance.

"That woulda scared the pants off of any feller, no matter how brave he thought he was."

Joe just nodded and wondered why Chuck felt as if he had to face a gunfighter. Maybe he was expecting to use the two-handed draw to protect his claim. He definitely wasn't planning on asking the sheriff about filling a deputy position. Oddly enough, before Chuck learned about the gold strikes, Joe thought he would have made an excellent lawman. Now he wasn't sure that the old Chuck even existed anymore. It was the opposite of Mary's sudden conversion from witch to friend.

Chuck continued firing until both pistols were empty. After he holstered his Colts, Joe relaxed, and Chuck walked back wearing the same grin.

"I don't see the wagons yet, so I'm gonna clean and reload my guns."

"I'll watch for them while you take care of your Colts. I imagine Bo's wagon will show up pretty soon."

Chuck nodded then walked to his saddlebags and removed a leather pouch and his slicker. After spreading the slicker across the ground, he sat down then set both pistols on the rubberized canvas.

As Joe watched for the wagons, he wondered if Chuck was going to become even more obsessed before they reached Idaho City. He couldn't imagine that it was even possible, but a few weeks ago, he never would have expected that Chuck would even think of leaving the wagon train before it reached Oregon.

Less than ten minutes later, he saw the top of Bo's wagon and said, "There're here, Chuck."

Chuck didn't look up from reloading his first Colt when he replied, "They won't get here for another hour or so. Then we can join 'em for lunch before we head out again."

Joe continued watching the wagons as he said, "Okay. I need to give Duke some water when we get back anyway."

Joe rubbed Duke's neck as Chuck continued to work in silence. The morning had already seemed to last an extra hour or two, and Joe suspected when they returned late in the afternoon, it would feel as if he'd spent a week in the saddle. At least he'd be able to talk to Faith after the wagons arrived. If Chuck hadn't used Duke's saddle horn as a hitching post, he would have ridden away already.

―――――

Two miles away, Bo turned to Nora and said, "I wonder why Chuck and Joe are just waiting for us. They should either be riding ahead or comin' back this way."

Nora replied, "Chuck is sitting down, so maybe his horse went lame, or he fell from his saddle."

"I don't think so. His horse is still standin' and if Chuck was hurt, Joe woulda helped him. I guess we'll find out when we get there."

―――――

Chuck stood, holstered both pistols then picked up his slicker and snapped it to free it from its accumulated dirt. The sharp crack startled Willy and the gray gelding jerked backwards sliding Joe's saddle akilter.

Chuck laughed as Joe quickly slipped it back into position, untied Willy's reins then let them drop before he tightened his cinches.

Chuck rolled up his slicker, tied it behind his saddle and said, "I ain't never seen Willy spooked like that before. Maybe I shoulda taken Max today."

Joe said, "Maybe so. I'm going to have lunch with Faith," then mounted and rode away.

Chuck quickly stepped into his stirrup, swung his leg over Willy and set off after Joe.

Nora quickly said, "It looks as if I was wrong. Now I wonder why Joe is out front. I hope they didn't have a fight."

"I wouldn't be surprised if they did. Chuck doesn't seem like himself since he heard about gold bein' found around Idaho City. It's been gettin' worse every day, too."

"Are you going to give him his full pay if he leaves early?"

"I'll probably pay him all of the two hundred dollars he signed up for. We'll only have a couple of weeks left after reachin' that turnoff, and I'd rather not make Chuck mad for ten bucks."

"You'll be down at least one scout if he leaves. Will that be alright?"

"I only had two when we started and most of the danger is behind us. It's kinda funny when you think about it. We may finish this journey with three scouts, and none of them will be the two men I hired for the job."

"And you aren't even paying the one who almost single-handedly saved the wagon train four times."

"Don't remind me. I musta asked Joe to take Mort's pay a few dozen times, but he always tells me about the promise he made to me when I first talked to him. He said that he'd do all he could to help and wouldn't ask for anything. I ain't even sure it was a real promise, neither."

"Before he leaves, you could give the money to Faith without telling him. She didn't make the promise, and you can tell her it's a late wedding present."

"I reckon I could do that, but Faith might still turn it down 'cause she knows Joe wouldn't take it. Maybe I'll just slip it into his saddlebag when they're not lookin'."

Nora smiled as she said, "That's a perfect solution, Bo."

Bo grinned then said, "It looks like we'll find out what happened soon enough. Go ahead and give that bell a ring, Nora."

Nora nodded then grabbed the clapper's rope and whipped it back and forth three times.

―――

As soon as she heard Nora ring the bell, Faith began crawling to the back of the wagon and as soon as it stopped, she slid off the tailgate. She spotted Joe but didn't walk towards him, as she knew that he and Chuck would need to talk to Bo first.

Joe was still twenty yards in front of Chuck when he heard the bell then watched the wagons come to a somewhat coordinated stop.

He was approaching from the west side of the wagons, so as soon as he spotted Faith, he greeted her in his traditional hat wave.

As soon as she waved back, he slowed Duke to let Chuck catch up.

When he did, Chuck loudly asked, "Why'd you take off like that, Joe?"

"I wanted to water Duke, and if there had been somewhere to tie off Willy, I would have headed back as soon as I saw the wagons."

Chuck grinned as he said, "I reckon you really just wanted to see Faith."

Joe smiled and said, "You know me too well, Chuck."

Chuck snickered but didn't say anything while Joe wondered if he understood the new Chuck at all.

As soon as they pulled up and dismounted, Bo asked, "Why were you boys just waitin' out there? Did you have trouble of some kind?"

Chuck replied, "Nope. I was just cleanin' and loadin' my pistols."

Bo looked at Joe who just said, "My saddle horn was being used as a hitching post for Willy."

"Okay. Go get some chow."

Joe nodded then waved to Nora before leading Duke away. He greeted Marigold who was preparing lunch then saw Faith waiting for him beside Mary's wagon.

When he reached her, Joe let Duke's reins fall then scooped her into his arms and kissed her as if he'd been gone for a month.

When their lips parted, Faith smiled and asked, "What inspired that?"

As he released his grip, Joe replied, "You always inspire me, Faith."

"And I'm always happy when you return. Go ahead and tie off Duke and I'll fix our lunch."

Joe nodded, said, "Yes, ma'am," then took Duke's reins and led him to the tailgate where he tied him to Duchess' saddle.

Will approached and asked, "Anything happen this morning, Joe?"

"Nothing much. Did you notice that Chuck turned his left-hand holster around?"

"Sorry. I musta missed that."

"When we lost sight of the wagons, Chuck decided to practice drawing and firing both pistols at the same time."

Will's eyebrows rose as he asked, "Why would he wanna do that?"

"I'm not really sure. When he told me he was going to do it, he sounded as if he planned on getting into a gunfight, but I can't imagine him getting into that sort of situation. But when he was practicing, I noticed that he was pulling back his hammers with his thumbs before the muzzles cleared the holsters. The right side wasn't too bad, but the left side was slower and more awkward. I was worried the gunsight might snag on the leather causing an accidental discharge, so when he said he was going to fire a few rounds, I moved the horses out of the away."

"Did he have an accident?"

"No. But his shots all hit the ground between twenty and forty feet in front of him."

"Did you tell him he was making a mistake?"

"Nope. I was pretty sure he wouldn't appreciate any criticism. If he does any more two-handed target practice, I'll just make sure I'm a few feet to his right."

Will nodded before Joe said, "I need to get some water for Duke, so I'll talk to you later."

"Okay."

As Will walked back to the front of the wagon, Joe walked to Nellie, pulled the sealed pot from her pack then carried it a few yards away and set it on the ground.

After taking off the lid, he returned to the horses, untied Duke and led him to the pot of water, wondering if the stallion would turn his nose away when he detected any scent of residual vinegar. Duke must not have noticed anything different or simply was too thirsty to care as he quickly began lapping the water.

When he'd drunk more than half of the water, Joe led him back to Duchess and tied him to her saddle.

As he was replacing the lid, Faith stepped close and said, "I heard what you told Will about Chuck. Do you still think he won't give you any trouble?"

Joe tightened down the lid and as he carried it to Nellie, he replied, "Chuck may have changed since he learned about the gold strike, but I still don't think he'll cause me any grief unless he accidentally shoots me. If anyone needs to worry about him, it's Pete. Chuck does seem to mention that last bushwhacker fairly often. Luckily, it's highly unlikely that he'll ever see the man."

After replacing the pot in Nellie's pack, he and Faith walked to the right side of Mary's wagon to share lunch with the Boones and their boys.

Twenty minutes later, Joe waved to everyone and rode Duke to the front of the line. Bo was talking to Chuck, but when he spotted Joe, he turned and waited until he arrived.

When Joe pulled up, Bo said, "After we finally got rollin', we covered more miles that I expected. I reckon we should be off this empty ground by midafternoon tomorrow. So, I was just tellin' Chuck that you should stay within eyesight."

Joe nodded as he said, "Okay, boss."

Chuck mounted Max before saying, "At least we ain't got any rivers or creeks to cross."

Bo said, "Even the ones we'll ford the next day won't be any trouble."

As Joe started to ride away, he heard Chuck say, "Then the day after that, me and Joe will be headin' off to Idaho City."

Joe didn't hear if Bo replied but didn't believe the wagon master would bother saying anything.

When Chuck caught up, he loudly said, "We're gettin' close to the turnoff, Joe."

Joe looked at him and said, "Only if you believe that sixty miles is close."

Chuck just snickered as they continued pulling away from the wagons.

After a few minutes, Joe looked back and said, "They're moving again, but we probably need to slow down."

Chuck glanced behind them then said, "I reckon I'm just too anxious to reach that turnoff," before slowing Max.

"I hope you don't get so excited that you keep going after we make that turn to the west."

"I ain't makin' any promises, Joe. But I reckon I'll be able to hold back until we start crossin' the Little Camas Prairie."

"I've never heard of it before. Where is it?"

Chuck grinned and replied, "It's after the Big Camas Prairie."

"That doesn't help, Chuck."

"The Big Camas starts after we cross the Wood River. It ain't that big, so we'll only take us a day to cross it. The Small Camas is about half that size, and we'll reach the turnoff twenty miles after we leave it behind."

Joe nodded and tried to picture the path in his mind but found it difficult to imagine as he didn't believe that the Camas Prairie resembled the Great Plains or the much smaller Laramie Plains.

They rode in silence for almost an hour before Chuck said, "Let's pull up. I want to practice some more, but I ain't gonna waste any ammunition."

Joe nodded and brought Duke to a halt before he dismounted. After Chuck tied Max's reins to Joe's saddle horn, he stepped away and began to practice.

As Joe studied his technique, he noticed that Chuck was improving, but only marginally. He still hadn't fully corrected his dangerous method of cocking the hammers using his thumbs before the pistols cleared their holsters and his left-hand draw was still noticeably slower. He still didn't mention it to Chuck but hoped sheer repetition would fix the problem before he shot himself.

IDAHO CITY

When Chuck holstered his pistols, Joe looked to the south and found that the wagons were within a mile, so he said, "I think we can start moving again, Chuck."

Chuck nodded then untied Max and mounted. After Joe stepped into his saddle, they headed north and began to rebuild the gap.

———

Joe's afternoon seemed to drag even more than his morning. So, when the sun finally neared the western horizon, he looked skyward and said a silent prayer of thanks.

When they started back, Chuck said, "I reckon they musta covered almost twenty miles today, even after crossing the Snake. We'll probably ford the Wood River tomorrow afternoon then we'll start crossin' the Big Camas Prairie."

Joe simply replied, "I reckon so," but had noticed the excitement in Chuck's voice. He began to suspect that Chuck was already planning to continue on to Idaho City as soon as they reached the Small Camas Plains.

———

That night, after sharing supper with Will, Mary and their boys, Joe and Faith ducked into their tent. For their first time, Joe lit their kerosene lantern. The nights were growing longer and colder, and even the low heat generated by the lantern was appreciated. Laddie seemed to have completely shifted his allegiance to John, so Faith would no longer benefit by having his body heat warm her left side.

After they'd generated their own significant amount of body heat, Faith snuggled close and asked, "If Chuck does leave before you expect, will you go with him?"

"It depends on how far away we are when he tells me. I suppose if we're almost across the Small Camas Plains, I'd keep going. But if he says he's continuing on before that, I'll just let him go."

"So, it's possible you may not return when I expected."

"I reckon so. You aren't worried, are you?"

Faith sighed then answered, "No, not really. I'm just annoyed with Chuck's behavior."

"So, am I. Have you talked to Marigold at all?"

"No. I haven't talked to Becky much either. At least Herm is riding on the driver's seat now."

"I noticed. I don't think he'll be ready to ride out front for another couple of weeks, though. Just about the time we cross into Oregon."

Faith began to ask, "Do you…" then stopped.

After a few silent seconds, Joe smiled as he asked, "Do I know where we'll stay or what I'll do?"

Faith quietly said, "I'm sorry, Joe. I should just trust that you'll keep your promise to provide a home for me and Kathleen Maureen."

"There's no reason to apologize, Faith. I ask myself those same questions at least ten times a day. I may not have found an answer to either of them, but I won't let it be the first promise I break. When we welcome our daughter into the world, she'll be warm and safe, just like her perfect mother."

Faith kissed him before saying, "Thank you, Joe. I won't ask again."

"It won't bother me if you do. So, are your journal entries up to date?"

"As of yesterday. Tomorrow, Mary and I are going to try to do some baking while the wagons are rolling."

"How can you manage to do it without setting her wagon ablaze?"

"We're going to build a small fire in one of her pots on the tailgate, then we'll put the dough in our Dutch oven and cover it with her washtub. It'll be an adventure trying to get it right, but we'll start with biscuits because they're faster. If we get it right, we'll be able to use some of Alice's strawberry preserves to make them special."

Joe smiled and said, "I hope it works because my mouth is already watering."

"I can make bacon biscuits for you, too."

"Now you're just torturing me, Mrs. Beck."

Faith laughed then kissed him on the tip of his nose before rolling onto her back and tugging the blankets up to her chin.

After she closed her eyes, Joe blew out the lamp then laid beside her. He stayed awake for a few more minutes as he wondered what the next few days would bring.

CHAPTER 6

The next morning passed much as it had the day before. Joe and Chuck stayed within eyesight of the wagons and Joe continued to suffer from Chuck's frequent comments about Idaho City, the turnoff and the time or distance they'd travel before they left the wagons behind. The only change was that Chuck didn't practice his double-draw technique as he seemed satisfied with his ability to pull and fire both pistols simultaneously.

Despite the fresh ruts left by the recent passing of the freight wagons, the wagons themselves never appeared on the horizon. So, Joe began to wonder if they alternated sleeping and driving and only stopped for short breaks to rest their teams.

When they returned for the noon break, Faith impressed Joe when she gave him a biscuit even though it was lacking any of Alice's strawberry preserves. Before he left, she promised to bake a dozen more by the time they stopped for the day.

―――

Three hours after Joe and Chuck left the wagons, they pulled up before the eastern bank of the Wood River.

Joe said, "I'll check the ford. The freighters didn't have any problems getting across, but I want to see how deep it is."

Chuck grinned and said, "Be my guest."

Joe nodded and walked Duke into the cold water. The river was about half the width of the Snake and the current wasn't nearly as fast as it had been when they crossed the wider, deeper river.

The crossing wasn't difficult, and the water level just lapped at his knees before receding. When he returned, Joe walked Duke to a nearby pine and dismounted. As he tied off Duke, Chuck arrived and stepped down.

Joe sat down and was pulling off his boots when he looked upstream and said, "This sure is pretty country, isn't it?"

Chuck replied, "It's gonna be a lot prettier when I see the gold shinin' back at me."

Joe dumped the water from his right boot as he said, "If they hadn't found that gold, I wouldn't mind living here. This country is nothing short of magnificent."

"I don't care if it looked like hell on earth as long as I find a lotta gold."

Joe didn't reply but just continued admiring the scenery while he upended his left boot then set it down and stripped off his socks.

IDAHO CITY

After wringing them out, he set them across the boots leaving enough space for the insides of the boots to dry. Then he took off his hat and set it down before stretching out with his hands behind his neck.

Chuck tied Max's reins to a pine branch then walked a few yards away and began to practice his double draw, but Joe didn't even bother watching.

He was about to nap when Chuck exclaimed, "I'm gettin' pretty good, Joe!"

Joe turned to look at Chuck then said, "I don't think you'll ever need to fire both of them at the same time, Chuck."

"Maybe so. But sendin' two bullets at the same time gives me a better chance of hittin' my target."

"If it ever becomes necessary to use a pistol, if a single .44 doesn't do the job, I imagine a second one won't be much help."

"You gotta be kiddin', Joe! Two slugs at close range would almost cut a feller in half."

Joe stared at Chuck for a few seconds before saying, "Only if he was as skinny as a hitching post."

Chuck snickered then said, "Or if he was like some girl I could mention."

Joe was startled that Chuck would even think of saying something like that about Faith but pretended he hadn't put a face on the girl he said he couldn't mention. Marigold was definitely more robust, but Faith was hardly thin enough to be called skinny. Even when she had been so concerned about her lack of a womanly figure, he never thought she was too thin. She'd been filling out almost daily as they journeyed west, and he suspected that if she'd been able to rest and eat more, even she would have noticed.

Chuck resumed his double-draw practice and was still slapping leather when Joe pulled on his damp socks and mostly dry boots.

After he stood, he walked to Duke, opened the flap to his left saddlebag and removed his spare gunbelt. He had no intention of wearing it but had never removed the knife from its sheath and wanted to inspect the blade.

Chuck never looked back at him as Joe slid the eight-inch-long knife from its leather home. It wasn't as well-maintained as his nine-inch blade and needed sharpening but was still a good knife. He returned it to the sheath then rolled the gunbelt and put it back into his saddlebag.

He patted Duke's left haunch then looked at Chuck and noticed that he didn't have a knife on either gunbelt. He had kept his own ammunition pouch but must have removed his knife when he decided to wear both pistols. He thought it was a bad idea but didn't ask Chuck about it.

IDAHO CITY

Joe looked to the southeast and just a minute or so later, the canvas roofs of the wagons began to emerge on the horizon, brightly illuminated by the afternoon sun.

He was focusing on the wagons when he said, "They'll get here in about an hour, Chuck. Do you want to head back?"

Chuck glanced at the distant wagons before replying, "Nah. Let's wait for 'em. I reckon Bo will pull up for the night after crossin' the river."

Joe thought about leaving but didn't want to make Bo think something was wrong if he returned alone.

———

When Bo spotted Joe and Chuck a few minutes later, he said, "They're waitin' for us near the Wood River, Nora. We made really good time crossin' these barren lands, so we'll be able to ford the river today. After we set up camp on the other side, we'll have some spare time to do some maintenance on the wagons."

"It wasn't as bad as I'd expected it to be. I imagined it to be more like a desert, and some of the oxen and mule would collapse from lack of water."

Bo grinned as he replied, "I reckon it's better to expect the worst and find it ain't so bad than expectin' it to be easy and learnin' otherwise."

Nora smiled and said, "You're right, Bo," then looked at the rugged mountains stretching across the horizon and asked, "It certainly is beautiful country ahead of us, isn't it?"

"It sure is. But before we reach Oregon, it'll get ordinary again until we reach the forests."

Nora looked at Bo and quietly asked, "What does our destination look like?"

"It's covered with pine forests and has a lot of rivers and creeks. There's good ground for raisin' crops and plenty of rain, too."

"Will we be able to see the Pacific Ocean?"

Bo smiled and replied, "Only if we want to make a two-hundred-mile drive."

Nora nodded before she refocused on the mountains. She'd never seen an ocean but began to think of making a home somewhere close to the majestic mountains.

A few wagons back, Faith said, "I imagine Joe is imagining building our home in a tree-filled canyon among those mountains."

Mary turned and looked north before asking, "Even if there isn't another person living within fifty miles?"

"I should have said that more clearly. I don't mean that he's thinking of building our home in those mountains, just that seeing them probably triggered Joe's imagination. Ever since we visited the canyon at the bottom of Cheyenne Pass, it's rare that Joe lets three days go by without talking about it."

"And how do you feel about living among the trees?"

Faith smiled as she replied, "As long as it's not isolated, I'd love it."

"If it's near a town, maybe we'd join you."

"That would make it perfect."

Mary nodded, then looked at Will and wondered what his reaction would be if she said she wanted to join Faith and Joe. But there was no point in asking, at least for a while as even Joe had no idea of where he and Faith would find a home. And with their long journey about to end, she knew how anxious Faith was about their uncertain future.

She knew of other women who had different concerns about what lay ahead because their husbands had expressed an interest in joining Chuck and Marigold when they headed to Idaho City. While the temperature of the gold fever had diminished somewhat over the past few days, she expected it to rise rapidly when Chuck and Joe returned from their visit to the town.

After his extensive study of the mountains, Joe had shifted his attention to the Big Camas Prairie on the other side of the river. While there were some similarities with the Laramie Plains, there were notable differences. It wasn't nearly as wide and was bracketed by mountains. He could already see streams passing through the grasslands and Chuck had told him that the Small Camas Prairie included marshlands.

He suspected that when they rode out tomorrow morning, Chuck would begin lobbying to continue on to Idaho City, which was still seventy miles away. If he did, Joe doubted if he'd be able to talk him out of it. His best argument would be to tell him that if he left, he'd be on his own for at least another day.

He was still looking west when he spotted something moving in the distance.

After studying the specks, he smiled and said, "Maybe the freighters had a problem with one of their wagons because I can see them now. They'll disappear again soon though because they're almost three miles away."

Chuck turned, looked to the west and after staring for almost a minute, he said, "I can't see 'em, Joe. Are you sure you didn't see a Shoshone scout?"

"I'm sure. The reason I think they needed to fix one of their wagons was that I didn't see them a few minutes ago. I guess they must have pulled off the road into the shadows to do the repairs, so they were almost invisible until they started rolling again."

"You ain't makin' all this up, are ya?"

"It's just a guess. But at least we know where the freight wagons are."

Chuck still hadn't seen a hint of the wagons as he said, "I wonder why we ain't seen a stagecoach full of gold headin' this way."

"Joe Oxnard said that most of the road traffic uses the new road. But maybe they don't even take the gold to Salt Lake City. They could just take it to the Snake, load it on a barge and then just let it and the Columbia carry them all the way to Astoria. Then they could load it onto a ship bound for San Francisco."

Chuck snickered then said, "You sure got a crazy way of lookin' at things, Joe."

Joe smiled as he replied, "I know, but it keeps me busy."

The freight wagons soon faded over the horizon, so Joe turned and walked back to their horses. Bo's wagon was less than half a mile away, so he untied Duke and led him out from under the pine before he mounted.

Chuck was about to say something then changed his mind and untied Max. When he was in his saddle, he waited until Joe started moving before he followed.

Joe avoided smiling as he closed the gap to the wagons. There wasn't a reasonable excuse for making the short ride, but after two days of putting up with the new Chuck, the minor act of annoying Chuck gave him a small measure of satisfaction.

After they reached the lead wagon, Chuck reported to Bo while Joe continued to Mary's wagon and was surprised when he didn't see Faith. But when Will saw him, he must have told her because just seconds later, she trotted around Bernie and waved.

Joe almost ripped his hat from his head, wagged it three times then pulled it back on before wheeling Duke around.

Just as he was dismounting, Faith arrived and said, "I thought you were just going to wait for us to stop."

Joe smiled as he replied, "I guess I'm supposed to say that I couldn't wait to see you. But to be honest, I just wanted to irritate Chuck."

"Has he been that annoying?"

"And then some."

"Did you try the ford across the Wood River?"

Joe nodded and replied, "Yes, ma'am. It was pretty easy compared to the Snake and many of the others we had to cross. How did your portable bakery work this afternoon?"

"I had to put some branches under the firepot to keep it from scorching the tailgate, but other than that, it worked almost as well as a cookstove's oven."

"I imagine the washtub and the pot will need a good scrubbing later."

"Are you volunteering for the job?"

"I'd be happy to if I'm paid in bacon biscuits."

"I think that's a fair arrangement. So, tell me why Chuck was so irritating."

Joe began detailing the annoying afternoon as the wagons rolled closer to the river. He was still talking when Nora rang the bell, and the wagons pulled to a fairly well coordinated stop.

Faith looked to the front of the line and was about to ask why they stopped when she saw Bo's wagon slowly enter the river.

She looked at Joe and said, "I'll stay with Mary until we reach the other side."

Joe nodded then kissed her quickly before she climbed onto the wagon. After she disappeared into the canvas cave, he mounted Duke again then rode to the riverbank. By the time he arrived, Chuck had already driven the flatbed into the water, so Joe just pulled up a few yards downstream to monitor the crossing.

As he watched the wagons roll onto the west bank, Joe thought about Fort Boise and the new town that had been established nearby. Corporal Oxnard had told him that the Boise River was east of the fort and the town, and that its source was up north in the Salmon Mountains. It was also fed by fast-moving creeks that flowed past Idaho City. That information was why he'd suggested that they could be moving the gold by barge rather than using the road to Salt Lake City.

But it wasn't the question of how they shipped the gold that was on his mind. He was thinking of Boise City. He didn't know how big it was but imagined it had fewer than a hundred residents. He suspected that it would grow quickly with the influx of folks heading to Idaho City in the hope of striking it rich. Many of them would soon realize that their dreams were in vain and return to the new town and the protection of Fort Boise.

Joe continued watching the wagons and wondered how long it would take before Chuck's gold fever subsided. It had better be soon as he'd have to make a home for Marigold before she had their baby. That thought instantly triggered his almost constant concerns about finding a home for Faith and Kathleen Maureen. *What could a sixteen-year-old do to support his wife and baby?*

He was still pondering his dilemma as Mary's wagon rolled out of the river and their four mares and Bernie rained water as they climbed onto dry ground. He was growing frustrated when he saw Faith stick her blonde head out of the back of the wagon. When she smiled and waved to him, Joe's somber mood vanished.

He pulled off his hat, waved back, and as he tugged it back on, he said, "I'll keep my promise to you and our baby, Faith."

Then Joe smiled as he said, "I hope I didn't guess wrong. I'd lose my air of mystique if we had a son. We haven't even thought of a boy's name. But if I am wrong, then he won't be a Joe Junior. He'll have a proper Christian name and a middle name, too. I imagine Faith won't want to give him her father's name, so I think she'd agree to christening him James after my father. I could live with James Joseph Beck."

Now that he'd settled his mind, Joe continued to observe the wagons as they forded the river. When the last one rolled out of the water, Joe walked Duke into the river.

Two minutes later, he dismounted as Faith stood beside Bessie just watching.

When he tied Duke's reins to Mary's left rear wheel, Faith stepped close and said, "After you empty the river from your boots, I'll trade you this dry pair of socks for your wet ones."

Joe grinned and said, "Thank you, Mrs. Beck," then sat on the ground and began pulling off his right boot.

"You need to oil your boots, or the leather will dry out and they'll just fall off your feet."

Joe tugged his left boot off and replied, "Yes, ma'am. I'll do that. But let me remind you I still have the second pair that Captain Chalmers gave to me."

"I haven't forgotten, sir. You still have your old work boots, too. Do they even fit anymore?"

"I haven't tried them on in months. They were too tight back then, so I imagine my toes would scream bloody murder if I tried to stuff my big feet into them now."

Faith laughed as she exchanged his dry foot covers for his seriously sodden socks.

As she wrang them out, she asked, "Why don't you give the work boots to someone with smaller feet?"

Joe grinned as he replied, "Everyone on the wagon train has smaller feet than I do. Maybe that applies to everyone in Idaho Territory, too."

"Maybe you're not finished growing."

Joe pulled on the dry socks then said, "That's a possibility, I suppose. But for you, it's a certainty."

Faith smiled but didn't reply as she slid her hands across her stomach.

After Joe's feet were enclosed in leather again, he stood and said, "I'll start setting up our camp. Do you want to stay here until it's ready?"

Faith glanced back before she replied, "No. I'll help you get it ready."

Joe nodded before they walked to their horses and after tying Duke's reins to Bernie, they released Duchess and Bessie and towed them downstream. They stopped two minutes later when they reached a small grove of river birch. Joe tied the hitching rope to one of the birch trunks then he and Faith separated the horses and Bernie and secured them to the rope.

Ninety minutes later, their camp was finished, and Faith was frying bacon while Joe scrubbed the inside of the scarred washtub.

After he returned the tub and pot to Mary and thanked her for letting Faith use it as an oven, he headed back to their camp.

As he and Faith shared their supper, Joe told her about his almost unending afternoon with Chuck, including the possibility that Chuck might decide to continue riding to Idaho City tomorrow.

But even as they turned in for the night, the one topic they hadn't discussed was the one that concerned them the most. Joe didn't want Faith to believe that he wouldn't be able to keep the promise he'd made to her, and Faith wasn't about to let Joe think she was worried about their future.

So, as they lay close together under their blankets, neither was soothed by the relaxing sound created by the flowing water just a few feet outside their tent.

After a light breakfast the next morning, they saddled and loaded their horses and Bernie then led them to Mary's wagon.

When Joe and Chuck rode out thirty minutes later, Joe had almost brought Bessie along in case Chuck decided to continue on to Idaho City. He decided against it because he thought that they'd at least return for lunch. But just in case he was wrong, he did have six of Faith's bacon biscuits in his food pouch.

As they followed the freight wagons' ruts across Big Camas Prairie, Joe scanned the horizons, but spent more time studying the mountains to the north. They were the source of the creeks and rivers and he wondered if he'd finally get to try feather fishing. As they were called the Salmon Mountains, he assumed that those waters would be highways for large bug-hungry fish.

They rode for almost thirty minutes before Joe realized that Chuck hadn't said a single word or touched his pistols.

He looked at Chuck and said, "This may be called the Big Camas Prairie, but it's not even half the size of the Laramie Plains."

Chuck seemed startled before he turned and replied, "You're right about that, Joe. I reckon it ain't very long, either. We could reach the Small Camas Plains by midafternoon."

Joe suspected that Chuck was about to suggest they continue on after reaching the Small Camas Plains, so he said, "We probably will, but those marshlands might slow the wagons."

"I've crossed it a couple of times and it wasn't any problem."

Joe knew he'd shot his wad, so he just nodded.

Then Chuck gave him a small opening when he grinned and said, "The last time I passed through there, I almost got thrown outta my saddle when Willy got spooked by a big snake. I thought it was a rattler and got off a shot. When he slithered away, I figured out it was a bull snake. I reckon Willy didn't know the difference."

Joe smiled as he said, "At least he wasn't a big snapping turtle. I imagine that much marshland is home to some real monsters. I hope I don't see one bigger than the giant I saw when I was a boy. That beast was almost four feet long when he stuck out his neck and opened his massive mouth."

Chuck stared at Joe before saying, "You gotta be makin' that up, Joe. I ain't never seen one half that size."

"You know I don't say things that aren't true or exaggerated, Chuck. If anything, my estimate of the first one was on the low side. Now the one Faith and I saw back in Dakota was only about three feet long, but he scared the daylights out of Faith."

Chuck looked ahead as if he expected to see a wagon-sized snapper lumbering towards them before he asked, "Do you really think there could be one that big in those marshlands?"

"I reckon it's possible because they don't have any natural predators after they've grown for a year. They can live for more than a hundred years and weigh over two hundred pounds."

Chuck's eyebrows shot up as he exclaimed, "You're kiddin' me!"

Joe said, "I didn't ask either of the ones I saw how old he was or how much he weighed, but I read about them."

As Chuck turned his eyes to the west, Joe was surprised when he'd seen Chuck's reaction. He hoped his tale had eliminated the possibility that Chuck would leave for Idaho City a day early. Then he silently confessed to stretching the range of the alligator snapping turtle by a few hundred miles. At least he hadn't exaggerated the lifespan or the potential size of the shelled amphibian.

But even as he'd made the claim, he began to question what he'd passed along to Faith what he'd read about the never-ending growth of the snapping turtle. He'd seen small snappers that grew much larger in just two years. So, if they lived for decades, they should be as big as a buffalo unless their rate of growth slowed with each passing year. He figured it didn't matter but still wished he hadn't told Faith.

After a couple of minutes of silent riding, Joe said, "I wonder how big Boise City is now."

Chuck looked at him and asked, "What's Boise City?"

"You were there when Corporal Oxnard told us about it, Chuck. Don't you remember?"

"I musta missed hearin' it."

"He said that after the army built the new Fort Boise, folks began arriving and established a town nearby. I reckon that it's not that big yet, but it's right on the Boise River, so I'm sure it'll grow."

"Maybe it will, but it ain't gonna be as big as Idaho City."

"At least not until the gold around Idaho City runs out."

"That ain't gonna be for years, Joe."

Joe noticed that Chuck's intensity had ratcheted up a notch, so he shrugged and decided to abandon the topic.

"After we cross the Small Camas Prairie, we'll reach that new road that goes south to Salt Lake City. I imagine we'll see a lot of traffic, too."

"I reckon they're all headin' to Idaho City to find gold, too."

Joe cursed himself for not choosing a subject that couldn't be so easily redirected back to gold but wasn't able to think of one that Chuck couldn't deflect. But even as he searched his brain for a solution, Chuck solved his dilemma when he began drawing his pistols.

Joe didn't stare at Chuck but stole periodic looks to see if he'd improved his technique. After a few minutes, he had only seen Chuck make the same mistake a couple of times. Yet Joe still relaxed when Chuck finally holstered his pistols for the last time. And if Willy understood that he would have been the likely victim of an accidental discharge, Joe believed the gelding would be relieved even more than he was.

―――

Whether it was because of Chuck's sudden fear of a giant snapping turtle or for some other reason, Joe was still pleased when Chuck had them turn back to the wagons before the sun reached its zenith.

But even as they made the U-turn, Joe knew that the real test would come late in the afternoon.

―――

After sharing a pleasant lunch with Faith and the Boones, Joe and Chuck headed west into Big Camas Prairie. Then, within an hour, they'd enter the Small Camas with its marshlands.

Joe began to suspect Chuck had no intention of returning when they lost sight of the wagons without slowing their pace but decided to wait. But after another half an hour or so, if they continued to extend their lead, he'd have to ask Chuck if he was planning to keep going.

Five minutes later, Chuck looked back then slowed Willy and said, "I reckon I musta been too anxious to see a giant snappin' turtle."

"At least you'll be able to shoot it if it opens its big mouth."

"Do they get big enough to bite off your foot?"

"When they're scared, they act as if they're going to bite but it's like a rattlesnake's warning to go away. Of course, all boys and most men have to jab at them with a stick to see how powerful their jaws are, but as long as you don't poke at him, he'll leave you alone."

"Do they make a noise like a rattlesnake?"

"They hiss when they first see you, but if they extend their necks to warn you off, they'll make a low roar."

Chuck stared at Joe for a few seconds before shaking his head and pulling Willy to a stop.

Joe thought he was going to head back already when Chuck turned Willy to the north, dropped his reins and began practicing his double draw. As he whipped his Colts from his holsters, Joe backed Duke away until he created a twenty-foot safety zone.

After four dry runs, Chuck suddenly fired both pistols which made Willy jerk but as soon as the gelding was stable again, Chuck pulled the Colts and fired once more.

When Willy didn't react the second time, Chuck holstered his pistols before he turned him west again.

Then he grinned at Joe and said, "I wanted to see what Willy did when he heard shots just inches from both of his ears."

"You're lucky he didn't throw you out of your saddle."

"I was ready in case he did, but I noticed you backed away before I even fired the first time. Did you know I was gonna do that?"

"Nope. I just didn't want to be behind you in case one of your gunsights snagged on a holster and you sent a slug my way."

Chuck snickered then said, "I mighta done that the first time I tried it, but I'm too good for it to happen now."

Joe nodded despite knowing that Chuck was far from being good enough to avoid an accidental discharge. Even if he told Chuck that he was still cocking his pistols too early, he doubted that Chuck would listen.

IDAHO CITY

Ninety minutes later, much to Joe's relief, they pulled up and dismounted to await the wagons.

After tying off their horses, Chuck scanned the landscape and said, "This seems dryer than it was the last time I visited this place."

"I'll take your word for it, Chuck."

"I don't see any snappers or much else out here except all of those birds."

Joe had been examining the large, diverse flocks and said, "That's quite a mix of waterfowl out there. There are ducks, geese, and I can even see some swans far off to the southwest. I reckon a lot of them will be heading south pretty soon. How cold does it get up here, Chuck?"

Chuck glanced at Joe and didn't ask how he could identify the types of birds at this distance before he replied, "I never had to stay here in the winter, but I heard it gets nasty cold, especially up in those mountains. But I don't care how cold it gets if I strike it rich."

Joe was watching a large flight of ducks begin to land as he said, "It's getting pretty cold already and it's not even October. I think I'll buy Faith a heavy coat, some fur-lined gloves or mittens and a heavy scarf for her birthday."

Chuck grinned and said, "Then she'll be the same age as you."

"Only for another hundred and eight days, then I'll turn seventeen."

"How did you figure that out so quick?"

Joe smiled as he said, "I didn't just figure it out. I came up with that number months ago when Faith said I seemed so much older than her."

He expected a rejoinder from Chuck, but he just turned his eyes to the south and lapsed into an extended silence. As Chuck continued to stare at the marshlands, Joe wondered what had triggered his almost melancholy mood.

When Joe had told him that he was just a few months older than Faith, it had reminded Chuck of the much larger age disparity between him and Marigold. When they first married, that almost six-year gap hadn't bothered him. But each time the wagons had stopped at a settlement or fort, he'd seen how other men looked at Marigold. Many of them were closer to her age too, especially the ones in uniform. That was bad enough, but Marigold was a lively girl who enjoyed the attention and he'd begun to worry that she'd leave him when their journey ended.

While he freely admitted to his intense desire to become wealthy and powerful, his fear of losing Marigold was a secondary reason for his obsession to find gold. He was convinced that if he struck it rich, Marigold wouldn't even think of leaving him. He also failed to realize that taking her to Idaho

City might exacerbate his worries. The fast-growing town was home to many unmarried men who had already made a fortune.

But if he had expressed his concerns to Marigold, he wouldn't have been worried at all and might not be so intent about leaving the wagons after they reached Fort Boise.

Joe continued to watch the flocks of birds for another ten minutes before he turned to study the mountain range that spread across the entire northern horizon. There was snow on some of the peaks already and he imagined those white caps would cover half of the mountains by the time spring arrived. But even in the dead of winter, the heat from the sun would melt some of the frozen water and keep those creeks flowing into the valleys.

Then he reminded himself to add a fur-lined hat to his list of Faith's birthday gifts. But the most important gift he needed to give her was one he was unable to buy. He had to find a home for her and their baby.

As he shifted his focus to the west, he was almost startled to find the sun so close to the horizon. So, he quickly looked to the east and was surprised again when he saw the wagons less than a mile away. It was as if he'd lost an hour or two.

He turned and loudly said, "The wagons are almost here, Chuck."

Chuck twitched as he emerged from his reverie and looked east before saying, "I shoulda seen 'em before they got that close. I reckon I was payin' too much attention to all those birds."

"They kind of snuck up on me, too. I was looking at the snow on the mountains."

Chuck glanced to the north then said, "There ain't much up there now, but there's gonna be a lot more in a few weeks."

"I wonder how deep the snow gets down here."

Chuck shrugged before he walked to their horses and untied Willy. By the time Joe released Duke, Chuck had already mounted.

After he was in his saddle, Joe waited until he saw Faith walking alongside Mary's wagon before he waved his hat over his head.

Faith had been watching Joe for a few minutes and was beginning to wonder if something was wrong. After he mounted and waved, she knew he was all right, but was curious about what had distracted him. She suspected it had something to do with Chuck and was sure he would tell her about it later. At least he hadn't needed to follow Chuck to Idaho City a day early.

It wasn't until they began setting up their camp when Faith finally asked, "Did Chuck try to convince you to keep riding to Idaho City?"

IDAHO CITY

"Nope. He often talked about the town and gold but didn't even suggest leaving early. When he told me about the marshlands, I described the giant snapping turtle I saw when I was a boy and it seemed to spook him. I don't know if that was the reason he decided to wait, but it doesn't matter. I'm sure he'll want to continue riding to Idaho City tomorrow, though."

"So, I won't see you for the next two nights?"

"Unless he suddenly changes his mind."

Faith pulled the skillet out of a pack and said, "I don't think there's much chance of that happening. I talked to Marigold this afternoon, and she was even more excited about the idea than she was before."

Joe nodded and asked, "Did you talk to Becky or Herm?"

"I did. Herm has lost much of his enthusiasm after being shot, and Becky seems to believe it won't be difficult to convince him to stay with the wagon train."

"That's something. Have you heard anything else about the others?"

"No. Will said that they don't talk about it much and believes that we'll only find out how many will head north when we reach Fort Boise."

Joe unraveled the first bedroll into the tent before saying, "If I find that Idaho City is a decent place, I won't be concerned about how many families take that road. Corporal Oxnard told me that besides the dozens of saloons, it had a lot of other normal businesses as well as six churches and a school."

Faith looked at him and asked, "You aren't thinking of making it our home, are you?"

Joe felt his stomach twist into a ball before he replied, "No. But I do have to find a home for you and our baby, Faith. I just don't know where it will be."

"If it's a decent town, I suppose it may as well be there."

"It's not likely that will happen because I promised Bo that I'd stay with the wagons until they reached their destination in Oregon."

Faith smiled as she said, "And you always keep your promises."

Joe nodded before he slid the first half of the buffalo robe onto the bedrolls and wished he hadn't made that promise. It wasn't that he was planning to stay in Idaho City but simply didn't want to limit his choices.

———

The lantern was providing light and heat as they slid under their blankets.

After their body heat made the space beneath the covers cozy, Joe blew out the lantern and asked, "Does Laddie even follow you anymore?"

"No. I think he's John's dog now. John, Albert and William are constantly petting him and sneaking him bits of food. Even Will gives him treats."

Joe smiled as he asked, "What does Mary think about their new guest?"

"You'd be surprised to know that she's pleased having him in their wagon because he keeps the boys busy."

"I assume he hasn't used the wagon as his personal privy."

"Not once. Mary said his behavior is quite gentlemanly. He simply walks to the back of the wagon, hops out of the tailgate and returns when he's finished."

"I imagine she prays for the day when Oscar follows Laddie's example."

Faith laughed then took a deep breath and asked, "We'll need to buy things for Kathleen Maureen before she arrives."

Joe simply replied, "I know," but felt another stab in his gut after being reminded that he needed to find a job before he could make a home for Faith and Kathleen Maureen.

Faith couldn't see Joe's face but still realized the unintended pressure she'd place on him by reminding him of their uncertain future.

She was about to apologize when Joe kissed her softly then said, "Goodnight, sweetheart."

Faith sighed before she replied, "Goodnight, Joe," then rolled onto her back and closed her eyes.

Joe tried to push aside his frustration but was unable to shake his anxiety. He looked at Faith and wished he could at least project more confidence.

Tomorrow morning, he'd ride away with Chuck and probably reach Idaho City late in the afternoon. What he found there could either diminish his concerns or make them much worse.

Joe finally closed his eyes and almost willed himself to sleep.

CHAPTER 7

Joe and Faith had a fairly routine morning until Joe tied their horses and Bernie to the back of Mary's wagon.

As Joe led Duke away, Faith followed until he prepared to mount his stallion then she took his hands and said, "Joe, it'll be alright. Don't worry about the future. I know you'll only do what's best for us."

Joe nodded then kissed her before saying, "I'll always try to do whatever I can to make you happy, Faith. The wagons should reach Fort Boise tomorrow afternoon, and I should be waiting there when you arrive."

Faith took a deep breath as Joe mounted then looked down at her. He smiled then slowly rode Duke away, and Faith suddenly felt as if she'd never see him again. The thought made her shudder before she quickly turned and looked at Duchess. For just a moment, she thought about climbing onto her mare and following Joe, but knew it was an irrational idea. She had to believe that there was no danger waiting for her husband in Idaho City.

———

After Joe collected Chuck, they rode west at a medium trot and soon lost sight of the wagons.

Chuck hadn't spoken much, but Joe could almost feel his excitement. In a few hours, Chuck would reach the focal point of his dreams of almost instant wealth while Joe was more interested in seeing Fort Boise and its similarly named town. But he was still curious about not only Idaho City, but the surrounding mountains, valleys and creeks. He still vividly recalled the canyon near Cheyenne Pass and wondered if there were any like it tucked in between those mountains. He suspected that if there were, they'd be populated by dozens, if not hundreds, of prospectors.

After losing sight of the wagons, Chuck said, "We oughta see the Boise River in another hour or so."

"We'll probably see Fort Boise at the same time, but we'll spot the new road even sooner."

Chuck nodded and just ten minutes later he pointed and shouted, "Look at that!"

Joe had noticed the cavalry column a minute earlier and had been counting the number of soldiers when Chuck yelled.

"There are twenty-two men in that column with another two riding way out front."

Chuck kept his eyes focused on the troopers as he said, "I guess they're from Fort Boise, but I can't figure out why they're ridin' south."

"I have no idea, but I think we'll find out soon enough because one of their scouts just pointed at us."

Chuck snickered then said, "I reckon one of 'em has eagle eyes like yours, Joe."

"Maybe so. The column just slowed down and the scouts are both heading this way."

"I can see that. At least they ain't pulled their rifles."

Joe didn't reply as they continued riding west to meet the scouts. While neither of the cavalrymen had yet to slide their carbines out of their scabbards, Joe wouldn't have been surprised if they did once they were within range. There had to be a reason for dispatching a column that size and those scouts would be expecting trouble.

When the cavalry scouts were about a quarter of a mile away, they suddenly pulled their rifles free, so Joe quickly said, "I guess their officer told them to play it safe."

Chuck was reaching for his Spencer when he stopped and asked, "Why do you figure?"

"That column must have been sent out to stop some trouble and need to make sure we aren't part of it."

Chuck forgot about his Spencer as he stared at the approaching scouts.

When the two pairs of scouts were about a hundred yards apart, Chuck said, "Let's hold up," then pulled Willy to a stop.

After Duke halted, the cavalrymen slowed their mounts until they were just twenty feet away.

The taller of the two asked, "Where are you comin' from?"

Chuck replied, "We're scouts for a wagon train that's a few hours behind us."

The soldier nodded then asked, "Have you seen any riders this mornin'?"

Chuck shook his head before answering, "Nope. You're the only ones we've seen since we started out."

"What's your name?"

"I'm Chuck Lynch and my young friend is Joe Beck. Who are you lookin' for?"

"Six men showed up this mornin' and shot the owner of a store in town then stole what they could and ran off. They crossed the river but by the time we were dispatched, we couldn't pick up their trail because they were mixed with all of the other tracks on the road."

Chuck asked, "They didn't go north to Idaho City?"

"Nope. That's where they came from. I reckon they used up all of their money without findin' any gold."

"Why didn't they try to rob a store in Idaho City?"

"Too crowded, I reckon. Is that where you're headed?"

Chuck grinned as he replied, "You bet."

The soldiers returned their Burnside carbines to their scabbards before the taller one said, "I hope you have better luck than them other fellers," then he and the silent scout wheeled their horses around and headed back to the column at a brisk pace to make their report.

Joe had hoped that Chuck might at least be less determined to stay in Idaho City after listening to the soldier. Those six men had resorted to theft and murder after failing to find any gold. Joe was sure that their fate as far more common than those who succeeded. But when Chuck had gleefully said they were going to Idaho City, Joe realized the story hadn't fazed him in the least.

Less than a minute later, Chuck said, "Let's get movin', Joe," then immediately had Willy moving at a fast pace.

Joe sighed before he pushed Duke to a slightly fast speed until he caught up. Before they reached the roadway, the column had begun moving south.

Chuck watched the cavalry for a few seconds then said, "I reckon they're gonna catch up with those fellers before sunset."

"They probably will. And I imagine any of them who are still alive after they're found will be brought back to Fort Boise and hanged. I wouldn't be surprised if that has become a bigger problem for the army than the Shoshone."

"I don't figure it like that, Joe. I reckon those boys musta done somethin' bad in Idaho City and had to skedaddle."

When he realized that Chuck wouldn't believe anything negative about his future home, Joe simply replied, "I suppose that's possible."

After a few more minutes riding west on the new road, they spotted Fort Boise and the Boise River in the distance and Chuck said, "We'll reach the turnoff in another thirty minutes or so."

"Do you want to have lunch at Boise City?"

"Nah. Marigold packed me somethin', and I'm too excited to eat anyway."

Joe wasn't surprised and was pleased that Faith had stuffed his pouch with bacon biscuits.

As they drew closer to the fort and town, Joe was surprised by the size of Boise City. Joe Oxnard had prepared him for the size of the fort, but he'd expected that the newly established town would have no more than fifty or sixty residents. As he continued to evaluate Boise City, he estimated that at least two hundred people now called it home. He could see figures moving between freshly built buildings and noticed more under construction. The river was about as wide as the Snake but he expected that the well-used ford would make it easier to cross.

Ten minutes later, Joe was able to perform an evaluation of the ford when he and Chuck walked their horses into the icy, fast-moving water. It took more than two minutes to reach the western bank, but when Duke clambered onto dry ground, Joe thought it had been a much easier crossing than the Snake or even some of the wide creeks.

Chuck didn't bother emptying the water from his boots before he turned Willy to the north. Joe followed, but still slid his right boot from the stirrup and pulled it off. After dumping out the water, he tucked it under his belt then put his wet sock covered foot into the stirrup before he yanked the left boot from his foot. It was an odd sensation to be riding without boots but after his left boot was secured under his gunbelt, he pulled off his left sock, wrang it out then quickly tugged the sock and boot back on.

Chuck was watching with a big grin as Joe removed and twisted the water out of his right sock.

After he pulled his right boot back on, he snickered and said, "I figgered you were gonna slide outa your saddle, Joe."

"I was more worried about dropping one of my boots onto one of those piles of horse manure."

"There sure are a lot of 'em. I'm kinda surprised we ain't seen more riders or wagons."

"I'm sure we'll see them soon enough."

Chuck nodded then focused ahead as if he expected Idaho City to magically appear.

Joe was studying the panorama that lay before them as the road began to rise into the mountains. There was a large creek that ran along the west side of the road and Joe hoped to see a trout or salmon leap from the water. Just a minute later, they passed a mid-sized forest on the right side of the road.

As the road continued its gradual ascent, Joe turned, opened his left saddlebag and pulled out his food pouch. Chuck glanced at him when he extracted a bacon biscuit, and Joe was about to ask if he wanted one when Chuck opened his own saddlebag.

They kept the same brisk pace as they ate, and five minutes later they were just riding. After an hour or so, the creek that had faithfully remained on their left suddenly veered to the east, so they had to slow to ford the twenty-foot-wide waterway.

As their horses waded through the cold water, Joe was startled when a large trout leapt out of the water a few feet downstream.

He grinned and asked, "Did you see the size of that trout, Chuck? He would have fed both of us."

"You can have all the fish you want, Joe. I want to find somethin' else in those streams around Idaho City."

"I know, but I still wish I had brought my feather fishing setup."

Chuck shook his head but didn't comment as they left the creek. Luckily for Joe, the water hadn't been deep enough to reach the tops of his boots.

Over the next two hours, they still hadn't seen any road traffic when Joe spotted a stream that emptied into the creek that was now flowing parallel to the road on the right side. He followed the stream until it disappeared into a pine forest and wished he could take time to trace its path but knew Chuck was growing more anxious, so he planned to explore the forest on his way back tomorrow.

A few minutes later, they spotted some riders ahead and Chuck asked, "Do you think they're those six fellers the army was lookin' for?"

Joe quickly replied, "Nope. The army only lost them after they cross the Boise River. Besides, there are only four of them, and they're moving a lot slower than we are, too. If they were worried about being chased by the soldiers, they would be checking their backtrail, but I don't think they've seen us yet."

"I reckon you're right. They seem kinda peaceful."

Joe let Chuck keep an eye on the riders as he continued to study the mountainous landscape. He knew they had to be close to Idaho City and had expected to see a lot of prospectors by now, yet he hadn't seen any evidence of eager gold hunters. Maybe the gold fields were north of Idaho City, so he tried to recall what Joe Oxnard had told him about the smaller towns surrounding Idaho City.

Joe had barely begun to create his imaginary map when Chuck exclaimed, "There's Idaho City, Joe!"

Joe quickly returned to the real world and looked ahead where he saw what appeared to be the spire of a church. The four riders picked up their pace as more of the town came into view. It wasn't as if the buildings rose from a distant horizon as they would on the plains. Each of them rolled into sight as they rounded the wide curve.

But the surprisingly large number of structures wasn't as impressive as the number of people, horses, mules and vehicles that mixed along the streets and boardwalks. Joe knew the town hadn't even existed for very long, but now it must have had over five thousand residents and hundreds of buildings.

As Idaho City continued to expand in his eyes, Joe began to examine each of the buildings. He noticed that the left side of the main street was blanketed by saloons and suspected that there were many more on the side streets.

IDAHO CITY

He spotted two churches and a large store before Chuck shouted, "Look at that place, Joe! It's a lot bigger than I expected."

"I'm surprised myself, and we can only see a small part of it."

"Look at all of them saloons! I ain't had a cold beer since we left Julesburg."

Joe nodded but continued studying the buildings and the people. As they reached the outskirts, he noticed the stone-walled courthouse and the large jail built alongside. And on the next block was another, equally impressive structure.

He was looking at the courthouse when a man wearing a badge exited the building and headed for the jail. Judging by his age, Joe assumed he was the sheriff.

The sheriff suddenly stopped when he seemed to notice him and Chuck. Joe didn't know why they had attracted his attention when there were so many riders in the streets, including the four men they'd been following. He glanced at Chuck but knew that he hadn't seen the sheriff as he was focused on the saloons.

When Joe looked back at the sheriff, he found the lawman staring back at them with his dark eyes focused on Chuck.

They were about thirty yards from the jail when the sheriff stepped down from the boardwalk and beckoned to Joe.

He nodded then said, "Chuck, I think the sheriff wants to talk to us."

Chuck quickly shifted his attention to the right side of the street before saying, "Why does he care about us?"

"I have no idea, but let's go find out."

When they pulled up a few feet in front of the sheriff, the lawman said, "I ain't seen you boys before. Who are ya?"

Chuck replied, "We're scouts for a wagon train that's headin' for Oregon. My name's Chuck Lynch and my young partner is Joe Beck."

"I'm Sheriff Tap Fulmer. If your wagons are headed to Oregon, then what brings you up here? Are you plannin' on lookin' for gold like a lot of young fellers?"

Chuck grinned and replied, "Yup," as Joe shook his head and answered, "No, sir."

Sheriff Fulmer looked at Joe as he asked, "If you ain't here to look for gold, what brings you to Idaho City?"

Joe began to answer when Chuck snickered and said, "He's been tryin' to talk me out of it, but it ain't worked. Now he wants to look around before he goes back and tells the other folks that they all should keep goin' to Oregon."

The sheriff said, "I asked your friend why he came here."

"He always said he wanted to be a lawman, so maybe you can give him a job. Of course, he's only sixteen."

Chuck's second interruption was obviously irritating Sheriff Fulmer, so Joe said, "I plan to explore your town before I report back to our boss. Is that alright?"

The sheriff nodded as he replied, "Sure. Why don't you step down and I'll tell you about the place before you start explorin'?"

As Joe began to dismount, Chuck said, "I'm gonna head over to one of the saloons and treat myself to a cold beer."

Sheriff Fulmer pointed across the street and said, "Hopper's House is a decent place."

Chuck waved then turned Willy and after finding the saloon with a sign that read Hopper's House, he walked his gelding away.

Joe watched him leave then said, "I apologize for Chuck. Ever since he heard about the gold strike, he hasn't been the same."

"That's the way it is for most men. But how come you ain't bitten by the gold bug?"

Joe shrugged then said, "I wish I could tell you, but I just never cared about it. I guess I'm immune to the disease. May I ask you why you wanted to talk to us? You must have dozens of strangers arrive each week."

"I see new faces every day, but your friend was wearin' two pistols and I figured he might be one of those pistoleros I keep hearin' about."

Joe smiled as he said, "I gave him the extra Colt a little while ago and he's been practicing drawing both pistols at the same time ever since."

"He any good at it?"

"He's alright, but he keeps cocking both hammers with his thumbs while the muzzle is still inside his holsters. So far, he's been lucky not to have an accidental discharge."

"Why'd you give him the extra pistol? You ain't wearin' one."

"I have a spare gunbelt in my saddlebag, but don't bother wearing it because I figure if it ever comes down to needing a second pistol, I'd have time to fetch it."

Sheriff Fulmer didn't want to know how Joe managed to get the two extra pistols but asked, "Are you really sixteen years old?

"Yes, sir. I'll turn seventeen next February."

As the sheriff prepared to ask another question, the unmistakable sound of a gunshot echoed from Hopper's House. Then before he even took a step, they heard a second shot followed by a loud shouting.

Sheriff Fulmer raced away before Joe quickly wrapped Duke's reins around the jail's hitchrail and chased after him. He had a sinking feeling that Chuck had been involved in the shooting.

His long legs allowed him catch up to the sheriff as he raced through the saloon's open doors.

Once inside, Joe saw two small crowds of men looking down at the floor. One was directly in front of them and the second was ten feet away near the northern wall. When the sheriff pushed his way through the men in the closer group, Joe felt his stomach drop when he saw Chuck rolling on the floor in a pool of blood.

Chuck was grimacing as he tried to stop the bleeding and hadn't seen Joe enter.

One of the men handed the sheriff Chuck's pistols, which he put in his coat pockets before he glanced at Chuck then looked at Joe and said, "Help your friend while I take a look at the other feller."

Joe nodded then stepped beside Chuck and took a knee. It didn't take long for him to realize that Chuck's wound wasn't fatal. The quick look also explained how he'd been wounded.

As he began ripping away the cloth around the bullet wound, Chuck finally recognized Joe and growled, "Who was the bastard who shot me?"

As he spread the canvas apart, Joe replied, "Nobody else shot you, Chuck. You shot yourself."

"That ain't possible!"

Joe looked up at the closest patron and asked, "Can you get me a bar towel, some water and a shot of whiskey?"

The man asked, "Do you need to steady your nerves?"

"No. I need to clean the wound and pour some whiskey on it to keep infection away."

The man said, "Oh," then hurried to the bar.

Joe was still clearing away the cloth when he heard Sheriff Fulmer say, "That ain't too bad, mister. Let's get you on your feet then take you to see Doc Wallace."

He was still focused on Chuck's bloody behind when he heard a familiar high-pitched voice whine, "He shot me for no reason, Sheriff! I didn't even touch my gun."

Joe quickly looked through the gawkers' legs where Sheriff Fulmer was helping Pete to his feet. He would have said something, but the patron returned, set the glass of water and a smaller glass of whiskey on the floor then handing him a bar towel.

Joe said, "Thank you, sir," and picked up the glass of water.

As he began pouring it onto Chuck's wound, the man said, "The barkeep said you owe him fifty cents."

Joe smiled as he replied, "Tell him I'll pay him before I leave."

Joe set the empty glass down and began patting away the blood with the bar towel when Sheriff Fulmer slowly passed behind him and said, "Have one of these fellers take you to Doc Taylor's then meet me in the jail after you drop him off."

Joe didn't look up as he replied, "Yes, sir," then heard the sheriff help Pete out of the saloon.

Chuck was looking at the floor when he snapped, "I shoulda killed that bastard!"

"You're lucky you only wounded him, Chuck. I'm about to pour some whiskey on your wound, so it'll hurt like hell."

Chuck smirked and said, "It won't be as bad as when you burned the wound that Mort gave ya."

Joe said, "Hold that thought, Chuck," then dumped the whiskey onto the large hole in his left butt cheek.

Chuck wailed and spasmed before he exclaimed, "*I'll bet you enjoyed that, didn't you?*"

Joe folded the bloody bar towel then stuffed it beneath Chuck's torn britches to cover his wound before he stood and said, "Not particularly. Let's get you on your feet."

He helped Chuck stand then asked the man who'd fetched the whiskey, "Can you help me take him to Doc Taylor's after I pay the bartender?"

"Sure."

Joe stepped to the long bar, set the empty glasses on the polished surface then handed the bartender the eight bits and said, "Thank you."

The bartender nodded then Joe returned to Chuck, plucked his hat from the floor and popped it onto Chuck's head before he pulled Chuck's left arm around his shoulder.

After he and the stranger brought Chuck out of the saloon, the man said, "We head left to the next street to get him to Doc Taylor's. My name's Jack Mallory, by the way."

Joe replied, "I'll let you be the guide, Jack. I'm Joe Beck."

Chuck muttered, "Quit chattin' and get me to the doctor."

As they started down the boardwalk, Joe asked, "How did you manage to shoot Pete, Chuck? I know your left pistol must have gone off when you were pulling it out of your holster, but I heard two distinct shots."

"You keep sayin' that I shot myself, Joe. How can you be so damned sure?"

"I saw the powder burn on your britches, and the angle of your wound crossed downward across your left butt cheek. If you don't believe me, take a look at what used to be your left holster. So, unless you shot Pete with your right-hand pistol before you tried to draw your other Colt, I can't understand how you got off both shots."

Chuck replied, "I don't remember how that happened. I was drinkin' my beer when I heard that girly bastard's giggle. When I turned around, I saw him playin' cards. I walked close and yelled at him then pulled my pistols. After that it gets kinda blurry."

Before Joe could ask another question, Jack said, "I saw what happened. Your pal caught my attention when he called the other feller a murderin' bastard. Then he drew both pistols and the one in his left hand went off when the gunsight musta caught on the holster's lip. His other Colt was almost level when he shot himself, so his trigger finger musta yanked back."

A line of rubberneckers stared at them as they half-carried Chuck along the crowded boardwalk, but Joe ignored them and asked, "Did you see where Chuck hit the other man?"

Jack nodded as he replied, "That slug creased the left side of his chest. I reckon he'll be alright."

They turned left and Jack said, "Doc Taylor's place is the brown house on the left side of the street."

As they continued walking to the doctor's house, Chuck grunted and moaned, but didn't say anything. After helping him up the porch steps Joe opened the door then he and Jack escorted him into the waiting room.

Doctor Ben Taylor had been talking to his wife when he heard them enter, then turned and quickly approached them and asked, "What happened?"

Joe said, "He's been shot in his left buttock. I cleaned the wound and poured some whisky on it, but I reckon you'll need to sew him up."

"Alright. Let's get him into my examining room."

After Chuck was prone on the doctor's examination table, Joe said, "Sheriff Fulmer wants to talk to me, but I'll be back as soon as I can."

Doctor Taylor peeled away the bar towel bandage before saying, "That's a pretty wide gash, so it'll take me about an hour to close it."

Joe nodded before he and Jack left the room.

When they reached the porch, Joe said, "I appreciate all of your help, Jack."

As they stepped down the four stairs, Jack replied, "No problem, Joe. It was kinda interesting."

Joe waved to Jack as he headed back to the saloon while he crossed the street. As he passed the large courthouse, he wondered what the sheriff would do about the shooting.

He soon entered the sheriff's office and was surprised by how well furnished and equipped it was.

As he closed the door, Sheriff Fulmer said, "Have a seat, Joe."

Joe nodded then took off his hat and sat down on one of the three hardwood chairs lined up before the desk.

The sheriff leaned back and said, "That Pete feller was screamin' bloody murder and wants your friend hanged. Now I don't reckon Judge Oliver will go that far, but he ain't gonna be leavin' town for a while, even if he could ride."

"Did Pete tell you why Chuck shot him?"

"Nope. He claims he never saw your pal before."

"He didn't see me, did he?"

"I reckon not."

"If Pete decides not to press charges, will you still arrest Chuck?"

"I don't see that happenin', but if you can get him to let it go, I won't arrest him."

"I'm sure it won't take long for me to convince him to change his mind."

Sheriff Fulmer stared at Joe for a few seconds before saying, "Let's head over to Doc Wallace's place. I'll watch while you're tryin' to get him to drop the charges, so don't even think of threatenin' him."

Joe said, "I wouldn't do that, Sheriff," then stood and waited for Sheriff Fulmer.

After leaving the jail, Joe asked, "Where are your deputies?"

"I only got one right now. I sent Eddie Pascal to Placerville to handle a spot of trouble."

"You only have one deputy?"

"I've been sheriff of this county for eight months and I've gone through six deputies already. I swore in Eddie three months ago and I ain't sure he's gonna last another month."

"Do you lose so many because of gold fever or lead poisoning?"

Sheriff Fulmer snickered then replied, "Mostly 'cause they get the itch to find yellow sand. One of 'em took a slug in the belly, but he kinda earned it."

"What did he do to deserve getting shot?"

"He had his britches down around his ankles when the blacksmith came home without warnin'."

"Oh. Can I assume that the blacksmith wasn't charged?"

IDAHO CITY

"He had a good reason for shootin' Deputy Nichols, so he never saw the inside of one of my jail cells. The odd thing was that he still lives with the woman as if nothin' happened."

Joe grinned as they turned down a side street, and Sheriff Fulmer pointed to a white house as he said, "That's the place."

"I'd heard about the dozens of saloons and your oversupply of lawyers, but I was surprised to see so many houses."

"Those lawyers and businessmen gotta live somewhere, Joe. Then the prospectors who find gold decide to build a house and become gentlemen. Then either their find goes bust and they leave or the gold mounts up and they build a bigger place. That means there's kinda a merry-go-round of empty houses. The ones who move up after they get rich don't even care how much they get for their first houses, either."

As they continued walking to Doctor Wallace's house, Joe said, "It seems that they're still building more houses, too."

"It ain't just houses, either. I swear those boys keep goin' after midnight with their hammerin' and sawin'."

"I've already counted four churches, but it looks as if you're building another one."

"I'm impressed that you noticed. It's the first Catholic church in all of the northwest. they're gonna call it Saint Joseph's when they're done."

When they turned down the short walkway to the house, Sheriff Fulmer said, "We got three hotels and two boardin' houses and four banks, too. Each of 'em has an assayer, but the territorial assayer has his office in the claims and property section of our new courthouse. That other big building is for the territorial offices, but the governor and legislature ain't arrived yet."

"So, the town will grow even faster, and you've only got one deputy. How many can you hire?"

"As many as I can get. There's talk of havin' a town marshal, but even the mayor knows that ain't gonna happen if I can't even have two deputies workin' at the same time."

Joe nodded, then said, "I expected to see the streets swarming with men carrying pickaxes and shovels. Where are all the prospectors?"

"Most of 'em stay close to their claims or live in the gold camps that are scattered to the west, north and east of here. There's a road that heads northwest at the other end of town that goes to Centreville and Placerville."

"And you and your deputy are the only law for those towns?"

"Yup. Them and all those gold camps. I hated sendin' one of my deputies to those camps 'cause there was a good chance they wouldn't come back after bein' bitten by the gold bug."

IDAHO CITY

When they stepped onto the porch, Joe opened the door to the doctor's office and after entering, Sheriff Fulmer continued through an open doorway and stopped before another door.

He rapped on the door then immediately swung it open.

Doctor Luke Wallace turned and said, "I figured you'd be stopping by, Tap."

Sheriff Fulmer looked at Pete who was stretched out on the examination table and asked, "How's he doin'?"

"I had to put in fourteen stitches, but he should be alright if he doesn't get an infection."

Pete didn't hear a word of what the doctor said as he stared at Joe.

Joe's eyes bored into Pete as the sheriff asked, "Can we talk to him, Doc?"

"Sure. I'm finished with him."

After the doctor left and closed the door, Sheriff Fulmer stepped back and watched as Joe approached Pete.

Joe stood over the small, wounded man, then smiled and asked, "Do you remember me, Pete?"

Pete nodded before he squeaked, "Yeah."

"Now I'm not going to make excuses for what Chuck did because it was stupid and reckless. He already punished himself by shooting himself in the butt. But as a personal favor, I'm going to ask you to not press charges. I'm sure you haven't forgotten how I treated you that night which put you in my debt. Do you understand?"

Pete glanced at the sheriff before replying, "Yeah, I understand. I'm willin' to let it go if you'll promise that he ain't gonna try to shoot me again."

"I can't make a promise for another person, and I'm not his boss, either. But he'll be laid up for a while and I'll talk to him before he's mobile. That's the best I can do."

Pete sighed then said, "Okay," then looked at Sheriff Fulmer and said, "I ain't gonna press charges, Sheriff."

"Okay. When you're up to it, you can pick up your pistol, but don't go tryin' to get revenge, either."

"I won't."

The sheriff nodded before he turned, opened the door and exited the room with Joe following closely behind.

Once outside, Sheriff Fulmer asked, "We'll stop by Doc Taylor's office, so I can tell your friend he ain't gonna be arrested. But I'll keep his Colts in my office for a while."

Joe nodded as the sheriff asked, "So, why did Pete figure he owed you enough to drop the charges?"

As they headed for the main street, Joe replied, "It's a long story, but basically, Pete and his three partners bushwhacked Chuck and another scout named Herm Berger. One of them shot Herm in the arm before they took them into a gully where they bound and gagged them. After I found Chuck and Herm, I hunted down Pete and his partners to retrieve Chuck and Herm's horses and rifles.

"It was late at night when I caught up with them and had them in my Henry's sights. I told them to take the percussion caps off their pistols, but one of them opened fire. I shot him, then the others grabbed their repeaters and began shooting, so I returned fire. After three of them were down, Pete dropped his rifle and surrendered. I let him take his horse, their pack animal and a spare horse before I headed back to the wagons. I took Chuck and Herm's horses, rifles and two more horses as a sort of reparation for being bushwhacked. I just reminded Pete that I didn't shoot him."

"You did a lot more than just let him go. Did you even let him keep his pistol?"

"Yes, sir. He wasn't a hard man like his partners, so I knew he wasn't going to try to shoot me. I was more worried that he might pee on himself."

Tap snickered as they began crossing the street and Joe asked, "Where can I board Chuck's horse?"

"Use Frank Smith's livery. It's right next to Jim Chilton's blacksmith shop. I board my horses there at county expense. Tell him I sent ya. You ain't thinkin' of leavin' today, are ya?"

"No, sir. The wagons should reach Boise River by mid-afternoon tomorrow, so I'll leave first thing in the morning."

"Then board your horse there, too. Frank won't charge ya, either."

"I appreciate it, Sheriff."

"Call me Tap, Joe."

Joe nodded but wasn't uncomfortable addressing the sheriff by his Christian name.

When they entered Doctor Taylor's office, the doctor was still repairing Chuck's torn behind, so the sheriff told his wife-nurse to let Chuck know he wasn't being charged and that Joe would be back to see him shortly.

After leaving the house, they walked to the front of Hopper's House and as Joe untied Willy, Sheriff Fulmer asked, "Before you head off to the livery, can I talk to you in my office?"

Joe nodded, said, "Yes, sir," then led Chuck's gelding across the street where he tied him next to Duke.

IDAHO CITY

Before they entered the jail, Sheriff Fulmer patted Duke's neck and said, "He's just about the best-lookin' horse I ever saw, Joe. Where'd you get him?"

"The wagon master sort of gave him to me, and I named him Duke."

Tap's eyebrows rose before they walked into the jail. Once inside, he took off his hat, tossed it onto his desk and sat down.

After Joe removed his hat and took his seat, Sheriff Fulmer asked, "Why would he give you such a great horse?"

"When we ran into a Crow war party, I helped to stop them, and the wagon master gave me Duke as a reward."

Tap suspected that Joe had done a lot more than just help and really wanted to hear the details. But he knew it would probably be a long story, so he just leaned back and looked at Joe.

Joe was relieved when the sheriff hadn't immediately asked about the Crows, and was about to stand up when Sheriff Fulmer asked, "Your friend said you wanted to be a lawman. Is that right?"

Joe's brief sense of relief evaporated as he nodded then replied, "Yes, sir. But he also told you that I'm only sixteen."

"How long you lived on God's earth ain't important. It's how you lived those years that matters. Eddie Pascal is only nineteen but behaves like a snot-nosed kid."

Joe shrugged but didn't say anything, so Tap said, "I'd like to have you join me as a deputy, Joe. Would you be willin' to stay in Idaho City and help me keep the peace?"

Joe thought about it for a few seconds before replying, "I appreciate the offer, Sheriff Fulmer, but I can't stay here."

"Why not? Don't you like our town? Or do you have some land waitin' for you in Oregon?"

"No, sir. I don't have a place waiting for me, and Idaho City impressed me much more than I expected. It's just that I promised the wagon master that I'd protect the folks all the way to Oregon."

"If it's just a matter of losin' your pay for scoutin', then you can set that worry aside. I'd pay you eighty dollars a month plus room and board."

Joe quickly asked, "Why so much? That's almost as much as a Union officer makes."

"The county knows they gotta pay my deputies more because it's hard to keep 'em. So, what do you say?"

"That's a tempting offer, Sheriff. But I still have to go back and scout for the folks."

"Ain't the wagon master gonna pay you anything if you leave? They'll reach Oregon in a couple of weeks."

Joe shook his head before answering, "No, sir. It's not that either. I'm not being paid at all."

The sheriff's eyes opened wide as he exclaimed, "*You're not being paid? Why not?*"

Joe took a deep breath then replied, "I wasn't a scout when I first saw the wagon train preparing to depart from Kansas City. I just asked the wagon master Bo Ferguson if I could follow behind. But after an incident with some Pawnee, he gave me a horse and asked me to help the scouts. That's when I promised to stay until they reached their destination in Oregon."

Sheriff Fulmer scratched his chin and said, "I thought you said he gave you the horse after you helped to stop a Crow attack."

"That's when he gave me Duke. He gave me his spare mare after I helped to avoid a dangerous situation with the Pawnee."

The sheriff slowly shook his head as he said, "You sure are ticklin' my curiosity bone, Joe. But I still wish you'd take my offer."

"I always keep my promises, Sheriff. But maybe I'll come back after the folks are settled in Oregon."

"I might not be here by then. I can't depend on Eddie Pascal to stick around 'cause he's always tryin' to improve his lot. And I ain't likely to find another deputy with your high morals and common sense. But seein' as how you're not leavin' 'til the mornin', why don't you join me and my family for supper?"

"That'll be okay. I'll take the horses down to the livery before I look in on Chuck, then I'll come back here."

"He's gonna need a new pair of britches."

"I think he has a pair in his saddlebags, but if he doesn't, I'll stop at a store."

"If you need to buy 'em, use Walker's. He's got better prices."

Joe smiled, said, "I'll do that," then stood and left the jail.

Once outside, he took a deep breath, pulled on his hat and untied Duke and Willy. He mounted Duke, then led Willy down the street. As he headed for Doctor Taylor's house, Joe was thinking about Sheriff Fulmer's offer. If he wasn't so adamant about keeping his promise to Bo, then he would have gratefully accepted. Of course, he'd have to ask Faith about it first.

After he dismounted and tied both horses to the nearest hitchrail, Joe looked in Chuck's saddlebags and was pleased to find his old pair of britches and even a pair of shabby underpants that were close to becoming gun-cleaning rags. The britches weren't clean, but they weren't covered in blood, either.

He carried them into the doctor's office and as soon as he entered, he heard Chuck loudly ask, "Where is he?"

Joe suspected that he was the 'he' who Chuck was demanding to see. As he crossed the waiting room, the hallway door swung open.

A young woman he assumed was the doctor's wife stopped and asked, "Are you the friend he's been asking for?"

Joe smiled then nodded and replied, "Yes, ma'am. I brought him some undamaged clothes. Can he walk?"

She shook her head as she replied, "No. We'll keep him overnight. I'll take the clothes, but please come inside and talk to him."

Joe handed her Chuck's spare britches and underpants then followed her into the hallway. She pointed to the examination room door then continued down the hall.

As soon as Joe opened the door, Chuck snapped, "It's about time you got here! I was beginnin' to think you already headed outta town."

Joe pulled up a chair and sat down close to the examination table then said, "The sheriff told you I'd be back shortly, Chuck. It's only been about a half an hour since we checked on you."

"I reckon it just seemed to be a lot longer. I ain't goin' anywhere for a while, so are you headin' back tomorrow to tell Marigold what happened?"

"I'll leave early in the morning."

Chuck quietly asked, "Is the sheriff gonna arrest me?"

"Nope. I talked to Pete and he's not pressing charges."

Chuck's brief period of calm vanished as he exclaimed, "I shoulda had him arrested!"

Joe didn't bother arguing the point but said, "I brought your spare britches, but the sheriff has your Colts in his office. You won't be needing them for a while, anyway. Do you need anything else before I leave?"

"I reckon not. When you talk to Marigold, don't make me look like a fool."

"That'll be hard to avoid, Chuck. I'll see you in the morning before I head back. Do you want me to escort Marigold to Idaho City?"

"I'd appreciate it, but I don't have any place to stay."

"That shouldn't be a problem, Chuck. They've got three hotels and two boarding houses."

"I ain't gonna be able to ride for a while, so can you have Bo give my pay to Marigold?"

Joe nodded, said, "Sure," then stood and slid the chair back to its original place.

He looked down and said, "Be nice to the doc and his wife, Chuck," then turned and left the examination room.

He didn't see anyone before he left the house and untied Duke's reins. He noted his stallion's long shadow before he mounted and headed to Frank Smith's livery.

He pulled up in front of the large barn two minutes later and stepped down. Before he led Duke and Willy inside, a tall, heavyset man approached him.

"That's a mighty fine stallion you got there, young feller. Tap told me you'd be comin' but didn't tell me about your horse."

Joe smiled, shook his hand and said, "His name is Duke. The gelding is my friend's horse. Can I leave my guns with you?"

"Yup. The sheriff leaves his rifles here and I ain't lost one yet."

Joe nodded then removed his saddlebags and hung them over his shoulder before saying, "I'll be leaving early in the morning."

"Tap said you were headin' back to your wagon train. I hope you come back and be a deputy. Tap's havin' a hard time and Eddie Pascal ain't the kind of feller you can trust."

"Thanks for taking care of Duke, and I'll see you in the morning."

Frank rubbed Duke's nose and said, "It'll be a privilege."

Joe nodded then turned and left the livery.

As he walked to the jail, Joe studied the town. The streets were still crowded, and he could hear the distant sounds of construction which meant the population would continue to rise. He had been surprised by the normalcy of the town after hearing so many bad things normally associated with boom towns, especially one with so many drinking establishments.

There were a lot of businesses that were unrelated to prospecting, but what truly amazed him was the number of women. He'd expected to see masses of grizzled, unkempt men packing the streets, but the streets he visited looked no different than the ones in Kansas City. But he'd only been in town for a few hours and suspected that soon those grizzled prospectors would be visiting the saloons, or they wouldn't be able to stay in business.

After he passed the courthouse, Joe stepped into the jail and found Sheriff Fulmer sitting behind the desk writing.

He took off his hat, sat down and waited until the sheriff finished.

But he stopped in mid-sentence, set his pencil down and asked, "How's your friend?"

"He's okay. He'll be staying at the doctor's tonight, and I'll visit him before I leave tomorrow morning."

"He'll probably stay there for another day, too. But he ain't gonna be walkin' for a while, so are you gonna have somebody come up here with a wagon to pick him up?"

"Maybe. He was planning on staying here, so it depends on what his wife says."

"He's married?"

"Yes, sir. And next spring, he'll be a father, too."

"And he wanted her to have the baby while he was lookin' for gold, is that right?"

"He believed he'd be rich before the baby arrived."

"Every one of those fellers who comes here lookin' for gold thinks they're gonna strike the mother lode, but not many of 'em find more'n a few ounces of dust."

Joe nodded then asked, "How long do you think it'll be before the gold dries up?"

"If you listen to those fellers, you'd think it'll just keep flowin' down those mountains like water. But Milo Truman, the territorial land officer, says that the gold will probably be cleaned out in a couple of years, if not sooner."

"I didn't see any prospectors when I was riding here from Boise City. Were they just out of sight?"

"Nope. They never found any gold in the streams south of the town."

"That's odd, isn't it?"

"Milo said that it's because of the kind of rocks in the mountains."

"I was impressed by the natural beauty I saw just a mile or so south of town. I guess God wanted to preserve some of his best handiwork."

Tap grinned as he said, "Maybe if you stayed, you'd be able to buy some of that land."

Joe just smiled before saying, "I always keep my promises, Sheriff."

"You oughta at least ask the wagon master if he'll let you go."

Joe shrugged before asking, "Where are your jail cells?"

The sheriff pointed to his left and said, "Behind that door. I've got six cells but they're all empty. I arrested some fellers last night for bein' drunk and disorderly but let 'em go this mornin'."

"I'm surprised you haven't already gone home for the day. Don't you ever get any sleep?"

Tap replied, "I do most nights. I usually let Eddie keep an eye on the town after dark, but he's in Placerville. I was thinkin' of lockin' up when I spotted you and your friend ride into town."

"Sorry. Are you going to lock up now?"

"In a couple of minutes, but before we go, I gotta ask you somethin'."

Joe hoped it wasn't about the Crow attack because it would take him longer than a couple of minutes to explain and it would probably inspire more questions.

So, Joe asked, "What would you like to know?"

"It sounds like you had some problems with Indians along the way, so what do think of 'em?"

Joe was surprised by his question, but quickly answered, "Their ways are different than ours, but I believe they have the same needs and desires that everyone has. They want to make their lives better and don't like it when someone tries to take what they have."

"So, you don't hate 'em like most fellers?"

"No, sir. My mother taught me that it's ignorant to hate a group just because of how they look, and I've learned to look past folks' appearance. The quality of a man's character isn't defined by the color of his skin or which church he attends."

Sheriff Fulmer stared at Joe for a few seconds before he quietly asked, "Have you ever talked to any Indians?"

Joe smiled as he replied, "My wife and I had an Ogallala Sioux woman staying with us for a while. I found her alone and afraid after she escaped from the Arapahoe. Her name was Hanepi Wi."

Tap focused on the second word in Joe's answer and asked, "You're married?"

"Yes, sir. I met Faith the same day I joined the wagon train."

Tap smiled then asked, "What happened to Hanepi Wi?"

"Her chosen husband had been searching for her after she'd been taken by the Arapahoe. I met him when I was scouting, so I brought him back to our camp where they were reunited. Just a few minutes later, he took her home. We haven't seen her since."

The sheriff nodded then said, "I reckon you're wonderin' why I asked about Indians. It's 'cause I didn't want you to upset my wife when you see her. I met her eight years ago when I visited her Nez Perce village. She was taught English and how to read and write by a Jesuit priest then became a Catholic. I had to become one myself before Father Benedict married us. She was really happy when she learned they were gonna build St. Joseph's."

"She must be a smart lady."

"She's real pretty, too. We got two young'uns. Joseph is six years old, and Grace just turned five."

"Our first is due next April."

"I hope you noticed that we've got two doctors in town, Joe."

Joe smiled as he said, "I noticed."

Sheriff Fulmer said, "Let's get outta here before somebody comes lookin' for me," then grabbed his hat, stood and stepped around the desk.

Joe quickly popped to his feet and followed the sheriff through the jail's door.

After the sheriff locked the door, they headed north along the boardwalk and Joe continued his inspection of the town but ignored the saloon-studded west side of the street. When they passed Frank Smith's livery and the blacksmith, Joe spotted a large shop with a sign that read D.M. Elliott's Firearms & Ammunition. While he wasn't surprised to find a gunsmith, he was impressed with its size.

As they continued walking, the saloons gave way to other businesses, including Walker & Sons General Store which Sheriff Fulmer had recommended.

By the time they turned right onto a side street, Joe didn't believe Idaho City had any more surprises for him but was soon proven wrong in that belief. After he saw the almost completed

Catholic church, on the left side of the street, he noticed that they were constructing an adjoining building.

He asked, "What is the building that's almost attached to the church?"

Tap replied, "That's gonna be the Catholic school and a home for the nuns who are comin' to be the teachers."

"They're sending nuns to live in Idaho City?"

"Yup. Father Burns told his bishop that he was gonna add the school and if the bishop sent the nuns, he'd build a convent."

"That's still odd, don't you think?"

"I thought so, but Mary's really happy about it 'cause Joseph will be startin' school next year."

Joe nodded and began to feel that Idaho City was seriously flirting with him in an attempt to make him to break his promise to Bo.

Joe was still looking at the half-built school when Sheriff Fulmer turned and began walking toward a nice two-story house.

Joe didn't ask him how he managed to buy the large house but suspected it had cost him less than it should have. Maybe the county bosses had given it to him as a bonus when he was sworn in.

IDAHO CITY

After climbing the porch steps, Tap opened the front door and shouted, "Mary, I brought a guest for supper."

Joe followed the sheriff inside, closed the door and set his saddlebags on the floor. He was removing his hat when Mary Fulmer stepped out of the kitchen.

Joe forgot about hanging his hat as he stared at her. She was a slim, five-foot-tall woman and could have been Hanepi Wi's twin sister.

She kissed her husband then smiled and said, "Hello. I'm Mary."

Joe quickly recovered and replied, "My name's Joe Beck. It's a pleasure to meet you, Mrs. Fulmer."

As Tap hung his hat on a coatrack, Joseph and Grace cautiously entered the main room.

Mary looked at her children and said, "Your papa invited Mister Beck to share our supper."

As Joseph and Grace slowly approached the tall, young stranger, Joe smiled and said, "You must be Joseph and Grace."

Joseph asked, "Is your name Joseph like mine?"

"No, sir. My father named me Joe because it was easier to spell. I don't have a middle name either, so it only takes seven letters to write my name."

As Joseph smiled, Joe asked, "Do you want to know what my wife's name is, Grace?"

"Is she named Grace, too?"

"Almost. Her parents named her Faith Hope Charity Virtue, but I'm sure if they'd added another name, it would have been Grace."

Grace giggled then said, "My middle name is Mary, but maybe mama will let me choose Faith for my confirmation name."

Mary smiled as she said, "I think it's a very nice name," then she looked at Tap and said, "Supper will be ready in about thirty minutes."

"That's fine, Mary. We'll wait out here and I'll spend that time tryin' to convince Joe to be my deputy."

Mary looked as if she was about to say something but just turned and left the room.

After Joe hung his hat, he and Tap walked into the parlor. Joe took a seat in an easy chair near the large fireplace while Tap sat down on the couch where he was joined by Grace and Joseph.

Joseph asked, "Are you gonna be a deputy?"

Joe glanced at Tap and was about to answer when someone began pounding on the door.

IDAHO CITY

Sheriff Fulmer exploded from the couch and raced to the door before Joe quickly stood and hurried behind him.

Tap yanked the door open, and a terrified man exclaimed, "Tap, three fellers just robbed the Landsman Bank!"

As the man turned and trotted away, the sheriff yanked his hat from the coatrack then ran out the door. Joe took his hat and automatically snatched his saddlebags from the floor before following.

Joe had just stepped onto the ground when he heard the sheriff ask, "What happened, Ira?"

Ira was still jogging when he replied, "I ain't sure how it started, but one of the robbers shot somebody before he got hit. The other two got on their horses and skedaddled south."

"Is anybody dead?"

"I don't know."

Joe's enhanced mode kicked in and as time slowed, he studied the panicked scene taking place on the main street. Men were running in all directions as they shouted, and some already had pistols in their hands. He hadn't noticed the Landsman Bank before but looked in the direction some of the men were pointing and spotted it just two buildings north of the intersection.

When they reached the main street, Tap slowed and pulled his Colt then turned towards the bank. Some of the men spotted him, and the crowd parted to let the sheriff pass. Joe followed closely behind but left his pistol in its holster.

Before the sheriff reached the open door, a tall, heavily bearded man approached him and loudly said, "Al Rochefort is dead, and the thief is wounded."

Tap asked, "Is he still armed?"

"I ain't sure. I saw him get hit in the leg before I got outta there."

Tap nodded then slowly approached the open door.

After stopping beside the doorway, he yelled, "I'm Sheriff Fulmer! Toss your gun to the door and I'll have a doctor fix you up!"

It took ten seconds before the wounded outlaw shouted, "You're gonna have to come and get me, Sheriff! I ain't gonna let you hang me!"

Joe stepped closer to Sheriff Fulmer and said, "I don't know the layout inside, but if I can get him to fire, you can shoot at his muzzle flash."

Tap looked at Joe and quietly exclaimed, "That's crazy, Joe! We'll just wait for him to bleed out."

"Okay. If it's alright with you, I'll head south to find his two partners."

"You ain't even a deputy, Joe!"

"I wasn't when I chased down Pete's bushwhacking friends, either. I can't risk letting those two outlaws cause trouble with the folks in the wagon train."

Tap let out a breath before saying, "I reckon I can't stop ya."

Joe nodded then turned and jogged towards Frank Smith's livery.

When he spotted the stable, he wasn't surprised to find Frank standing at the door watching the excitement, so he pointed to his chest then to the south.

Frank got the message and quickly entered his barn. By the time Joe passed the wide doors, Frank was already tossing Joe's saddle onto Duke's back.

Joe dropped his saddlebags near his stallion as he stepped past Frank and picked up his rifles.

Frank was tightening the cinches when he asked, "Why are you goin' after those two bastards?"

"The sheriff is waiting for the wounded robber to bleed out and I don't want those two killers reaching the wagon train."

"Did he swear you in as a deputy?"

"Nope. Just tell the sheriff that if I catch up with them more than halfway to Fort Boise, I might just leave them there overnight."

Frank tied down Joe's saddlebags as he said, "It sounds like you ain't even worried that they might get you first."

"Worrying never helps, Mister Smith."

"I reckon it doesn't. But you're gonna lose your light pretty soon."

Joe hung his Spencer on the left side of his saddle and said, "I know," then attached his Henry on the right.

After he mounted, he looked down at Frank and said, "Tell Tap I can't break my promise."

"What promise?"

Joe smiled as he replied, "He'll know which one I meant," then tapped Duke's flanks and walked him out of the livery.

After turning his stallion to the south, he started Duke moving at a fast trot. His enhanced mode quickly evaluated the landscape ahead and despite the multiple ambush locations, Joe was certain that the two outlaws weren't lying in wait.

He soon left Idaho City behind and entered the shadowed road that he'd just ridden with Chuck. So much had changed in those few hours and he wondered what would happen before the day ended.

Even at his fast pace, he picked up the trail of the two escaping outlaws. They'd been pushing their horses which left deep, sharp prints that marked their passing.

After he rounded a curve, he slowed Duke and angled to the left. He had to reduce his stallion's speed again before the horse reached the creek that ran alongside the roadway. Once on the eastern side of the creek, Joe kept his focus on the ever-darkening path ahead of him.

The mountains on both sides not only blocked the setting sun but also greatly reduced his line of sight as the road wound its way down to Fort Boise.

As Duke carried him across the rugged ground, Joe began thinking like the outlaws. He was sure that they knew they were being chased, but probably expected the followers to be a large posse. There wasn't a telegraph line between Idaho City and Fort Boise, so they wouldn't be concerned about the army. But they had probably exhausted their horses and would need to let them rest. But when they pulled up, they'd have to stay out of sight in case the posse arrived before their horses recovered.

Joe rode for another thirty minutes without any signs of the two outlaws and was about to recross the creek to check the road for their tracks when a fox suddenly raced out of the trees and onto the road's surface. He pulled Duke to a stop and watched until the fox disappeared back into the trees on the west side of the road.

The fox had appeared about four hundred yards away when Joe first spotted him, so he suspected that the two outlaws had disturbed the fox when they'd entered the forest to rest their horses.

He slid his Henry from its scabbard but didn't lever in a live round as he focused on the spot where he'd seen the fox appear. He wasn't sure if he'd been spotted yet but had to assume they'd seen him. Even so, he wasn't about to move and attract their attention. He didn't dismiss the possibility that he could be completely wrong, and they could still be riding. But he wasn't about to break his much more important promise to Faith. He wasn't going to risk being shot again even if it meant letting the outlaws get away.

So, he decided to wait for a few minutes. If they didn't ride out of the trees by then, he'd return to the road.

He began to sing Kathleen Mavourneen in his mind as he continued to watch the dark pine forest. The moon hadn't risen high enough to cast its light onto the road, so even if they fired from those trees, it would be an extremely difficult shot. But it was possible that if they already knew where he was, they could circle back in the trees and have a much closer shot. He had to depend on the critters who called the forest home to loudly protest their invasion.

He was still listening to his brain's serenade when a shadow emerged from the trees. Joe's extraordinary night vision soon watched the outlaws slowly return to the road and after taking a brief look towards Idaho City, they turned their horses south. Joe wasn't surprised that they hadn't seen him as his black horse and dark clothing rendered him almost invisible.

After they rode away at a medium trot, Joe slid his Henry back into its scabbard then started Duke moving at a slower pace alongside the creek.

When he lost sight of the riders, he shifted Duke to the right and entered the creek. He stopped halfway across to let his stallion drink but soon started moving again and reached the road.

He didn't match the outlaws' speed yet as they had to ride for another three hours or so before reaching level ground and Fort Boise. Joe decided to continue following at the slower pace in the hope that they'd become complacent.

―――

About a half a mile ahead, Orville Tucker asked, "Why do you figure they didn't send a posse after us?"

Jimmy Black loudly replied, "Beats the hell outa me. They could still be back there but I'm beginnin' to think they ain't comin'."

"I think so, too. Maybe they figure we didn't get a chance to take any of those gold bars. After Billy shot that feller, nobody cared what we were doin'."

"We shoulda stayed to help Billy, Tuck. He might be mad enough to tell the sheriff what we got in our saddlebags."

Tuck replied, "Maybe I shoulda shot him before we took off. But I don't reckon he's gonna get a chance to say one word to anybody. He knows they're gonna hang him, so he'll shoot anybody who walks through the door until his Colt's empty or he's dead."

"I guess so. We got more'n two hours before we get to Boise City, so do we keep goin'?"

"Let's pull over in an hour or so to make sure nobody's comin'. If the road's clear, we can keep ridin' until we spot the Boise River. Then we set up camp and get some shuteye."

"Okay. I still wish we took the time to add more gold bars to our saddlebags."

"I ain't complainin'. We each got a couple of bars, and every one of 'em is worth around fifteen hundred dollars."

Jimmy snickered as he stared at the dark road ahead and began to imagine what he would buy with all that money.

———

Back in Idaho City, Billy French knew he was close to passing out when he fired his last bullet through the wall near the door in a show of defiance. He slowly lowered his empty

Colt to the floor before he rolled onto his back and closed his eyes.

Sheriff Fulmer had been counting the shots but wasn't sure the outlaw didn't have another pistol, so he shouted, "This is your last warnin'!" but didn't expect to hear a reply.

Even if he wanted to shout his defiance, Billy French was well beyond being able to yell back.

Tap waited another minute or so before he quickly waved his pistol in front of the open door. When no more shots rang out, he dared to take a peek into the dark bank.

After seeing the outlaw's body on the floor, he turned to the few men who were standing a safe distance away and said, "He's dead. I need one of you to tell Lucas he can pick up the bodies."

He watched a couple of the men run off then entered the bank. He picked up the dead outlaw's pistol and stuck it under his belt before walking to Al Rochefort's body. He shook his head before he plucked the Smith & Wesson Model 2 from the floor and set it on Al's desk.

As he headed for the door, Tap wondered what had become of Joe Beck. But he wasn't worried that Joe wasn't going to accept his offer. He was almost sick thinking that Joe's wife might be a young widow and their baby would never know him.

He left the bank and began walking home. He'd sent someone to his house to let Mary know why he'd left so abruptly, but that was almost an hour ago. So, he needed to tell her what had happened since then and that Joe wouldn't be joining them for their postponed supper.

Joe had added some speed when the almost full moon appeared over the mountains. It gave him a much better view of the road, and he hoped to spot the outlaws within an hour.

He continued to focus as far ahead as the terrain allowed and soon crossed the creek when it shifted to the other side of the road.

Shortly after the quick crossing, he resumed the same pace just before he rounded another curve then immediately spotted the two riders.

He quickly pulled Duke to a halt and hoped that they hadn't seen him. They were still more than a thousand yards away, and even with the moonlight he knew it would be hard for them to pick him out of the background. What had surprised him was that they were no longer riding away from Idaho City. They were coming right at him.

He still didn't pull his Henry because he didn't want to increase his visibility by pulling the steel barrel into the moonlight. As he watched them draw closer, he began to wonder if they were heading back to make an attempt to rescue their partner.

For another very tense thirty seconds, the two criminals continued their slow approach until one of them said something and they pulled up. After a brief discussion, they wheeled their horses around and soon disappeared from Joe's view.

Joe exhaled, patted his stallion's neck and said, "I'm glad they weren't riding mares, Duke."

He remained motionless for a couple of minutes before he tapped Duke's flanks. As soon as he started, Joe figured that they had no intention of returning to Idaho City but had been ensuring that no posse was behind them. He kept the same pace knowing that they were satisfied that they'd made a clean escape.

Just a couple of minutes later, he spotted them again for a few seconds before they disappeared around a curve. He slowed Duke slightly to maintain the same gap in case they turned around again.

For another forty minutes, Joe played cat and mouse with the outlaws as they popped into view then vanished again which made him adjust Duke's pace.

While he wasn't as tired as he should have been, he suspected that the two bank robbers were close to exhaustion by now. Boise City was less than an hour away, and Joe wondered what they would do once they spotted the town. While the new settlement didn't have any lawmen, they did have a large army contingent that was there to keep the peace. The army's presence made him believe that the thieves would want to get well past the town before they stopped to get some sleep.

He glanced at the moon overhead before he started to plan how to capture the two outlaws. Ideally, he could sneak up on them while they were sleeping. But he knew that by then, he might be too tired himself and be more likely to make a mistake.

He kept his focus on the road as he whispered, "What do you think I should do, Faith? I don't want to shoot them if I can avoid it, but I don't want to give them the chance to shoot me, either. I've already thought like they do, but it won't help me now."

He didn't expect to hear Faith's imagined reply but felt better just by thinking of her. Then he remembered her bacon biscuits that were still in his saddlebag. After pulling his food pouch from the saddlebag, he quickly devoured the four remaining biscuits. They were a bit dry, but Joe still appreciated the flavor. After returning the empty pouch to his saddlebag, he grabbed one of his canteens and almost emptied it before hanging it back on its hook.

As he luxuriated in the bacon's aftertaste, Joe said, "Thank you, Faith. I think I'll just let them answer the question of how to take them down."

As it happened, he didn't have to wait much longer before they provided the answer. Just as he spotted the Boise River shining in the moonlight, the two riders suddenly turned to their left then pulled up near a small forest where they dismounted. He quickly pulled back on his reins and watched.

He thought they were just stopping to water their horses until they began removing their saddlebags. He continued to watch them strip their tired animals but still couldn't believe they hadn't continued riding until they were on the other side of the river.

Ten minutes later, they stretched out on their bedrolls and closed their eyes. Joe suspected that they might be playing possum to lure him within rifle range, but he needed to dismount to quiet his screaming bladder.

After adding a tinge of yellow to the creek's clear water, Joe led Duke closer to the apparently sleeping duo. He stopped when he was about four hundred yards away and tied Duke to a pine branch. He pulled out the Henry and quietly started walking toward the small forest.

He kept his eyes on the men and their horses, but still glanced down to ensure he didn't trip or make any noise. He was soon within the Henry's hundred-yard effective range but didn't lever a cartridge into the firing chamber. He doubted if he'd get near enough to use it as a club but wanted to be so close that they'd know he couldn't miss.

His enhanced state allowed him to hear the soft crunch of each of his footsteps above the background noise of the creek's rushing water and the occasional squawks or coos of the night birds.

He froze when he was just fifty feet away when one of them snorted and rolled onto his side. Joe didn't pick up his left foot until the rolling man hadn't moved for another thirty seconds.

When he resumed his stealthy approach, he checked their horses and was both surprised and relieved to find that they were also sleeping.

Joe altered his path slightly to his left so the closer one wouldn't block his angle of fire. When he was just twenty feet away, he expected one of them might suddenly awaken and had to force his heart to slow down.

They still hadn't opened their eyes when he was close enough to slam his Henry's barrel into their heads. He finally stopped when he stood just three feet above their heads. For just a moment, Joe thought about sliding their pistols from their holsters, but soon realized that he'd be stretching his luck. All he had to do now was to let them know they'd been caught.

But after he recalled the unnecessary shooting fiasco when he'd caught up with Pete's bunch, he decided not to say anything. He rotated the Henry, then raised the repeater and quickly brought the butt down on the head of the man who'd just altered his sleeping position. The fairly loud crack disturbed the other outlaw's peaceful sleep, but when he sat up in total confusion, Joe whacked his noggin with the bottom edge of the stock.

After the second outlaw collapsed onto his pal, Joe quickly stripped off their gunbelts and tossed them aside. He rolled each of them onto his belly then stepped to their saddlebags. When he opened the first one to find something to bind them, the moonlight reflected off a gold bar. He didn't take time to admire the expensive chunk of metal before he quickly moved to the second bag. He didn't find any cord but pulled out a pair of socks and a flannel shirt.

It took him ten minutes to tie their wrists and ankles with socks and the cloth from the shirt which he'd sliced into ribbons.

When he was satisfied that they weren't going anywhere even if they woke up, he picked up his Henry and headed back to Duke.

After he tied Duke to the same tree that served as a hitching post for the outlaws' horses, Joe began unsaddling his stallion.

The outlaws were still unconscious when he finished, so Joe picked up their gunbelts and rifles then piled them on the ground before sitting on his saddle.

When he pulled one of the rifles from its scabbard, he saw the dual triggers and realized it was a Frank Wesson carbine. He had only heard of them and wondered how the outlaws had come to possess the newer models.

Once he held the carbine in his hands, he released the catch and bent the barrel down, which exposed the breech. It was loaded, but the Frank Wesson didn't used a percussion cap. He slid the brass cartridge from the breech and held it in the moonlight. It was a .44 caliber rimfire, and while it was the same diameter as his Henry's cartridges, it was much longer because of the amount of powder it contained.

After putting the cartridge into his coat pocket, he closed the carbine and checked the second. It was the same model and bore, so after unloading its cartridge, he returned both empty carbines to their scabbards. He quickly examined their Colt Navy pistols then put them back into their holsters and rolled them up before setting them on the ground.

He stood, checked on his prisoners, then returned to their saddlebags. Even though he knew each of them contained gold bars, he was more interested in finding cartridges for the Frank Wesson carbines.

He found two boxes of the treasured cartridges before he searched for the gold. He moved the four bars into one saddlebag and the two boxes of .44 caliber cartridges into the other saddlebag. He carried the valuable leather pouches back to his saddle and set it on the ground before sitting down.

Joe knew he should be close to passing out from exhaustion, but his mind was too busy to grant him sleep. The predawn should arrive in less than two hours and by then, the outlaws should be awake. He planned on taking them to Fort Boise then riding to meet the wagons where he'd have to tell Marigold about Chuck.

As he sat on his saddle, he started to think about Sheriff Fulmer's offer again. It was a lot more money than he could have imagined. He liked Sheriff Fulmer, too. And while he hadn't protected anyone by capturing the two outlaws, he did feel the same satisfaction he'd experienced when he'd prevented Mort from shooting the Pawnees, and after the other incidents.

But in addition to his promise to Bo, having Chuck gone and with Herm still out of action, he felt an even greater obligation to ensure the folks reached their destination. He had no doubt that he'd return to Idaho City after the wagons reached Oregon but recalled Sheriff Fulton saying he might not be there by then. If that wasn't bad enough, meeting Mary, Joseph and Grace only increased his desire to help the sheriff.

He sighed and asked, "What do you want me to do, Faith? I know you want a home even more than I do. If I tell you about Idaho City and Sheriff Fulmer's offer, will you plead with me to leave the wagons?"

He stood and began to follow a small racetrack around the campsite as he pondered his dilemma.

While Joe paced, Faith slept in Mary's wagon. It had taken her hours to finally fall asleep because she was worried that something might have happened to Joe. She realized that there was no rational reason for her concerns, but she couldn't shake the feeling.

She'd spoken to Marigold and Becky earlier. And while Marigold was even more excited about what Chuck would tell her when he returned, Becky was noticeably subdued.

Mary had tried to convince her that Joe would return tomorrow with nothing but good news, but Faith could only pretend to agree.

She had finally placed the blame on her motherly condition before she'd drifted into slumber.

Tap Fulmer had stayed outside a little longer after he learned that the two outlaws had stolen four bars of gold. He couldn't have cared less about the gold but just hoped that Joe would safely return. He finally managed to get some sleep when the predawn was just three hours away.

CHAPTER 8

The stars were beginning to fade, and Joe was about to end his pacing and sit down when one of his prisoners moaned and slowly opened his eyes.

Jimmy Black started to struggle when he spotted Joe and mumbled, "What…who…what the hell happened?"

Joe stepped closer, looked down and replied, "I followed you boys from Idaho City and aim to take you back after your pal wakes up."

Jimmy glanced at his unmoving partner and said, "I gotta pee."

"Alright, but don't make me put you out again."

Joe stepped beside Jimmy, bent over and untied the sock binding his wrists. After pulling him to his feet, Joe stayed behind him and held onto his gunbelt.

"Go ahead and relieve yourself."

"I'm too wobbly!"

"Then you'd better be careful where you aim."

Jimmy continued to grumble as he unbuttoned his britches.

When he finished, Joe said, "Put your wrists behind you and I'll sit you down on your bedroll."

Jimmy would have tried to throw an elbow but was too unsteady, so he put his wrists behind his back and Joe bound them with the same dirty sock.

After he lowered him to a sitting position on his bedroll, Joe said, "I'm going to saddle the horses. I'll keep an eye on you, so don't make me shoot you."

"Ain't you kinda young to be a deputy?"

"I'm not a deputy. I'm a scout for a wagon train that should reach Fort Boise this afternoon. I was just visiting Idaho City when you and your friends robbed a bank."

"If you ain't a deputy, why'd you chase us down?"

"I didn't want the likes of you and your pal paying a visit to the folks on the wagon train."

Jimmy quickly said, "Look here, kid. You ain't gotta bring us back. I can make it worth your while to let us go and nobody will be the wiser."

Joe shook his head and started to turn away when Jimmy said, "I'll give you a five-pound gold bar if you let us go. It's worth fifteen hundred dollars, and I reckon that's more money than you'll make for the rest of your life."

"Maybe so. But those gold bars belong to the bank, not you. Your partner murdered a man in the bank and you two brave souls abandoned him after he'd been shot. I wouldn't let you go for all four of the gold bars in your saddlebags."

Jimmy's tone changed when he asked, "Is Billy dead?"

"If you're referring to your wounded partner, I can't give you a definite answer. Before I left, he was alive. But he refused to surrender, so the sheriff was going to let him bleed out. He'll probably be buried by the time you get back."

Before Jimmy could ask anything else, Joe stepped quickly to the horses and began saddling Duke.

He had just finished preparing one of the outlaws' geldings when the other one groaned.

As Joe began saddling the last horse, he kept an eye on the pair and listened to their conversation. Before he tightened the cinches on the third horse, the second outlaw loudly announced his need to moisten the ground.

Five minutes later, both outlaws were sitting on their bedrolls while Joe gave each of them water from one of their canteens. The sun still wasn't peeking over the horizon, so Joe figured he could return the outlaws and gold to Idaho City and make it back before the wagons arrived.

Twenty minutes later, Joe was riding back to Idaho City leading his two prisoners.

Joe had managed to secure them in their saddles without any problems other than having to listen to their almost constant offers of gold bribes in return for their freedom.

Despite the incline, he had Duke moving at a fast trot to ensure that he'd be able to return before the wagons arrived.

The sun was up, but the road was blanketed in the mountains' shadows as he made his way back to Idaho City. His lack of sleep was finally catching up to him and the rhythmic clopping of the horses' hooves wasn't helping. He began to worry that he'd fall asleep and simply fall out of his saddle. Then he'd lose his prisoners and maybe his life if they could get to his guns.

He shook his head then began to boisterously sing Das Esellied. When the words of the German beer hall song echoed back from the mountains, Joe felt as if his father had joined him in his effort to stay alert. Soon, his drowsiness faded away as Duke carried him through the chilly mountain air.

When he stopped singing. he looked back at his prisoners and found them both staring at him as if he'd sprouted a pair of massive buffalo horns. After Joe turned his eyes back to the front, his stomach loudly growled reminding him of his neglect.

He patted his belly, said, "Sorry," but there was nothing he could do to satisfy his hunger until he reached Idaho City. He wasn't concerned about the outlaws' stomachs.

Just a few minutes later, Joe rounded a wide curve and spotted a rider heading towards him at a fast pace. He was about to reach for his Henry when he recognized Sheriff Fulmer, so he pulled up to let Duke rest.

As the sheriff continue his rapid approach, Joe checked on his prisoners again and noticed that they were focused on the rider heading their way.

When he loudly said, "That's Sheriff Fulmer," they almost shrunk in disappointment.

Just a couple of minutes later, Tap pulled his tan gelding to a stop and exclaimed, "I thought you were dead, Joe! *Are you okay?*"

"Yes, sir. I was going to drop these two off at Fort Boise but changed my mind when I was able to leave earlier than I expected. What happened after I left?"

"The one in the bank bled out like I expected. How'd you catch those two?"

"I followed them for a few hours and waited until they were sleeping. Then I snuck up on them, conked them on their heads and tied them up."

Tap glanced past Joe at the outlaws before asking, "Did they have any gold on 'em?"

"Each of them had two gold bars in his saddlebags, but I moved them into one bag that I have on top of mine. The other saddlebag has their pistols and two boxes of ammunition for their rifles. You might want to keep those Frank Wesson carbines, too."

As Joe turned to untie the extra saddlebags, Tap asked, "Are you comin' back with me?"

Joe pulled the saddlebags free and replied, "Only if you need my help. But I'm pretty tired and need to tell Chuck's wife what happened."

"I can handle those two. Are you gonna bring his wife to see him?"

"That's my plan. I should get back later this afternoon."

Tap smiled then said, "Mary will want you to stay for supper this time."

Joe replied, "I'll try, but I'm not making any promises, Sheriff," then handed him the weighty saddlebags.

Tap tipped forward and almost dropped them before hanging them over his saddlebags and lashing them down tightly.

After Joe untied the trail rope and handed it to the sheriff, he waited until Tap secured it to his saddle then waved and started back.

Joe continued watching for another minute or so before he wheeled Duke around and headed south.

As he descended toward the Boise River, Joe began debating about what he would do when he got there. He desperately needed sleep but wanted to cross the river then ride to meet the wagons. And it wasn't just to let Marigold know about Chuck. He had even more to tell Faith and wanted to hear her thoughts. *But how lucid would he be if he didn't get a couple of hours of sleep?*

The silent debate soon ended when he slid his fingers across his chin and felt the hard stubble. He'd get some sleep then wash and shave before riding east.

―――

Before the wagons started rolling that morning, Faith had decided not to stay with Mary.

So, as Joe was approaching the small forest where he'd found the outlaws, Faith was riding Duchess alongside Bo's wagon with Bessie, Betty, Nellie and Bernie trailing behind her black mare.

Even though Joe had told her not to expect him to return until late this afternoon, Faith hoped to see him before she spotted the Boise River.

As Duchess walked beside the lead wagon, Faith conversed with Nora to keep her illogical concerns about Joe at bay.

After some routine banter, Faith was surprised when Nora asked, "Have you and Joe decided where you'll make your home?"

Faith paused before shaking her head and replying, "Not yet, but I'm sure Joe will provide for me and our baby."

"I'm sure he will, but I was just wondering if he was planning to stay with us all the way to Oregon."

"He promised Bo that he would, and Joe never breaks his promises."

Bo leaned forward, looked at Faith and said, "He never really promised me to stay with us all the way to Oregon, Faith. He said he'd help protect the folks, and he's done more than anyone could've imagined."

"I think that Joe sees it differently. I imagine he feels even more obligated now because Herm's injured and Chuck is probably going to stay in Idaho City."

IDAHO CITY

"That don't matter, Faith. After we cross the Boise River, we'll only have a couple of more weeks to go, and all of the danger will be behind us."

"I'm not sure you'll be able to convince Joe that he's free to stay in Idaho City, but I guess it doesn't matter because I don't think he'll be bitten by the gold bug."

Nora said, "Maybe that town isn't as bad as the rumors made it out to be. Then there's that new town that's growing near Fort Boise, too."

"I guess I'll find out when Joe returns this afternoon."

Bo turned his eyes back to the front before saying, "I reckon so, but I wonder if Chuck will come back with him."

Nora quickly looked at him and asked, "Do you think he'd stay there and leave Marigold behind?"

"He might stay there and expect her folks to bring her to join him. Once a feller is infected with gold fever, there's no tellin' what he's gonna do."

Faith let out a long breath then focused on the road. Her repressed worries returned with a vengeance with the added concern about Chuck's influence. Before they heard about the gold strike, she never would have believed that Chuck would ever cause any problems for Joe. While she still trusted that Joe wouldn't be bitten by the gold bug, she couldn't predict what Chuck might do to keep him in Idaho City.

Joe didn't unsaddle Duke before he stretched out on his bedroll and closed his eyes. He wasn't in the same spot the outlaws had used but had moved to the center of the small pine forest. He imagined that the road would soon be busy with wagons and riders heading to Idaho City and didn't want to be spotted while he slept.

It was a passing stagecoach that awakened him, and he wasn't sure how long he'd slept. He slowly stood, grabbed his saddlebags and walked east to the riverbank. After leaving the trees, he looked at his shadow and estimated he'd slept for less than three hours. It wasn't much, but he felt much better.

He washed and shaved in the cold water then returned to Duke, hung and secured his saddlebags, then untied his stallion and mounted. When he walked Duke out of the small forest, he scanned the roads and spotted four riders approaching from the west. He headed southwest until he reached the road and picked up Duke's pace. He didn't focus on them as he rode toward the curve in the river, and they didn't seem to be paying him much attention, either.

Before they reached the intersection, Joe had turned east to cross the river. As Duke waded across the powerful current, Joe avoided having his boots fill with water again by lifting his stirrups above the swirling surface.

IDAHO CITY

After reaching the east bank, Joe lowered his stirrups and set Duke to a medium trot before taking a quick look back to see if the riders had headed north. He knew it was highly unlikely that they'd follow him but wanted to avoid even the tiniest chance of being bushwhacked. When he spotted them, he only saw the hind ends of two of their horses before they disappeared behind the forest on their way to Idaho City.

When he looked ahead again, he chuckled then said, "You're getting a bit too nervous, Mister Beck. Maybe you should have slept a little longer."

He hadn't expected to see the wagons for at least another hour, so he was surprised when Bo's wagon suddenly appeared from behind some low hills only a mile or so away.

He was about to ask Duke for more speed when he spotted Faith riding beside the wagon and quickly pulled off his hat. He only waved it once overhead to let her and Bo know that there had been some trouble. After Faith waved back, he tugged it back on.

After she brought her hand down, Faith looked at Bo and exclaimed, "I'll find out what happened!"

She quickly rode away without waiting for Bo's reply. She was concentrating so much on Joe that she wouldn't have heard it anyway.

Faith was intensely focused on her husband as she tried to imagine what had happened. She wished she had his eagle eyes because she couldn't see any blood on any of his clothes. She hadn't even noticed that he was returning without Chuck.

After she'd gone, Bo said, "I reckon Chuck musta stayed in Idaho City after all."

Nora asked, "Would Joe warn Faith of trouble just because Chuck decided not to return?"

Bo stared at Joe as he replied, "Maybe not."

———

Faith still hadn't seen any signs of injury when Joe pulled up beside her just a couple of hundred yards in front of Bo's team.

She quickly asked, "What's wrong, Joe? Are you hurt?"

Joe smiled as he replied, "I'm fine. I just have a lot to tell you. But I need to talk to Bo, too. So, let's wait for Bo to get here. Have you seen Marigold?"

"She's riding on her new horse on the other side of Bo's flatbed."

"Good. When Bo gets here, can you ask Marigold to ride closer to hear what happened?"

"Did something happen to Chuck?"

Joe was about to answer when Bo's team reached them and Bo loudly asked, "What happened, Joe?"

IDAHO CITY

Faith dropped back to fetch Marigold while Joe made a U-turn then slid him closer to the wagon.

After Joe was riding close to the driver's seat, he finally replied, "After we reached Idaho City, Chuck went into one of the saloons for a beer and spotted Pete, the surviving bushwhacker. He got shot and…"

Just as Marigold and Faith arrived, Bo exclaimed, "Don't tell me he's dead! Say it ain't so, Joe!"

Joe shook his head and loudly replied, "No! No! He's not dead, Bo. He'll be walking around in a week or so, but he won't be riding for at least a month."

Before he could explain any further, Marigold angrily asked, "Who shot him, Joe? Was it that bastard you let go?"

Faith glared at Marigold as Joe said, "No, Marigold. Pete never even pulled his pistol. Chuck was so mad when he spotted Pete that he was going to shoot him with both of his Colts. When he drew, his left-hand pistol got caught on his holster and went off while it was tilted backwards. The bullet cut across his left butt cheek and as he fell, he fired his other pistol and hit Pete in the chest."

While Marigold stared at Joe, Faith asked, "Did Pete die?"

"No. The slug didn't even penetrate his chest, but as you might expect, he was pretty mad. The sheriff was going to arrest

Chuck, but I reminded Pete that he owed me a favor, so he dropped the charge."

Marigold finally asked, "Where is Chuck now?"

"He's in the doctor's house until tomorrow. I told him I'd escort you to Idaho City."

"Can we leave today?"

Joe glanced at Faith before replying, "After we stop for the noon break. I need to get something to eat."

Bo said, "We made good time this mornin', so we'll stop as soon as we reach the river. I reckon we'll get there in less than an hour."

Joe nodded as he looked at Faith and asked, "Do you want to go ahead with me?"

Faith smiled as she replied, "Do you think I'm going to let you out of my sight again?"

As they started riding away, Joe expected Marigold to tag along but she didn't. He looked back and saw her talking to Bo but couldn't hear what she was saying.

Faith asked, "Now can I hear the news you needed to tell me?"

"There's a lot but let me start by describing Idaho City. It's a crowded, busy town but not nearly as unsavory as I expected it to be. As soon as Chuck and I arrived, we were stopped by the sheriff because Chuck was wearing two pistols and looked like trouble. Chuck wanted to have a beer, so he left while I talked to the sheriff."

"Then Chuck tried to shoot Pete."

"Yup. Anyway, after that mess was settled and Chuck and Pete were being treated by different doctors. I had a long talk with the sheriff."

Faith's eyebrows rose slightly as she asked, "Was it an interesting conversation?"

"It was very interesting. Before he left, Chuck told him that I wanted to be a lawman but only to get a rise out of me. Then the sheriff told me he had a hard time recruiting and keeping deputies because men without a trade would rather hunt for gold."

"How many deputies does he have now?"

"Just one. His name's Eddie Pascal and he's only two years older than I am, but the sheriff described him in less than glowing terms. I didn't meet him because he was in Placerville."

"It sounds as if the sheriff was trying to talk you into staying and becoming his second deputy."

Joe hesitated before replying, "Um, he even made me an offer."

Faith quietly asked, "Did you accept it?"

"No. I told him that I promised to stay until the wagons reached Oregon and I always keep my promises. Besides, I'd never make a decision like that without talking to you."

"It's funny that you told him about that promise. This morning, when Nora asked me what we planned to do after we reached Oregon, I told her about your promise. Then Bo told me that you never promised to stay with the wagons all the way to Oregon, only that you'd do the best you could to protect the families. He even told me that you did that better than anyone could have imagined."

Joe looked at her before saying, "I guess Bo's right about what I said. But now that he lost Chuck and Herm, I still feel obligated to stay with the wagons."

Faith smiled as she said, "That's what I told him. He said that there's little danger ahead and they only have two more weeks to go."

After they'd ridden another hundred yards, Joe asked, "What do you think?"

"I don't know enough about the job or the town yet."

Joe asked, "Do you want to come along this afternoon?"

"I just told you that I wasn't going to let you out of my sight, Mister Beck."

Joe grinned as he said, "Yes, you did. So, before we reach the river, let me tell you more about the job and the town."

Joe decided to give Faith a balanced report of the town rather than taint her opinion with the very positive impression it had made on him. So, he began describing Idaho City by telling her about the line of saloons that lined the west side of the main road.

He was about to add weight to the good side of the scale when Faith asked, "Did the sheriff tell you how much the job pays?"

"I was surprised when he told me that it was eighty dollars a month plus room and board. That's almost as much as a Union lieutenant makes."

Faith's eyes widened as she exclaimed, "*Eighty dollars a month?* I would have been impressed with thirty! Is it that dangerous?"

"I think it's a lot less dangerous than what we've experienced so far. I expected to find the streets filled with hardened men in a perpetual ruckus, but it was far from that. If anything seemed constant, it was the construction of new buildings. Another surprise was the number of women in town."

"So, the gunfight between Chuck and Pete was an oddity?"

"I wouldn't call it a gunfight, but I don't think it was an oddity, either. I think it'll probably get worse because the population will continue to expand until the gold runs out. Sheriff Fulmer is a good man, but he needs more than two deputies to keep the peace."

Faith looked at Joe before saying, "It sounds as if you're thinking of accepting his offer."

"I'll admit that it would be the answer to my only serious concern, the one about finding a home for you and Kathleen Maureen. So, I'd rather wait to make that decision until you've seen the town. You might find it too hectic to be our home."

Faith smiled as she said, "I doubt if it would be more frightening than watching that enormous herd of buffalo stampeding at us."

Joe grinned as he started telling her about the churches.

———

Sheriff Fulmer reached the outskirts of Idaho City and focused on the jail. He wondered if Eddie Pascal had returned and almost wished that he hadn't. When he'd told Joe about his deputy, he hadn't given him a full description because it would have sounded as if Eddie was just a product of his imagination.

In addition to his questionable character and constant bootlicking, Eddie, like many young men, chose to emulate a man he admired. For most of them, it was his father. Some tried to dress and behave like generals or heralded Indian fighters like Kit Carson. But just recently, the famous man Eddie chose to copy was the President of the United States, Abraham Lincoln. Unfortunately, Eddie didn't mimic the many admirable characteristics of the president, just his appearance and use of the language.

He wore a dark suit with a long black coat and had grown a full beard on his thin face. But last month, when he bought a tall beaver stovepipe hat to complete his Lincoln ensemble, it had turned him into a laughingstock. Tap had tried to convince him to wear his normal hat while on duty, but Eddie had been so pleased with the stovepipe that he'd never wanted to be seen without his Lincolnesque lid.

He had almost reached the jail when Eddie, complete with the beaver stovepipe hat perched on his head, stepped through the door and smiled at him as he gripped the lapels of his black coat.

Tap groaned then pulled up and dismounted.

As he was tying off his gelding, Eddie gushed, "You caught 'em! I knew you would, Sheriff. You're the best lawman in the territory."

Tap didn't bother telling Eddie that Joe Beck had captured them because he knew Eddie wouldn't listen anyway, so he just said, "Help me get them into the cells, Eddie."

"Yes, sir."

Tap was helping Jimmy Black from his saddle and as Eddie approached Orville Tucker the outlaw burst into laughter.

Sheriff Fulmer waited until his deputy had pulled Tuck from his horse and escorted the still laughing outlaw into the jail before he led Jimmy Black inside.

After locking each man into his own cell, the lawmen headed back to the front office where the sheriff said, "I've gotta see Mister Blanton then return the gold to the bank."

Eddie nodded then walked to the desk and sat down without removing his stovepipe hat.

Tap headed to the open door but just before he left the jail, he looked back and said, "Leave the beaver hat on the desk, Eddie. You're indoors now."

Eddie grinned then reverently removed the ten-inch-tall black chapeau and carefully set it on the desktop.

Tap rolled his eyes and left the jail. He removed the heavy saddlebags from his horse and hung them over his left shoulder. Before he walked to the courthouse to meet with the county prosecutor, Drew Blanton, Tap looked at the Frank Wesson carbine hanging on Jimmy Black's saddle. He smiled when he recalled how Joe had seemed to be more interested in the rifle than the four heavy bars of gold.

IDAHO CITY

As he began walking to the courthouse, he tried to think of a new incentive he could add to convince the extraordinary young man to take a deputy's badge.

———

When Joe and Faith pulled up before the Boise River, Faith said, "Fort Boise is even bigger than I expected, and Boise City seems to be growing quickly."

"That's what I thought, too. I imagine after the gold runs out around Idaho City, a lot of the folks might move to Boise City because of the fort."

Faith saw a pair of wagons taking the road to Idaho City and asked, "Did you see a lot of road traffic?"

"Not as much as I thought I would."

As Faith continued her visual exploration, Joe looked back and noticed that the wagons were just a half a mile away. They had pulled up a good hundred yards north of the road, in case Bo decided to ford the river and continue to Boise City rather than stopping for an early noon break.

———

Sheriff Fulmer set the four gold bars on Jerome Brown's desk and said, "I reckon you musta figgered you'd never lay eyes on those expensive doorstops again, Jerry."

The banker was close to tears as he slid his fingertips across the cold, shiny metal and said, "You're right. I thought that I'd never see the gold again, Tap. But I'm really surprised that the young feller who caught up with those murdering bastards didn't even shave off any of the gold."

"If you'd met Joe Beck, you wouldn't have been surprised at all. He's only sixteen, but he's looks like he's a few years older and thinks like a man a few decades older."

"You say you asked him to be your deputy, but he hasn't accepted?"

"Nope. I could tell he was impressed with the town and almost shocked by the pay, but he said he had to stay with the wagon train. He doesn't even know where he's gonna find a home for his wife, either."

"He's sixteen and he's already married?"

"He said she's gonna have a baby come springtime, too. He said he'd come back after the wagons reached the end of the trail, but I really wish I could change his mind when he comes back this afternoon with his friend's wife."

Jerome leaned back and said, "Maybe he would if you added a sweetener to your offer."

"I was tryin' to come up with somethin', but ain't got a clue what would work."

"I might. We're still holding a mortgage on the Snider house, but I'd be willing to rip up that mortgage and give the deed to Mister Beck if it would be enough to convince him to accept your offer. After all, I was already looking at a six-thousand-dollar loss if the gold hadn't been returned. So, I think that the three hundred and forty-five dollars remaining on that mortgage would be a sufficient reward for Mister Beck as well as a very powerful argument for him to become your deputy."

Tap wasn't surprised that the banker knew the exact balance on the mortgage, but grinned as he replied, "I reckon so. He said he'll be comin' back this afternoon to escort his friend's wife. I'll add your sweetener to the offer and hope it works."

Jerome stood, picked up the twenty pounds of gold and said, "Good luck, Tap."

Sheriff Fulmer nodded then turned and left the banker's private office wondering if telling Joe about the Snider house would convince him to stay in Idaho City. It was a really nice place just one block north of his own home. He'd never been inside the house, but knew it had its own barn in back which should please Joe. But he hoped that when he returned in a few hours, he'd be accompanied by his young wife. If she was with him, he had no doubt that when she heard about the house, she would want to make it their home.

―――

Joe was wolfing down one of Faith's biscuits when the wagons rolled to a stop. He was still chewing as he and Faith walked to Bo's wagon.

Bo quickly clambered down just before they arrived and said, "We're gonna cross the river after a short break. Can you and Faith help Marigold get ready to go?"

Joe nodded then asked, "Is she going to bring the flatbed to carry Chuck back or is she planning on staying with him in Idaho City?"

Bo glanced at the back of his wagon before replying, "She's plannin' to stay with Chuck. She needs help loadin' her mule and Max with all of their things. I already gave her Chuck's pay, too."

Joe wasn't surprised about Marigold's decision when he said, "Before we leave, I need to talk to you for a few minutes."

Bo smiled as he said, "I figgered you might need to bend my ear."

Joe looked at Bo for a few seconds before he took Faith's hand and they began walking to the flatbed where Marigold was pulling a bag from the back of Bo's wagon.

Bo looked at Nora who nodded before they quickly walked down the right side of the line of wagons.

IDAHO CITY

When Marigold saw Joe and Faith, she loudly asked, "Can you help me load Max and my mule?"

Joe replied, "That's what we're here for, Marigold."

After Marigold set the bag on the ground with two other heavy bags, she asked, "Do you have any spare room on your horses and Bernie for our heavy packs?"

Joe nodded then asked, "Which ones are the heavy ones?"

"They're still in Bo's wagon, but they're not all packed yet."

"Alright. You and Faith can hang those bags on your mule and Max while I head back and get our horses. Then I'll start shifting the loads on the mares."

Marigold quickly said, "We have a lot of stuff, Joe."

Joe replied, "I suspected as much," then walked away to retrieve their horses.

They didn't have that much spare room in their packs, but they did have some empty burlap bags he could fill and drape over the panniers.

By the time he returned to the flatbed, the mule already had four bags hanging over its sides and Faith and Marigold were hoisting another pair to load onto Max. There were still two bags on the ground, and he suspected that Marigold had enough cast iron cookware and other heavy items in Bo's wagon to fill all of his burlap bags. He just hoped she wasn't bringing any furniture.

As Marigold and Faith hung the first pair of bags over Max's saddle, Joe tied Duke's reins to Bo's wagon and walked to the tailgate.

He peered inside and was surprised by how much he saw piled near the back of the wagon and wondered if it all belonged to Marigold.

He was about to ask her when she hurried to the tailgate and said, "My parents gave me everything I need to set up my kitchen."

"So, you're bringing all of that with you?"

"Of course, I am. It belongs to me."

Joe sighed then strode back to his mares and grabbed the six burlap bags hoping they would be large enough to fit all of it without ripping apart.

Even with Marigold and Faith's help, it still took almost an hour to load and balance all of Marigold's possessions.

As soon as they were ready to leave, Joe said, "I need to talk to Bo before we cross the river."

Marigold was about to mount her horse when she turned and said, "I hope it won't take too long, Joe."

Joe glanced at Faith hoping she didn't pull her Colt before he said, "I'll be back in a minute," then quickly walked to the front of the wagon.

Bo had been talking to Nora when he spotted Joe heading towards them, so they turned just before he arrived.

When he reached them, Nora said, "I need to talk to Faith," then quickly hurried away.

Joe smiled and said, "Faith told me that you felt I was under no obligation to return and escort the folks to Oregon, Bo. I can understand why you might believe that, but I still don't want to leave you shorthanded. Herm can't help and even if Chuck returns, he won't be able to sit in the saddle."

"I figgered that's what you wanted to talk to me about, Joe. But I've crossed this trail four times before, and I'm tellin' ya that there ain't a lick of trouble between here and where the folks wanna go. So, if you and Faith wanna settle in Idaho City, it's alright with me."

Joe said, "I'll admit that I was tempted to stay in Idaho City, but I'd still feel guilty if I did."

Bo smiled and said, "Faith told Nora that you were concerned about finding a home for her and the baby and was sure that she was even more worried about it. If you can find that home in Idaho City, then she won't worry anymore. Isn't that more important to you than riding with us for another two weeks?"

Joe slowly smiled as he said, "I guess so."

Nora returned, looked at her husband and nodded before Bo said, "I think I convinced Joe that it'd be okay if he stayed in Idaho City."

Nora smiled and said, "I'm sure Faith will be happy to hear it."

Joe said, "Thank you for everything, Bo."

Bo nodded then Joe shook his hand then kissed Nora on the cheek before he turned and walked away.

When he reached Faith he grinned and said, "I think Bo just fired me."

As Faith laughed, he mounted Duke and waited for Faith and Marigold to step into their saddles then began riding to the river bank. As they passed Bo and Nora, he tipped his hat and Faith and Marigold both waved. Joe didn't notice Nora wink at Faith.

Faith was riding Duchess on his right and Marigold was on his left as their horses stepped into the cold water. Marigold's horse was leading Max and her pack mule while Joe had attached all of their heavily burdened mares and Bernie to his saddle. He left Duchess untethered even though she carried the lightest load because Faith was too precious to endanger. He was grateful when Faith hadn't pointed it out before they reached the river but wouldn't have cared one bit if Marigold had mentioned it.

IDAHO CITY

Shortly after reaching level ground, they made the right turn onto the road to Idaho City. Joe looked back at the wagons and saw many of their folks looking at them, so he pulled off his hat and waved it high over his head. Marigold and Faith were watching as the crowd of settlers waved back just before their view was blocked by the trees at the edge of the forest.

Joe felt a twinge of guilt after losing sight of the wagons and wondered if Faith felt sad about leaving Mary and her children behind. He imagined she'd miss Becky, too. He freely admitted that leaving the only friends he'd found since his family died was part of the reason that he hesitated to take Sheriff Fulmer's offer. But his promise to provide for Faith and Kathleen Maureen was paramount.

As they began the long climb, Faith asked, "Did you tell Bo about the sheriff's offer?"

Joe shook his head as he replied, "I never got around telling him. It didn't matter anyway."

Marigold quickly asked, "What did the sheriff offer you, Joe?"

"He asked me if I wanted to be a deputy."

Marigold smiled as she asked, "Does he know you're only sixteen?"

Before Faith had the chance to answer the question with greater intensity, Joe quickly replied, "Chuck told him how old I was before he went into the saloon and shot his ass off."

Faith managed to block the giggle that was threatening to erupt when Marigold sharply asked, "How bad is it? You said it wasn't that bad when you first told me about it."

"It was a large hole, but it's not that bad because of its location. There aren't any large blood vessels, bones or joints that could cause serious problems."

Marigold simply said, "Oh," before lapsing into silence as she thought about her husband's injury.

When Joe looked at Faith, she smiled but knew she couldn't ask him more about the sheriff's offer.

She was searching for a different topic when Joe said, "In about an hour, the creek that's on our left will cut across the road and then continue north. The first time I crossed it, a large trout leapt out of the water and was close enough that I could have caught him with my hands if I knew he was ready to jump."

Faith was finally able to release her laughter before saying, "It's too bad that your feather fishing pole passed on two weeks ago, but I'm sure you can make another one if you want to try your luck."

Joe smiled as he said, "Maybe I will."

Marigold asked, "Where can I stay after I see Chuck?"

Joe replied, "There are hotels and boarding houses, but you'll need to find someplace to store all your things and board your horses and the mule."

"Chuck won't be able to do that, so could you and Faith stay for a day or two to help me?"

Joe looked at Faith who replied, "We'll do all we can to help, Marigold."

Marigold smiled then said, "I was worried you might just leave me on my own now that Joe is the only scout they have left."

Joe wasn't sure why Marigold hadn't simply said 'thank you', but her reply still tweaked his unreasonable sense of guilt. He'd finally become comfortable with accepting Sheriff Fulmer's offer, but now Marigold had reminded him that the folks no longer had a functional scout.

Faith had seen Joe's reaction, and despite having never seen Idaho City, she looked at Marigold and said, "We're not returning to the wagon train. Bo all but fired Joe before we left, so Joe is going to be a deputy sheriff."

Joe was startled and stared at his smiling wife as she looked at him with her dancing blue eyes.

Marigold giggled then said, "I never heard of a sixteen-year-old lawman. Are you sure the sheriff wasn't joking, Joe?"

Joe turned to look at her before he replied, "If he was then he should have been a famous actor instead of a sheriff."

Faith asked, "What's he like, Joe? Does he have a family living in town?"

"He's a lot like Bo, and his family lives in a nice house just a block north of the new courthouse."

"Did you meet them?"

"I was about to share supper with them when there was a problem that required the sheriff's attention. His wife is named Mary and when you meet her, you'll notice her strong resemblance to Hanepi Wi. She's Nez Pearce and speaks English better than her husband. They have a six-year-old boy named Joseph and an almost-five-year-old daughter named Grace."

Faith smiled as she asked, "Did you tell her all of my names?"

"How could I not tell her my wife is named Faith Hope Charity Virtue?"

Marigold asked, "What else can you tell me about the town?"

Joe began describing Idaho City with more of a positive emphasis because it was going to be Marigold's home and now theirs if he could find a place to live. But at least he'd have a steady job.

IDAHO CITY

As they entered the stream when it crossed the road, Faith said, "I don't see any fish, Mister Beck."

"Maybe I was just dreaming, Mrs. Beck."

The fast-moving current wasn't deep enough to cause any difficulty for their horses, mule and lone donkey, but they took advantage of the creek's change in direction to let their animals satisfy their thirst in the cold water before they continued the ride.

As they neared Idaho City, Joe pointed to the stream that flowed out of the trees and emptied into the creek.

"I was surprised that there weren't any prospectors panning for gold in that stream, so I asked the sheriff about it. He said they did when they first got here, but soon figured out that all the gold was spread across the north of town."

Faith asked, "Is it like that canyon we found near Cheyenne Pass?"

"I don't think it's a big enough to be called a canyon. If you look at the mountains, that forest can't be more than a few hundred yards deep. I'd still like to enter those trees and do some exploring."

Marigold grinned as she said, "I thought you weren't going to look for gold, Joe."

"I don't expect to find any gold, Marigold. But I might try my hand at feather fishing in that stream."

Faith asked, "How close are we to Idaho City?"

"When we round the next curve, you'll see a church steeple."

"Is it the new Catholic church you told me about?"

"No, ma'am. I think it's the Methodist church. St. Joseph's church is hidden behind the county courthouse."

"And that's just a block north of the territorial offices."

Joe nodded as he said, "It is. But the governor or legislature haven't arrived yet. I guess the appointed bureaucrats need to get settled in first because they're more important, or at least think they are."

Marigold was focusing on the curve in the road ahead and tried to imagine what her new home would look like. She'd been living in an exotic, exciting dream world ever since Chuck had told her of his decision to leave the wagons to find gold. But now that her dream was about to become a reality, her excitement was suddenly replaced with fear and uncertainty.

Faith and Joe were still admiring nature's beauty and hadn't noticed Marigold's collision with reality. When they did turn their eyes back to the roadway, they were approaching the long left-hand curve.

IDAHO CITY

Sheriff Fulmer had just turned back onto Main Street after exploring the Snider house. It was even larger than his home and was fully furnished, too. In addition to the good-sized barn and corral, there was one other feature of the property that made it unusual. The large lot still had six tall pines in the back yard. When Bill Snider had the house built, he wanted the trees to remain because they reminded him of his home in Michigan.

He remembered how excited Bill Snider was when he had the place built for his future wife. He'd found a good amount of gold on his claim and used most of it to build and furnish the house then sent the rest to his fiancée to pay for her passage. When he returned to his claim to gather more gold, he only found a few more ounces of gold before it played out. He needed more money to file another claim, so he took out a mortgage on the house. He bought the claim but didn't find enough gold to fill a small pouch.

Then, less than a month ago, to add insult to injury, he received a letter from his mother letting him know that his future bride had used the money he'd sent to run off with another man. So, a frustrated and heartbroken Bill Snider suddenly packed up and left town. He said he was going back to Michigan, but Tap suspected he was heading to California to try his luck in their larger gold fields.

Sheriff Fulmer was still smiling when he spotted riders approaching the town trailing a large convoy of pack animals. He was passing the courthouse when he recognized Joe's tall black stallion then realized Joe was accompanied by two women. He grinned knowing that one of them must be Faith and suddenly his prospects of swearing Joe in as his deputy improved significantly.

Marigold was stunned by the size of the town while Faith was making a quick visual inspection when Joe spotted Sheriff Fulmer and said, "There's the sheriff," then waved with just his hand.

After the sheriff waved back, Faith said, "He seems excited to see you, Joe."

"I think he's more impressed when he saw you riding beside me, Faith."

Faith said, "I imagine he'll be smiling even more when you tell him you've accepted his offer."

Joe looked at her and asked, "Are you sure, Faith? Don't you want to spend a day or so just exploring the town?"

"I made up my mind before we left, Joe. Now that I've seen Idaho City, I'm even more convinced that it will be a good home for us."

Joe smiled as he said, "Alright. But we won't have a real home for a while. We'll be living in a boarding house until I save enough of my pay to buy a house. But the good news is that the sheriff told me that there are always some available at a good price."

"I'll be happy even if we have to live in a cave, Mister Beck."

Marigold then asked, "Where is the doctor's house?"

Joe said, "We'll go to Doctor Taylor's house after I talk to the sheriff for a minute."

He expected Marigold to insist on going to the doctor's office immediately, but she simply replied, "Alright."

After they pulled up in front of the jail, they all dismounted and as they tied off their horses, Joe said, "Sheriff Fulmer, I'd like you to meet my wife Faith, and Chuck's wife Marigold."

Tap smiled, pulled off his hat and said, "It's a pleasure meetin' you ladies, but call me Tap. I told Joe to do that, but he must think I'm more like his grandpa 'cause he still calls me sheriff."

Faith smiled as she said, "Well, I won't mind calling you Tap. But I have to confess that I've never heard anyone use that name before."

"I never heard anyone else use it either. I was named Patrick after my father, but my kid brother started callin' me Tap, and it kinda stuck."

Marigold asked, "How is my husband?"

"I ain't checked on him today 'cause I had to go lookin' for Joe before sunrise. But I'm sure he's okay."

Faith looked at Joe but didn't ask why the sheriff had been searching for him. She suspected that he knew the reason, but Marigold's presence had prevented him from telling her.

Joe said, "We need to bring Marigold to Doctor Taylor's house, but can we leave our horses here?"

Sheriff Fulmer glanced at Marigold before replying, "Sure. I'll keep an eye on 'em. When you come back, I need to talk to you again. I can introduce you to Eddie Pascal, too. He's inside the jail watchin' the two prisoners."

Joe smiled, said, "Thanks, Tap," then took Faith's hand before they started walking along the boardwalk.

Faith was looking at the county courthouse when Marigold asked, "Where did Chuck get shot?"

Joe bypassed the more humous, anatomical reply as he looked across the street and pointed as he replied, "It was in Hopper's House."

Marigold glared at the barroom as if it was to blame and was still staring at the saloon when Joe started angling across the busy street.

After entering the side street, Marigold said, "I can't imagine how that many saloons can stay in business. But there are more houses than I expected."

Joe nodded as he said, "I haven't been in town after sunset, but I think those saloons will be crowded with prospectors and other working men after dark. I expected the sheriff's jail cells to be stuffed, but I think he just lets the drunks sleep it off before letting them go in the morning."

As they turned onto the walkway to the doctor's house, Faith asked, "Where did they take Pete after the shooting?"

Before Joe could answer, Marigold snapped, "I hope they carried him to the cemetery!"

They stepped onto the porch and Joe replied, "They took him to Doctor Wallace's house, but I don't think he's still there because he could walk."

Marigold was still steaming as Joe opened the door then waited until she and Faith entered before following them inside.

As soon as he closed the door, Mrs. Taylor said, "I see you've brought Mrs. Lynch along, Mister Beck."

Joe took off his hat then replied, "Yes, ma'am. How's Chuck doing today?"

"His wound doesn't show any early signs of infection, and he's anxious to leave. I'll take you to see him."

Marigold hurried to join Mrs. Taylor while Joe and Faith slowly walked behind them.

When Mrs. Taylor stopped before an open door, Marigold quickly entered the room then rushed to Chuck's bedside.

As Faith and Joe passed the doctor's wife to enter the room, she smiled at them before she walked away.

Marigold pulled a stool close to Chuck, sat down and asked, "How are you doing, sweetheart?"

Chuck replied, "I'm doin' as good as can be expected, I reckon. I gotta get outta here, though. Did you bring a wagon?"

Marigold seemed confused as she shook her head and replied, "I didn't need to bring a wagon. We just loaded everything we owned onto our horses and the mule. Bo gave me all of your pay, so we can move you to a boarding house."

Chuck quickly said, "I won't be able to start prospectin' for at least a couple of months and then winter will stretch it out until springtime. Then you'll have our baby, and I won't be able to provide for you and our kid."

Marigold stared at Chuck in stunned silence for a few seconds before she quietly asked, "You want to go back to the wagon train?"

"It's all I can do now. That's why I was hopin' you brought a wagon."

Marigold glanced at Joe before she asked, "Why didn't you tell Joe that you changed your mind?"

"I only figgered it out last night."

Then he looked at Joe and asked, "Is Bo gonna stay at Fort Boise for the whole day tomorrow?"

"That's what he told me before I left. Do you want me to borrow a wagon to take you back?"

"That'll be okay. I reckon I'll have to stay here another night, though."

Marigold looked at Faith and said, "I'll stay with Chuck while you and Joe try to find a wagon."

Faith replied, "If you need to find us before we return, go to the jail and ask the sheriff."

Marigold nodded before Joe and Faith left the room. They stopped to ask Mrs. Taylor if Chuck could stay for another night, and after she agreed, Joe thanked her before they left the house.

Once outside, Faith asked, "That was a big surprise, wasn't it?"

"I was almost as surprised as Marigold. Chuck was so obsessed with finding gold that I believed it would take at least six months of failure to make him realize what really mattered. I guess shooting himself in the ass served the same purpose, only much faster."

Faith smiled as she asked, "Are you going to drive the wagon?"

"Let's ask the sheriff about a wagon first. Maybe he'd rather have Deputy Pascal drive the wagon in the hope he didn't return."

"Is he that bad?"

"I never met him, but Tap made it sound as if he behaved like a spoiled kid. I guess we'll meet him in a few minutes."

After winding through the street traffic, they stepped onto the boardwalk in front of the courthouse then as they turned right, Joe saw the empty hitching rail and asked, "What happened to our horses?"

Before Faith could reply, Joe answered his own question when he said, "I'll bet that the sheriff took them to Frank Smith's livery, but let's see if he returned to the jail yet."

Faith nodded as Joe opened the jail's door and let her enter.

As soon as she stepped into the office, Faith froze and stared at Deputy Pascal while Joe closed the door.

Deputy Sheriff Eddie Pascal rose to his full five foot and six inches of height crowned with his tall, beaver stovepipe hat and said, "Good afternoon. How can I help you, citizens?"

Despite the deputy's comical appearance, Joe was able to smile normally before replying, "I'm Joe Beck. Sheriff Fulmer wanted to talk to me, but I can't find him or our horses."

"Oh. He said if you showed up to tell you he'd be back shortly. Please have a seat."

Joe nodded, said, "Thank you," then took Faith's elbow and guided her to a chair.

Faith had recovered before she sat down and tried not to stare at the deputy.

Deputy Pascal waited until Joe took a seat before slowly returning to his chair but still didn't remove his cylindrical chapeau.

Joe took off his own hat before asking. "Did you have any trouble in Placerville?"

"Not as much as the sheriff encountered yesterday. I heard that you were the one who captured the two surviving outlaws."

Faith quickly looked at Joe as he replied, "It wasn't a dangerous situation. I just waited until they fell asleep before I tapped them on their noggins."

Eddie grinned before saying, "They still aren't very happy about it, either. Their trial is scheduled for Thursday at ten o'clock. I imagine you'll be called to testify."

Joe was about to reply when the door opened and Sheriff Fulmer said, "Glad you're back already, Joe. Why don't you and Mrs. Beck come with me, and I'll show you where I left your horses."

As Joe and Faith rose, Deputy Pascal stood and said, "I'll keep an eye on our prisoners, Tap."

Tap nodded then after Joe and Faith left the jail, he stepped outside and closed the door.

When they started walking north along the boardwalk, Sheriff Fulmer grinned and said, "I reckon I shoulda warned you about Deputy Pascal."

Joe asked, "Is it my imagination, or is he trying to look like President Lincoln?"

"It ain't your imagination, Joe. A couple of months ago, the paper printed a copy of his Gettysburg address complete with his picture. It took Eddie a couple of weeks to find the stovepipe hat and the black frock coat, and a little longer to grow the beard. Now he even likes to pose by hangin' onto his lapels."

"Why did you even hire him?"

"I was desperate, and he seemed okay for a while. I figure he'll move on pretty soon, especially if I can convince you to stay on as my deputy."

Joe was about to tell the sheriff that he was going to accept his offer when they reached Frank Smith's livery. But when he glanced inside, he didn't see any of their animals.

He missed a step before the sheriff said, "I didn't leave 'em with Frank, Joe. Let's keep walkin'."

Joe glanced at Faith before saying, "Okay."

Tap was enjoying himself immensely as he headed for the Snider house. He had planned to take Joe to the bank and let Jerome Brown tell him about the house. But after seeing the line of pack animals with their heavy loads, he decided to take them to the barn then add the sweetener himself.

After passing the sheriff's street, they turned right at the next intersection, but Joe had no idea where the sheriff was leading them because he couldn't see any liveries on the street. All he saw were nice houses before the street bumped into a tall foothill about a half a mile away.

Faith was equally puzzled but still studied the houses. She hoped that before Kathleen Maureen arrived, Joe would be able find a home, even if it wasn't as nice as any of the ones that lined the road.

Tap was still smiling when he turned right then pointed and said, "There they are, Joe."

As they continued walking, Joe stared down the gravel drive and saw the barn filled with horses while the two outlaws' horses and Marigold's mule were standing in the attached corral.

He looked at Sheriff Fulmer and asked, "Why'd you leave them there, Tap? That barn isn't really big enough for all of them."

"I figgered you'd move 'em around when you got time."

"But who owns this place? Don't they have their own horses in there?"

"You're right, Joe. Most of those horses belong to the folks who own the house."

Joe stopped and said, "Tap, you're not making much sense."

Tap grinned then said, "I reckon I did kinda take this too far. Let's take a seat on the rockin' chairs on the porch and I'll try to explain what happened after I got back this mornin'."

Faith looked at Joe who simply shrugged before they followed the sheriff onto the back porch. Joe glanced through a back window expecting an angry resident to charge through the back door with a shotgun before each of them sat in one of the four rocking chairs.

Tap said, "After I locked up those two robbers, I visited Landsman's Bank to give 'em back the gold bars. When I set 'em on the desk of the bank president Jerome Brown, I swear the man was close to tears when he looked at 'em. He figgered he'd never see 'em again and was surprised that you hadn't even shaved off any of the gold."

"Why would he be surprised about that?"

Sheriff Fulmer snickered before replying, "You might be the only feller I ever met who'd ask that question. Anyway, I told him I was tryin' to get you to stay on as my deputy, so he said to give you this house if you'd take the job."

Faith's eyes expanded into saucers as Joe said, "I was going to tell you that I was going to accept your offer anyway, Tap."

Faith was horrified when she thought Joe was about to turn down the offer of the house but was instantly relieved when he just smiled and said, "But I'm not about to look a gift horse in the mouth. Did Mister Brown own this house?"

"Nope. He held a mortgage on the property and was happy to just give you the place. When you visit him tomorrow to do the paperwork, just be careful he doesn't kiss ya."

"Why did the owner fail to pay the mortgage?"

"That's a long story and you got a lot to do, so I'll tell to you when you and Faith after you settle in."

As Joe nodded, Faith quietly asked, "Can we stay here tonight?"

Tap smiled as he replied, "It's your home, Faith. It's got everything you need, too."

Then he looked at Joe and said, "I'll swear you in on Friday mornin'. Did Eddie tell you about the trial on Thursday for those two bank robbers?"

"Yes, sir. Mister Lincoln let me know."

Tap snickered then said, "I've gotta get back to make sure he doesn't decide to head back to Washington City to tell his generals how to fight the war."

As he stood, he pulled a key ring from his pocket and said, "Here are your keys."

Joe stood, accepted the keys then said, "Thank you for everything, Tap."

"You earned it, Joe. Oh, and those two outlaws won't be needin' their horses or gear, so you can keep 'em."

As Joe looked at the barn, Sheriff Fulmer tipped his hat to Faith, then stepped down from the porch and walked back down the gravel drive.

Joe slowly sat back down in the rocker next to Faith with the key ring still in his hand and said, "I can't believe all this just happened. Just a few days ago, I was worried about our future. I didn't know where we'd find a home or what I could do to provide for you and Kathleen Maureen. Yet, here we are, sitting in rocking chairs on the back porch of our own house. In three days, I'll be a deputy sheriff and making eighty dollars a month, too."

Faith smiled as she said, "I'm still shaken by all of the changes in our lives. We have to start moving things out of the barn and into our house, but before we even do that, I have to give you this."

Joe watched as Faith slid a thick envelope from her coat pocket and said, "While we were helping Marigold pack, Bo and Nora visited the folks and told them that we were going to Idaho City and might not return. He knew that you wouldn't accept any pay for scouting, so each of the families donated some money as a going away gift."

When she handed him the envelope, Joe just looked at it and asked, "Do you know how much is in here?"

"I didn't count it, but Nora said it was four hundred and thirty dollars."

Joe stared at the envelope then gave it back to her and said, "You can find someplace to put it when you explore our home and I'll start moving our packs into the house."

Faith nodded then asked, "What about Marigold's things?"

Joe snapped his fingers and exclaimed, "I forgot to ask Tap about a wagon!"

Faith stood and said, "I told Marigold to see the sheriff if we didn't get back before she left the doctor's house. I think you'll be able to find one before then."

Joe smiled as he rose then said, "I'll go ask Tap about the wagon then visit Marigold and Chuck."

Faith looked to the east and said, "I wonder why the man who built this place left those pine trees."

"I don't mind having them in the yard, but we'll have plenty of time to make any changes."

Faith took a deep breath and was about to turn to the back door when Joe wrapped her in his arms and kissed her.

When their lips slowly parted, Joe whispered, "We found our home."

Faith sighed then simply nodded before Joe released her then trotted down the porch steps.

Faith unlocked the door and entered her new kitchen. She took one step before closing the door then slowly revolving in a complete circle, letting her mind accept what her eyes revealed.

There was a large cookstove with two brick boxes of firewood. There was even a sink with a pump. *A pump was inside the kitchen!* There was a large table and six chairs, but what attracted her attention even more were the shelves that held stacks of porcelain plates, matching cups and lots of glassware.

The counter near the sink had four large ceramic jars labeled for flour, sugar, salt and coffee. She lifted each of the lids and was relieved when she realized they had never been filled.

She crossed the shellacked floor as if it was a thin coating of ice and opened one of the three tall cupboards. She gasped when she saw the wide array of cookware and utensils and was almost afraid to open the next cupboard.

When Faith did open it, she laughed when she saw two oak buckets, a broom and a mop. There was a shelf at the top that was filled with soap, sponges and towels.

The last and largest cupboard turned out to be the pantry. It was mostly empty but still contained a tin of tea.

After closing the door, Faith suspected that the owner who'd defaulted on the mortgage had built and furnished the house for a bride who never arrived. As she walked to the hallway, she was anxious to hear Tap tell them their home's story.

While Faith was being overwhelmed by her kitchen, Joe was leading Duke out of the crowded barn. He knew it would take him at least an hour to strip the animals and move Marigold's things to a wagon, but he had to find the wagon first.

He mounted Duke then rode down their gravel drive. As he turned onto the street, Joe reminded himself to ask about the address, so he could write to Captain Chalmers.

He soon pulled up before the jail, dismounted and tied Duke's reins to the hitchrail. When he entered the sheriff's office, Sheriff Fulmer immediately ended his conversation with Deputy Pascal and stepped toward him with a big grin on his face.

"I didn't expect to see you back so soon, Joe."

"I forgot to tell you that Chuck decided to head back to the wagons in the morning, so I have to find a wagon to take him to Fort Boise."

"I ain't about to let you leave now, Joe. I'll have Bert Smith drive his wagon to take Chuck and his missus to Fort Boise. He's Frank's younger brother and he'll be more'n happy to do it. Just tell Chuck he'll be there after breakfast."

"I need to load their things onto the wagon first, Tap."

"That ain't a problem. I'll have him swing by your place before he goes to Doc Taylor's house."

Joe smiled then said, "I guess I'll just head over to the doctor's house and tell Chuck and Marigold."

Tap nodded before saying, "Maybe you and Faith can join us for supper tomorrow."

Joe said, "We'll be there," then turned and left the jail.

After mounting Duke, he turned him north and headed for the doctor's house. As he approached the intersection, Joe hoped that Chuck hadn't changed his mind again after talking to Marigold.

Faith had finished her preliminary inspection of their house and was still in awe of all that she found. All it would need to make it ready was to do some light cleaning and add linen to the beds. One of the upstairs bedrooms was empty, and the other three were only furnished with a bed and a dresser, but Faith wasn't about to complain. The two downstairs bedrooms were much more complete and the largest bedroom, which she had already claimed for herself and Joe, even had a small dressing table with a triple mirror. When she first laid eyes on it, Faith felt a pang of compassion for the man who'd bought it expecting to see his bride's excited reaction.

Before she left their bedroom, Faith laughed and said, "Maybe he was just trying to impress some working girl to move in with him."

The parlor had the largest of the three fireplaces in the house and was furnished with easy chairs and a large sofa. The last room she found was just off the large parlor. When she opened the door, she wasn't surprised to find a large desk and three chairs. There was a heavy cabinet in the corner and empty bookshelves lined the two of the walls.

As she scanned the room, she said, "I imagine Joe will fill those bookshelves within a couple of years. but we'll store our journals and our Bible in the desk."

Before she left the room, she decided to use the desk as their temporary vault and deposited the envelope in the center drawer.

After she left the office, Faith stepped onto the front porch hoping to see Joe mixed in with the other street traffic, but he wasn't there. So, she returned to the parlor and closed the door. Before she returned to the kitchen, Faith checked each of the downstairs lamps and wasn't surprised to find them empty because there had been no kerosene in the lamps upstairs, either.

She soon walked into the kitchen and after taking a quick look into the cold room, she left the house and sat down in a rocking chair.

Faith felt the soft blanket of serenity cover her, so she slid the fingers of her right hand across her abdomen then slowly began to rock. They hadn't moved any of their possessions into the house, yet she already felt at home.

———

The wagons were pulled into a long semicircle just northeast of Boise City and many of the folks had gone into town to buy supplies for the final leg of their long journey.

IDAHO CITY

Bo was looking at the young settlement and large fort as he said, "I gotta admit that I was kinda surprised that nobody else is stayin'. I figgered that Arv was gonna build a new store in Boise City and was expectin' Will and Mary to join Joe and Faith."

Nora replied, "We haven't left yet. They have a whole day to do maintenance on their wagons, so some could still change their minds tomorrow. When we start out on Thursday morning, we might be losing a few families."

"I reckon we could at that. I'm just real happy for Joe and Faith. I hope they find a good home in Idaho City."

"You're going to miss them, aren't you?"

"Yeah, I will. It's kinda funny. It seems like I've known Joe all my life, but it's been less than six months."

Nora smiled as she said, "You feel as if you're his father. And any man would be proud to call him his son."

Bo simply nodded as he looked at the road that disappeared into the northern mountains.

Joe entered the doctor's house and saw Mrs. Taylor talking to a patient. When he closed the door, she held up a finger then after a few seconds, the man nodded then walked to a chair and sat down.

Mrs. Taylor then said, "Mrs. Lynch is still talking to her husband, but I believe she's about to leave."

Joe nodded as he said, "I'll just need to talk to her for a few minutes."

"I believe you know the way, Mister Beck."

Joe smiled as he said, "Yes, ma'am," then entered the hallway.

As he approached Chuck's temporary bedroom, he heard Chuck say, "It'll be okay, Marigold. Besides, you'll have your family with you, too."

Joe rapped on the doorjamb before he stepped into the room.

Marigold quickly stood and asked, "Did you find a wagon?"

Joe was relieved that they hadn't decided to stay and replied, "I asked the sheriff where I could borrow one and he arranged to have a driver take you and Chuck to Fort Boise in his wagon tomorrow morning."

Joe expected Chuck or Marigold to ask why he wasn't driving the wagon, but Chuck simply asked, "When is he gonna show up?"

"He'll be here after breakfast, but I'll load your things into his wagon first and tie on your three horses and your mule."

Marigold said, "Mrs. Taylor said I could stay with Chuck tonight. I imagine you have a lot to do, but will you and Faith see us before we leave?"

Joe nodded and replied, "Of course, we will."

Chuck smiled and said, "I reckon that layin' on that bouncin' wagon is gonna be my punishment for tryin' to draw both pistols."

Joe nodded then said, "That reminds me I need to get your pistols from the sheriff before you leave."

"He can keep that messed up holster."

Joe replied, "I'm not sure he wants it either," then said, "I'll see you in the morning," before turning and leaving the room.

Joe had noticed that the new Chuck was fading away and briefly thought about asking him if he wanted to stay. But the notion quickly died when he realized what would be the most likely consequences if he remained. He suspected that if Chuck heard about the house, he and Marigold would move in and after he was mobile, the gold fever would infect him again.

After mounting Duke, Joe rode back to the sheriff's office to retrieve Chuck's two Colts and his gunbelt with the undamaged holster.

When he entered the jail, Sheriff Fulmer smiled and asked, "Anxious to start work already, Joe?"

Joe replied, "I'm ready to start, but I need to pick up Chuck's pistols. He didn't want the gunbelt with the ripped-up holster."

Tap opened the bottom desk drawer, pulled out the two gunbelts and handed them to Joe as he said, "You can do what you want with it. I already talked to Bert, and he'll stop by your house in the mornin'."

"Thanks, Tap. Faith and I will go with Bert to see Chuck and Marigold off. Have you heard anything about Pete?"

"Yup. As soon as he left the doc's house, he packed up and headed to Placerville. Why'd you ask?"

"I don't want to give the pistols to Chuck in the off chance he'd run into Pete again."

"At least he wouldn't be able to shoot his other butt cheek."

Joe smiled as he said, "I wouldn't put it past him."

Tap grinned and said, "You'd better head home and start movin' your things."

Joe said, "Yes, sir," then turned and left the jail.

———

Faith was carrying one of the lighter packs out of the barn and immediately set it on the ground when she saw Joe turn onto the drive.

Joe smiled, ripped off his hat and waved it three times overhead and barely had time to yank it back on before he pulled Duke to a stop and dismounted.

Faith smiled and said, "I was beginning to believe I'd never see you do that again."

Joe kissed her before saying, "It may be the last time, at least for a while. The good news is that I won't have to drive the wagon to Fort Boise tomorrow. Sheriff Fulmer arranged to have the liveryman's brother use his wagon to take Chuck and Marigold back to the wagons. He'll stop here first, so I can load some of their things onto the wagon. I'll pack most of their things onto their horses and the mule."

"That's wonderful news. Are you going to sacrifice some of our bedrolls now that we no longer need them?"

"I will be more than happy to make Chuck's journey more comfortable, but I'm not about to give up our buffalo robes."

"I didn't think you would. Let's start moving our things into our new home."

"Alright, but I don't want you doing any heavy lifting."

Faith asked, "Why should I?" then took his arm before they walked down the drive.

———

After moving most of their things into the house or just leaving them on the back porch, Faith stayed inside to cook their supper while Joe began stripping the rest of the horses. When he found Willy inside the barn, he was grateful that Tap had picked him up from Frank Smith's livery because he had completely forgotten about Chuck's gelding.

The sun had already set when Joe entered their house for the first time. As soon as he'd opened the door, he was greeted by the welcoming aroma of Faith's cooking. She had also filled some of the lamps and two were already burning as he hung his hat on a brass hook near the door and removed his gunbelt.

He smiled and said, "It smells pretty good in here."

She turned and said, "Now you can make use of the pump next to the sink to wash up."

As he walked to the sink, he scanned the kitchen and wished he'd been there when Faith discovered the full shelves.

When he began pumping water into the sink he said, "I'm surprised that the man who built this place left so much behind. Are the other rooms furnished?"

"All except one of the four bedrooms upstairs. The other three on the second floor only have a bed and a dresser, but our bedroom down the hallway even has a dressing table with three mirrors."

Joe took a bar of soap from the small tin shelf and began working up a lather before saying, "You can give me a short tour after supper."

"I was amazed when I walked through the house, and I'm sure you'll be impressed, too. But we have a lot to do, too. We'll need to buy linen and stock the pantry."

Joe picked up a towel and was drying his hands as he said, "At least we have a lot of money to buy what we need. I still have more than eighty dollars in the wallet Captain Chalmers gave me."

Faith smiled as she said, "Bo was worried that you wouldn't accept the money, so he had Nora slip it to me while you were talking to him about staying in Idaho City."

Joe hung the towel and said, "He was probably right."

He then began setting the table as Faith carried the food to the table. After they sat, Joe took Faith's hand and said grace before sharing their first meal in their new home.

―――

Joe was as impressed as Faith had been when she first explored their house.

When they entered the office, Faith said, "I put the envelope in the center desk drawer. I think we should put the journals and our Bible in the desk as well."

Joe nodded as he said, "We'll buy some pens and ink because you'll be adding entries to the journal and our Bible. I need to store something else in the desk, too."

Faith was about to ask what it was when Joe slid his great-grandfather's watch from his pocket, smiled at her then carried it to the desk. After opening the center drawer, he set it inside before slowly sliding the drawer closed.

As he walked away from the desk, Joe said, "When I left the Quimbys, I wondered where my father's watch would find a home."

Faith didn't say anything. She simply smiled and took his hand before they left the office.

After completing their joint tour of the house an hour later, Joe and Faith entered their bedroom.

The bed was in transition as its unused feather mattress was covered with their buffalo robes and their heavy woolen blankets.

Joe set the lamp on the bedside table, took Faith into his arms and asked, "Are you happy, Faith?"

She kissed him softly before replying, "I've been happy every day we've been together. But now, I'm more content than I could have imagined."

IDAHO CITY

Joe smiled then began unbuttoning her dress. Faith quickly began undoing the buttons on his shirt and hoped their new bed was as strong as it looked.

CHAPTER 9

The house was freezing when Joe awakened early the next morning and he wished he could stay warm beneath the blankets with Faith but knew he had a lot to do before Bert Smith arrived with the wagon. So, he slipped out of bed, grabbed his discarded clothing and boots then tiptoed out of the room into the dark hallway.

After hurriedly dressing, he made a dash into the even colder outside before returning to build a fire in the cookstove. Once it was ablaze, he quietly walked to the parlor and started a much bigger fire in the enormous stone fireplace.

Faith was still asleep when he washed and shaved in the kitchen sink then filled the new coffeepot with water and set it on the stove.

He donned his heavy coat, hat and gloves then left the house to saddle and load Chuck and Marigold's horses and mule.

He finished saddling Willy, Max and Marigold's horse and had begun getting the mule ready when Faith hurried out of the house to visit the privy.

Two minutes later, she trotted back to the house just as quickly and waved before she reentered the warmer house to wash and dress properly.

As Joe loaded the horses with their lighter packs and bags, he looked at the heavier burlap bags and estimated how many he could fit on the wagon's bed and leave enough room for the bedrolls.

He was going to saddle Duke and Duchess when he realized it wasn't necessary. He patted his stallion on the neck then made a trail rope for Chuck and Marigold's animals and two minutes later, he led them out of the barn.

After tying them off on the small back hitchrail, he moved their heavy burlap bags to the ground near the end of the gravel drive. The sun was rising when he returned to the barn and retrieved two of his undamaged bedrolls and carried them to the burlap bags. His breath was still creating clouds when he entered the kitchen and closed the door.

As he pulled off his gloves, Faith said, "I'm sorry I didn't help you, but I thought I'd be more useful making breakfast."

Joe smiled as he hung his hat on a hook and replied, "If you'd come outside to help, I would have sent you right back inside to stay warm. After we see Chuck and Marigold off, we'll visit Walker & Sons General Store. We'll buy whatever we need, but you will buy yourself a much heavier coat, a warm hat and fur-lined gloves or mittens."

"I'm not going to argue, Joe. It was pretty cold this morning and I'm sure it'll get much colder before long."

"We have a lot to do today, but I can't forget to have a full cord of firewood delivered."

"We need to know where to find everything, too."

Joe stepped close, kissed her then said, "We have time to discover every nook in Idaho City. It's our home town now, Faith."

Faith smiled as Joe began setting the table for their light breakfast.

———

Thirty minutes later, Bert Smith arrived. Joe was surprised to see that he was driving a heavy freight wagon which made the question of bed space moot.

After introductions were made, Joe and Bert quickly loaded the heavy burlap bags along one side of the wagon's bed before Joe stretched out the bedrolls on the other side. There was still plenty of room if Marigold wanted to ride with Chuck, so Faith brought their wool blankets from the house. Joe suspected they'd be buying more blankets and quilts later that morning.

While Joe tied the trail rope to the back of the wagon, Bert clambered onto the driver's seat.

When Faith climbed up next to him, Bert grinned and said, "I ain't never hauled a feller who shot himself in the behind before."

Faith laughed lightly before saying, "And I don't believe you'll ever have another butt-shot passenger."

Bert was still snickering when Joe climbed onto the wagon. He snapped the reins and the four massive Percheron draft horses stepped away as if they were just taking a morning stroll.

After Bert turned the wagon onto the street, Joe asked, "Where'd you get the Percherons, Bert?"

"Frank got 'em for me. I was only gonna use two of 'em but Frank wants me to pick up a load at Fort Boise while I'm down there."

"They're magnificent horses."

"They're like family. Your stallion is a mighty fine horse too, Joe. When I saw him in the livery, I figgered some king or prince musta been visitin'."

Joe chuckled before saying, "The only royalty I know is my stallion and Faith's mare. We named them Duke and Duchess."

"I imagine Duchess must be quite a lady to be paired with Duke."

Faith nodded and said, "She is quite the lady. And we expect her to add a prince to the household next summer."

Bert didn't slow when he turned onto the already busy main street, but the heavy traffic miraculously parted to grant right of way to the muscular Percherons. Bert seemed to accept it as normal, but Joe smiled at Faith and wiggled his eyebrows in appreciation of the deference shown to the kings of the freight world.

When Bert pulled up in front of Doctor Taylor's house, Joe stepped down then helped Faith to the ground before saying, "We should be back shortly, Bert."

Bert said, "I'm gonna turn the wagon around while you're gone."

Joe smiled and nodded before he and Faith began walking to the doctor's house.

Faith asked, "You don't think Chuck could have changed his mind again, do you?"

"It's possible, but we'll find out soon enough. I just hope we don't have to keep Bert waiting for more than a couple of minutes."

Faith nodded as they stepped onto the porch and Joe opened the door.

After Faith entered, Joe closed the door and was removing his hat when he heard Chuck say, "I'll be glad to get outta here, Joe."

Joe looked quickly to his left and saw a fully dressed Chuck standing next to Marigold.

"I'm impressed, Chuck. I thought we'd have to carry you to the wagon."

"It ain't any fun to walk, but I can manage."

Marigold said, "We've been waiting for ten minutes and were beginning to believe you'd forgotten about us."

Faith replied, "Joe had to get your horses and mule saddled and load all your things."

Marigold looked at Joe and said, "Oh. Thank you, Joe."

Joe smiled an said, "You're welcome. Now let's get you out to the wagon."

Chuck nodded then looked at Mrs. Taylor and said, "Thanks for all your help, ma'am. And tell the doc I appreciate him fixin' my behind, too."

Mrs. Taylor said, "You're welcome, Mister Lynch. Just don't make a habit of shooting yourself."

Chuck grinned then said, "No, ma'am," before he put his arm over Marigold's shoulders and stepped slowly across the waiting room.

Joe yanked his hat back on then opened the door. Faith hurried through and continued across the porch before Chuck and Marigold passed him. Then he waved to Mrs. Taylor before leaving the house and closing the door.

Faith was waiting on the ground as Joe helped Chuck down the steps. After he reached the walkway, Faith hurried to the wagon's tailgate and removed the blankets.

When they reached the wagon, Joe said, "Bert Smith volunteered to drive you to Fort Boise using his wagon and team."

Chuck looked up and said, "I appreciate it, Bert."

Bert nodded then watched as Joe helped Chuck into the back of the wagon where he laid on his right side. Marigold climbed in next to Chuck and Faith handed her the blankets.

Marigold covered her husband with one of the blankets then sat down near his head and wrapped herself in the second blanket.

After Chuck and Marigold were settled, Joe climbed onto the wagon bed, looked down at Chuck and said, "I put your pistols in your saddlebags, Joe."

"Okay. Are you and Faith gonna ride along?"

"I wish we could, but we have a lot to do."

"I reckon so. I hope things work out for you and Faith."

Joe shook his hand as he said, "I wish the best for you and Marigold, too."

Then Chuck grinned as he said, "Maybe we'll come back and visit one of these days."

Joe smiled, said, "Maybe so," then shook Marigold's hand and jumped back to the ground.

Even if Faith wanted to climb onto the wagon's bed to make her farewells, she wasn't given the opportunity when Bert snapped his reins, and the four draft horses quickly pulled the wagon away.

Joe rested his arm across Faith's shoulders as they waved to Chuck and Marigold. Chuck and Marigold waved back before the wagon turned onto the main street and disappeared.

Joe stared at the intersection and hoped that the gold ran out before Chuck and Marigold returned but suspected that he'd never see them again.

When he looked at Faith, he expected to see some sadness in her blue eyes, but he was wrong.

Faith smiled at him then said, "Let's go shopping."

As they began walking, Joe said, "We have to visit Landsman's Bank first to pick up the deed to our house first."

"I hope that Sheriff Fulmer didn't just tell you it was ours to make you accept his offer."

Joe laughed before he replied, "If he did, then I'm sure the man who owns the place will be angrily surprised when he returns to find us living there."

Faith had only been joking but now began to wonder if the sheriff hadn't just borrowed the property. The unexpected gift of the large, furnished house was almost too good to be true.

Her concerns were short-lived when just minute later, they were escorted into the bank president's office and met a beaming Jerome Brown.

Joe said, "Mister Brown, I'd like you to meet my wife, Faith."

The banker smiled as he said, "It's a great pleasure to meet you, Mrs. Beck. Please have a seat."

Faith smiled and said, "I'm happy to meet you as well, Mister Brown."

After Joe pulled out a chair, Faith sat down before he took the chair beside her.

After he sat down behind his exquisite oak desk, Jerome gushed, "Mister Beck, I can't tell you how surprised I was when Sheriff Fulmer entered my office and set those four stolen gold bars on my desk. After he told me how you'd tracked those thieves in the night and captured them without a shot being fired, I was truly amazed. And it was a testament to your integrity that not one tiny sliver of gold had been shaved from any of the bars."

Joe shifted uncomfortably in his chair as the banker continued.

"When the sheriff told me that he was trying to convince you to become his deputy, which he desperately needs by the way, I immediately offered the Snider property as an incentive to accept his offer and a well-deserved reward."

Joe finally spoke when he said, "I am very grateful for your generosity, Mister Brown. But I do have one concern. I'm only sixteen and was wondering if it's legal for me to own the house."

"Despite our overpopulation of lawyers, your age isn't a problem out here. This isn't Philadelphia or New York."

Joe smiled then said, "Just to be honest, I believe you should know that I was going to accept his offer before he showed us the beautiful house."

"It doesn't matter. I'm not about to change my mind. I think our city is in great need of a young man with your character and obvious talents."

Joe smiled and said, "Thank you, Mister Brown. The sheriff told us to see you before we registered the deed at the land office."

Mister Brown said, "Oh, of course. I've already signed the deed over to you," then opened the middle drawer and pulled out a large envelope.

As he slid it onto the desktop, he said, "The paperwork is all inside and the taxes aren't due until next April."

Joe picked up the envelope and glanced at the address before saying, "Thank you again, Mister Brown. My wife and I have a lot to do today to start turning the house into our home, but we'll be back soon to open a bank account."

Jerome rose from his chair, and after Joe and Faith stood, he shook Joe's hand and bowed slightly to Faith before saying, "If you need any help with your finances, feel free to see me, Mister Beck."

Joe replied, "We'll do that, Mister Brown," then he and Faith turned and left the office.

Once outside the bank, Faith laughed before saying, "I thought Sheriff Fulmer was only joking when he said that Mister Brown might kiss you. But I thought he was close to giving you a big wet buss when we met him."

Joe grinned as he replied, "So, did I. Let's stop at the land office and get the deed for 15 Third Street registered."

"That's the address?"

"Yes, ma'am. When I get a chance, I'll write a letter to Captain Chalmers and his wife. Hopefully, I'll get a reply soon and learn that the captain is all right."

"Maybe I'll write one, too. If it wasn't for the captain, I never would have met you."

As they started to cross the street to the county courthouse, Joe said, "It wouldn't have mattered, Faith. We were destined to find each other."

Faith tightened her grip on Joe's arm as they wound their way through the traffic.

―――

After the short visit to the land office, Joe and Faith spent almost two hours in Walker & Sons buying everything they needed and some they didn't. Faith found a heavy, wool-lined coat that reached below her knees, a pair of thick sheepskin gloves, and a cap lined with fox fur that covered her ears. Joe's protection against the elements took the form of three pairs of woolen Union suits. Their final clothing additions were four heavy scarves they could share to keep their necks and faces warm.

After arranging for the large order's delivery, they stopped at Pritchard's Butcher and Greengrocer to buy some fresh food. Joe had expected it to be a much shorter stop, but Faith's insatiable hunger kept them in the store for forty minutes. Joe paid the hefty bill and draped two heavy sacks over each shoulder before they headed back to the house.

After reaching Third Street, Joe said, "Now I feel more sympathetic to Bernie and our mares for having to carry their burdens for hundreds of miles."

Faith smiled and said, "I did offer to carry one of the bags, Joe."

"I know, but you're already carrying a much more important package. Besides, carrying all four is more balanced."

Faith rubbed her stomach as they approached their house and said, "I'll make lunch before the big order arrives."

Joe replied, "I need to sort the horses, too. After we unload the order and put everything away, if I have enough time, I'll see about the firewood."

"Do we have enough to keep us warm for a day or two?"

"I think so, but I don't want you to have to step out of bed into a cold room again if I can help it."

Faith smiled as she said, "It won't be so bad after you lay the buffalo robes on the floor along both sides of our bed."

"They did come in handy, didn't they?"

As they stepped onto the front porch, Faith asked, "Where are you going to put all of the other things that we accumulated along the way but no longer need?"

Joe opened the door and after Faith entered, he followed her inside, closed the door then replied, "I was going to put most of it in the unfurnished bedroom upstairs. I'll store the bayonets, Arapahoe knives and the Crow headdress in the closet, but I'll need to have some shelves and racks made for all of the guns."

Faith nodded before they continued down the hallway to the kitchen where Joe set the weighty bags of food onto the large table.

As they began emptying the bags, Faith asked, "Are you going to keep all of the guns and ammunition?"

"I'll keep most of them, but I'll see if Sheriff Fulmer would like one of the Frank Wesson carbines and a box of cartridges."

"What about all the horses? We won't be riding very much now, and hopefully, we won't need to use pack horses either."

Joe set the thick package of beefsteaks on the table then answered, "I think we'll keep Duke, Duchess, Bessie and Bernie. If Sheriff Fulmer doesn't want any of the others, I'll sell them to Frank Smith at a very good price. I should give one to Bert for taking Chuck and Marigold to Fort Boise, too."

"That's a good plan. I'd hate to lose Duchess. And I know how you feel about Duke and Bernie. Bessie and Duchess will probably foal in the summer, too."

Joe nodded as he continued to unpack the bags and hoped that Duchess didn't drop a mule foal.

Their order arrived shortly after noon, but it was almost three o'clock before they finished finding a place for all of their purchases. But it left Joe with enough time to find the sawmill and place his order for a cord of seasoned firewood.

By the time he returned to the house, Faith had finished making their bed with the new pillows, sheets, three new blankets and a heavy quilt.

Chuck and Marigold's return hadn't surprised Bo as much as it had many of the others. He suspected that the embarrassing wound he'd inflicted on himself made him unable to pursue his dream of sudden wealth. He assumed that Chuck would rather recover with his friends than in a strange town. He also mistakenly believed that Marigold had pressured him to return because she missed her family.

He had hoped that Joe and Faith had also returned but understood why they hadn't when Chuck explained that Joe was going to be a deputy sheriff.

As the sun began to kiss the western horizon, the families gathered for a large communal supper. Everyone was in a celebratory mood knowing that their long journey was almost done.

IDAHO CITY

Before they turned in for the night, Bo looked at Nora and said, "I'm surprised that no one is stayin'."

Nora smiled as she said, "It's ironic, isn't it? Over the past two weeks, the only ones who we were sure would stay with the wagons were Joe and Faith. Tomorrow, when we start rolling, they'll be the only ones staying in Idaho City."

Bo nodded as he replied, "I'm happy for 'em, but I still wish…"

When he abruptly stopped talking, Nora kissed him and said, "So, do I."

―――

There was no need to saddle Duke and Duchess as it was just a short walk to Sheriff Fulmer's house which also allowed Faith to wear a dress. They didn't even follow the streets but walked past their corral, cut across an empty lot and arrived at the Fulmer home just three minutes after leaving their house.

Joe knocked on the front door and just seconds later, Tap swung it open, smiled and said, "Come on in. You're right on time."

Faith entered and Joe followed her inside.

As they were removing their coats, Tap asked, "Did you visit Jerome Brown at the bank?"

Joe smiled as he replied, "We did and your warning about a potential wet smooch was appreciated. I was a bit worried about being able to legally own the house at my age, but he said it was alright."

"I wouldn't have let him give it to ya if it wasn't legal, Joe. But I'm impressed that you asked him about it. Between that and returnin' the gold bars without a sliver removed is a tribute to your honesty. I'm really happy you'll be workin' with me."

As Joe and Faith hung their coats, Joe replied, "I'm more than happy about it, Tap. Almost as soon as I joined the wagon train, I wanted to be a lawman but thought it wasn't possible until I was at least eighteen."

When they started walking slowly toward the hallway, Tap asked, "Why did you wanna be a lawman? Was your pa a sheriff?"

"No, sir. He was a farmer. I was inspired by the deep satisfaction I felt by helping to protect the families on the wagon train."

Tap looked at Joe and said, "That's the only reason a man should wear a badge."

Joe nodded as they followed Tap down the hallway and heard Mary sharply command, "Sit down and behave, both of you!"

Faith laughed lightly just before they entered the warm, bright kitchen.

Tap stopped, turned and said, "Faith, I'd like you to meet my wife, Mary. And those two troublemakers who are now quietly sittin' in their chairs are Joseph and Grace."

Faith smiled as she said, "It's a pleasure to meet you, Mrs. Fulmer."

Mary stepped closer, took Faith's hands and said, "I'd be pleased if you would address me as Mary."

"I'm honored and please call me Faith. I'm sure Joe told you my full name."

Mary smiled as she nodded then said, "After he was introduced to Grace, he said he was surprised that your parents hadn't added it to your other virtuous names. Please have a seat and I'll start serving."

"I'll help you, Mary. I'd like to feel useful."

Mary said, "Alright," then she and Faith walked to the cookstove.

Tap nudged Joe with his elbow and said, "We menfolk get to sit down with the young'uns where we can't do much damage."

Joe was grinning as he and Tap took their seats at the large table.

Joe's backside had barely touched the wooden seat when Joseph asked, "Are you gonna be my papa's deputy, Joe?"

"Yes, sir. He'll swear me in and give me the badge on Friday."

Grace asked, "Are you gonna dress like Mister Lincoln, too?"

Tap chuckled and Joe smiled as he replied, "No, ma'am. I figure one make believe U.S. President in town is more than enough."

Joseph happily exclaimed, "Maybe you can dress like a general!"

Joe glanced at Faith and Mary who were both smiling before he said, "Nope. I'd rather be a sergeant than a general anyway. Besides I don't have a soldier suit. I could pretend to be a Blackfoot war chief, though."

Tap's eyebrows rose as Joseph excitedly asked, "How could you do that?"

"Well, a couple of months ago, I was sitting on my saddle when a big Blackfoot war party came charging out of a forest at me. I knew if I ran away, they'd catch me, so I just sat there and watched. I guess they thought I was either really brave or really stupid because they just turned and rode back to their village. The next day, I met their war chief, and he gave me a feathered bonnet."

Joseph stared silently at Joe with wide eyes for a few seconds before he quietly asked, "Really? Do you still have it?"

"Yes, sir. It's in a closet in our new home. When you come to visit, I'll show it to you if you'd like."

Joseph vigorously nodded as he exclaimed, "I wanna see it for sure!"

Mary and Faith had been setting platters of food on the table while the tall Joe and the short Joseph talked.

So, as soon as they took their seats, Mary asked, "Why didn't the Blackfeet attack your wagons?"

"It's a long story, so I'll start telling it while we're having supper."

Mary nodded then looked at Tap who bowed his head and after a short pause to allow Joe and Faith to do the same, he gave thanks to God for their bounty.

After loading their plates with food and filling their glasses with fresh buttermilk, they started the nutritional purpose of the meal and Joe began narrating the story of the failed Blackfoot attack.

―――――

By the time Joe and Faith expressed their gratitude and said their goodnights to Joseph and Grace, Joe had been pushed into telling the story about the Crow buffalo attack, which impressed Tap as much as it awed Joseph.

As they were pulling on their coats to leave, Tap said, "Come to the office in the mornin' before the trial."

Joe nodded and said, "Yes, sir. Do you need any help with the prisoners?"

"I might ask you to help me walk 'em to the courthouse if I can't convince Eddie to leave that damned stovepipe hat at the office. It'll make Judge Oliver mad if he wears it in the courtroom."

Joe asked, "Do you think I'll have to testify?"

"Nope. I talked to Mister Blanton today and he said it wasn't necessary 'cause you weren't there when they committed the crime."

Joe nodded and said, "Then I'll see you in the morning, Tap."

Mary smiled as she said, "I'm sure Joseph will want to visit you soon, Joe. I imagine you have more stories to keep him entertained, too."

Faith replied, "He has too many of those kinds of stories, Mary. And I'm pretty sure he'll add more of them."

Joe grinned, said, "I hope not," then opened the door and waved to Tap and Mary before he and Faith left the house.

They were holding hands as they walked through the dark open field when Faith said, "You were right about Mary. She could be Hanepi Wi's sister."

Joe said, "I hope she doesn't attract a tornado like Hanepi Wi did."

Faith laughed before saying, "It wasn't Hanepi Wi who pulled that twister from the sky, Mister Beck."

"I know. Besides, I don't think they get many tornadoes in the mountains for some reason. But Mother Nature has other ways to torture us up here that might make us yearn for those days on the Great Plains."

"I don't think so. It's just so beautiful here, isn't it?"

"It's very impressive and maybe one of these days, we'll be able to buy the land in that semi-canyon where I can try my luck at feather fishing."

Faith smiled as she replied, "I'm just happy that we have such a nice house already."

Joe pointed ahead and said, "And there it is."

After building a fire to ward off the cold night, Joe and Faith were snuggling between their new sheets under the layers of wool blankets and the thick quilt.

Faith's head was resting on Joe's shoulder when she said, "This morning, when we helped Chuck and Marigold into the wagon, I was relieved that they hadn't decided to stay. But when I watched them wave as they rolled away, I suddenly felt empty knowing we might never see them again. Do you think that anyone else from the wagon train will come here or stay in Boise City?"

Joe kissed her on her forehead before replying, "I have no idea what they will do. But if they all go to Oregon, I know we'll miss the many friends we've made since we began our journey. But this is our home now and we'll make new friends here, beginning with the Fulmer family. But I want you to continue adding entries to your journals because now we've started a new chapter in the long story of our lives."

Faith sighed then closed her eyes. While she wished that some of their friends decided to come to Idaho City, she understood that Joe was right. They were home and their life together was just starting. She'd keep writing in her journals and in the spring, she'd make her first entry in their Bible.

IDAHO CITY

TRANSITION

By the time Joe arrived at the jail the next morning, all of the wagons were already rolling past Fort Boise.

Eddie Pascal remained in the jail while Sheriff Fulmer and Joe escorted the two prisoners to the new courthouse. Two hours later, they were returned to their cells which they would occupy until they were hanged the next morning.

On Friday, Joe was wearing his new badge when he and Tap led the condemned men to the scaffold behind the courthouse. They were the first men to end their lives on the newly constructed gallows. Later that day, they invited the Fulmer family to dinner. Before they had supper, they walked to the unfurnished bedroom where Joe gave Joseph the thrill of his young life when he let him wear the Blackfoot war bonnet. Then he entrenched himself as Joseph's best friend when he gave the boy one of the Crow arrows.

On Saturday, Joe posted the long letter to Milton and Alice Chalmers which also included Faith's two-page missive. By the following Tuesday, he'd reduced the barn's excess horse population, and Tap was grateful for the spare horse and the Frank Wesson carbine.

On the fourth of October, Joe surprised Faith with a birthday cake he'd ordered from Sanderson's Bakery. The Fulmer family joined the celebration as well. When they were alone, he gave her the only gift he'd bought which was really for both of them. He presented her with a wedding band made of gold from the nearby creeks. After he slipped it onto her finger, he handed her his matching ring which she slid onto his much larger ring finger.

Joe quickly settled into his new position and read everything he could about the law he was required to uphold. Over the first two weeks on the job, when he needed to intervene in the fairly common but potentially dangerous situations, he managed to quell the disturbance without pulling his pistol.

They received a reply from Alice Chalmers because her husband had been taken prisoner. She thanked him for what he'd done and promised to write again when she learned more of her husband's fate. Joe immediately wrote another letter expressing his concerns and prayers for Captain Chalmers' safe return.

In late October, before the cold weather arrived for a long stay, Deputy Eddie Pascal turned in his badge and left town after being seriously humiliated by Southern sympathizers.

Tap was able to hire his replacement just two days after he'd gone primarily because of the much more positive image of the sheriff's office presented by Deputy Joe Beck. Ezra Baker was almost as old as Tap and had no lawman experience. But he was willing to learn, and Joe suddenly found himself acting as a mentor to a man who was almost twice his age.

Joe and Faith began attending Mass with Tap and Mary at the recently completed St. Joseph church. It was there that they started expanding their circle of friends.

Faith was beginning to show when the snows arrived in earnest. While she was in good spirits, she couldn't wait for spring and Kathleen Maureen to arrive.

An early blizzard was buffeting the house as Faith and Joe kept warm beneath their blankets.

Joe was sliding his fingers across Faith's bump when she said, "When we left the wagons, I'll admit that I was concerned about what was waiting for us in Idaho City. But even in my most optimistic dreams, I could never have imagined how wonderful our life has become in our new home. I'm so very happy, Joe."

Joe kissed her softly before saying, "I'm happy, too. But none of this would matter to me if you weren't here, Faith. This is nothing but a house without you. You are my home."

Author's Note

I'll let Joe and Faith age for a bit while I spend some time in Nevada Territory. I'll blame the constant argument I have with my wayward brain. I'll be doing some research and find an interesting piece of history that triggers a plot for a new story. And as much as I try to ignore it, I know the only way to push it out of my mind is to write the book.

Hopefully, I'll return to Idaho Territory by April and find out what Joe and Faith have been doing while I was vacationing in the warmer climate of Nevada.

IDAHO CITY

BOOK LIST

1	Rock Creek	12/26/2016
2	North of Denton	01/02/2017
3	Fort Selden	01/07/2017
4	Scotts Bluff	01/14/2017
5	South of Denver	01/22/2017
6	Miles City	01/28/2017
7	Hopewell	02/04/2017
8	Nueva Luz	02/12/2017
9	The Witch of Dakota	02/19/2017
10	Baker City	03/13/2017
11	The Gun Smith	03/21/2017
12	Gus	03/24/2017
13	Wilmore	04/06/2017
14	Mister Thor	04/20/2017
15	Nora	04/26/2017
16	Max	05/09/2017
17	Hunting Pearl	05/14/2017
18	Bessie	05/25/2017
19	The Last Four	05/29/2017
20	Zack	06/12/2017
21	Finding Bucky	06/21/2017
22	The Debt	06/30/2017
23	The Scalawags	07/11/2017
24	The Stampede	08/23/2017
25	The Wake of the Bertrand	07/31/2017
26	Cole	08/09/2017
27	Luke	09/05/2017
28	The Eclipse	09/21/2017
29	A.J. Smith	10/03/2017
30	Slow John	11/05/2017
31	The Second Star	11/15/2017
32	Tate	12/03/2017
33	Virgil's Herd	12/14/2017
34	Marsh's Valley	01/01/2018
35	Alex Paine	01/18/2018

36	Ben Gray	02/05/2018
37	War Adams	03/05/2018
38	Mac's Cabin	03/21/2018
39	Will Scott	04/13/2018
40	Sheriff Joe	04/22/2018
41	Chance	05/17/2018
42	Doc Holt	06/17/2018
43	Ted Shepard	07/16/2018
44	Haven	07/30/2018
45	Sam's County	08/19/2018
46	Matt Dunne	09/07/2018
47	Conn Jackson	10/06/2018
48	Gabe Owens	10/27/2018
49	Abandoned	11/18/2018
50	Retribution	12/21/2018
51	Inevitable	02/04/2019
52	Scandal in Topeka	03/18/2019
53	Return to Hardeman County	04/10/2019
54	Deception	06/02.2019
55	The Silver Widows	06/27/2019
56	Hitch	08/22/2019
57	Dylan's Journey	10/10/2019
58	Bryn's War	11/05/2019
59	Huw's Legacy	11/30/2019
60	Lynn's Search	12/24/2019
61	Bethan's Choice	02/12/2020
62	Rhody Jones	03/11/2020
63	Alwen's Dream	06/14/2020
64	The Nothing Man	06/30/2020
65	Cy Page	07/19/2020
66	Tabby Hayes	09/04/2020
67	Dylan's Memories	09/20/2020
68	Letter for Gene	09/09/2020
69	Grip Taylor	10/10/2020
70	Garrett's Duty	11/09/2020
71	East of the Cascades	12/02/2020
72	The Iron Wolfe	12/23/2020

IDAHO CITY

73	Wade Rivers	01/09/2021
74	Ghost Train	01/27/2021
75	The Inheritance	02/26/2021
76	Cap Tyler	03/26/2021
77	The Photographer	04/10/2021
78	Jake	05/06/2021
79	Riding Shotgun	06/03/2021
80	The Saloon Lawyer	07/04/2021
81	Unwanted	09/21/2021
82	reunion	11/26/2021
83	The Divide	12/28/2021
84	Rusty & Bug	01/21/2022
85	The Laramie Plains	02/15/2022
86	Idaho City	03/16/2022

Made in the USA
Columbia, SC
26 July 2022

64053331R00213